If it's not magic, she asked herself, what is it?

She had no answer.

Giving in to impulse, Annja held the sword in both hands high over her head. Almost immediately, lightning reached down and touched the tip in a pyrotechnic blaze of sparks. For a moment, the blade glowed cobalt blue.

Annja dropped the sword, grateful she hadn't been electrocuted.

When she inspected the sword, it was unmarked. If anything, the blade seemed cleaner, stronger. Energy clung to the weapon. She felt it thrumming inside her.

Soaked and awed, Annja stood for a moment in the center of the city and knew that no one saw her. She was invisible in the night. No one knew what she held. She didn't even know herself. She breathed deeply, smelling the salt from the Atlantic and knew she'd somehow stumbled upon one of the greatest mysteries in history.

"Why me?" she shouted into the storm.

There was no answer, only the rolling thunder and lightning.

ROGUE ANGEL

Alex Archer

DESTINY

A GOLD EAGLE BOOK FROM

WORLDWIDE.

TORONTO • NEW YORK • LONDON
AMSTERDAM • PARIS • SYDNEY • HAMBURG
STOCKHOLM • ATHENS • TOKYO • MILAN
MADRID • WARSAW • BUDAPEST • AUCKLAND

First edition July 2006

ISBN-13: 978-0-373-62119-4
ISBN-10:   0-373-62119-1

DESTINY

Special thanks and acknowledgment to
Mel Odom for his contribution to this work.

Printed in U.S.A.

DESTINY

PROLOGUE

Rouen, France
30 May 1431

Out of breath, feeling as though the hounds of Hell pursued him, Roux whipped his horse mercilessly. The beast barely kept its feet on the muddy road. Bloody slaver covered its muzzle, streaking its neck and chest.

Straw-thatched houses lined the road, interrupted by the occasional stone building. He guided the horse between them, yanking the bridle hard and causing the animal to stumble.

"They're going to kill her," Durand Lassois had reported only a few days earlier. The big warrior had tears running down his scarred face and trickling through his black beard. "It's the damned English, Roux. They're trying her as a heretic. They're going to convict her and burn her at the stake. There's nothing we can do."

Roux hadn't believed it. The girl was marked for important things. She was a guardian of innocents, a true power to be reckoned with in the mortal world. The English were greedy bastards and fools besides.

He still didn't believe the girl would be killed now. He'd sensed the strength within her. Seventeen years old and she'd led men into battle at the besieged city of Orléans two years ago.

That had been the beginning of a string of victories that had lifted the English yoke from French necks. Her efforts, her conviction and her leadership brought the crown to the dauphin and allowed him to be crowned Charles VII.

Hypnotized by the power and a chance to negotiate peace, the new king had failed to act quickly and lost the tide of the war. The girl had been wounded during the attack on Paris. The French army never regained its momentum. She was captured during the attempt to lift the siege at Compiegne in May of last year. For the ensuing twelve months, the English at Rouen had held her.

Another half-dozen turns and traffic choked the roads leading to the market. Oxen-pulled carts, horses and asses stood in disarray. French peasants who had buried their hatred of the English in fear for their lives and armored English soldiers who pursued French maidens shared the road.

Roux jerked the reins and brought his horse to a stop. The flashing hooves threw mud over bystanders as the exhausted animal sagged to its rear haunches. Roux vaulted from the horse and landed in the mud.

Garin brought his mount to a similar sliding halt inches shy of colliding with Roux. The younger man's dismount was not nearly so elegant. His foot caught in a stirrup and he tumbled into the mud. When he rose, he was covered. He cursed in German as he tried to brush the muck from him.

Four inches over six feet in height, Roux's apprentice drew immediate attention because of his size. His straight black hair hung to his broad shoulders. Handsome features and his square-cut jaw, devoid of a beard because he was vain about his looks, drew a second glance from every female in the crowd. Magnetic black eyes held challenge and ferocity.

Gathering his riding cloak about him, Roux strode through the crowd. Grudgingly, people parted before him. He carried himself like a lord, though he was no such thing.

He looked like an old man, with white hair and a white goatee. His skin was fair, red from the sun and the wind during the long ride. Though not of the best quality, his clothing—pants, blouse and knee-high boots—showed signs of being well kept. At his side, he carried a saber with a worn handle.

Garin trailed Roux, swaggering through the crowd. He wore a long broadsword scabbarded down his back so the hilt jutted up over his right shoulder.

Only a moment later, Roux stood at the front of the crowd.

The English had tied the maiden to a pillar in the market-place. She stood atop a pile of wood and more logs were piled up to her calves. Her executioner had also outfitted her with faggots, small bundles of sticks and straw that were tied to her calves, thighs, hands, torso and hair.

Her death was intended to be cruel and painful.

Sickness twisted Roux's stomach. Steeling himself, he watched with grim expectation.

She will not burn, he told himself. She will not die.

This is not her destiny.

Still, for all that was in him to believe, he doubted. The young woman had always been stronger in her convictions. Her faith was one of the things that had drawn him to her. That, and the raw, unbridled power that clung to her. Roux had never been able to withstand the pull of that force.

As she faced death, clad in the same male clothing she'd worn so proudly in battle, she stood solemn and unshaken.

She didn't come here to die, Roux told himself. She's going to be all right.

"We can't just stand here and let them kill her," Garin said softly at his side.

"What do you propose, apprentice?" Roux demanded. "Should we rush in, you and I, and slay all the English warriors and free her?"

"No. We can't do that. They would only kill us." Garin's answer was immediate.

Pierre Cauchon, the presiding judge, stepped forward and read out the charges. Stern and dogmatic, he accused the warrior maiden of heresy and of being opposed to the church. He went on to add that she was a bloodthirsty killer and demon possessed besides. No mention was made of his own part in the bloody Cabochien Revolt in 1413 or his defense of the assassination of the duke of Orléans in 1407.

At the bailiff's command, soldiers lit fires along the pyre. Flames eagerly leaped up and twisted through the jumble of wood. The stench of smoke filled the air.

The young woman cried out, but not for help. She asked only that her friends hold up a crucifix so that she could look upon it. Two men did. In a strong, brave voice, the maid prayed to her Savior, asking for the aid of the saints.

You can't just let her die, Roux thought. Not like this. She's meant for more than this. His promise to her and to himself haunted him.

Unable to stand anymore, Roux surged forward. "Enough!" he cried, and he put all the long years of command he'd learned into his voice.

Heads turned in his direction. Several townspeople drew

back from him fearfully as the English soldiers converged on him with drawn swords and maces.

Roux drew his saber with a rasp of metal. "Set her free!" he thundered. "By God, you'll set her free or you'll know the fiery pits of Hell yourselves for judging her so harshly!"

Before he could take another step, something crashed into the back of Roux's skull. The English soldiers took away his saber and kicked him dozens of times, breaking his ribs and the fingers of his right hand. They stopped short of killing him.

While Roux was being beaten, the English commander took the maiden warrior's famed sword and raised it high. The broadsword, plain and unadorned, gleamed in the firelight. He put the tip against the ground and his foot at the center of the blade.

The broadsword shattered, falling into fragments in the mud.

Peasant and soldier pushed forward and snatched the shards from the trampled mud. The commander tossed the hilt deep into the crowd.

Smoke obscured almost everything by then, but Roux still saw her. She continued praying until the end, until finally the flames climbed her body and she sagged against the restraints.

Roux wept, barely hanging on to consciousness.

"Did you see it?" an English soldier shouted suddenly. The frantic note in his voice drew the attention of his comrades away from Roux. "Did you see the dove? A white dove left her body at the moment she died!"

Consternation filled the crowd. They drew back from the blazing pyre. The French separated from the English. In that moment, Roux couldn't hold on any longer. He sunk into familiar inky blackness.

1

Lozère, France
Present Day

She was being followed.

Annja Creed knew that from experience. She'd been followed before. Stalked, actually. On two occasions—once in Venice and once outside Berlin—the experience had ended in violence.

"Wait," Annja told her young guide.

Avery Moreau, seventeen years old and French, his hair a thick black shock and his demeanor sulky, stopped. Thin and lanky, dressed in his American jeans, red pullover and gray Nike hoodie, he didn't look as if he'd be particularly helpful in a physical encounter.

"What's wrong?" he asked.

"I want to look at this." Annja stood in front of the shop window and gazed with interest.

The young man glanced at the window, then back at her. "You're thinking about going fishing?"

For the first time, Annja took her attention from the reflection of the two men following her and really looked at the shop window. Pierre's Rods And Flies was written in French.

It was funnier, Annja supposed, in English. Kind of an unintentional double entendre. But it was a bad cover to stop and check out the guys following her.

"In case I stay up on the mountain," Annja said.

"You're going to stay in the mountains?"

Actually, Annja wasn't planning on that. She had a day hike in mind. But she was getting a later start than she'd have liked. Finding provisions and supplies in Lozère was proving more difficult than she had expected.

"I'm not planning to," Annja replied, "but I've learned to be ready for anything."

The two men following her were in their early twenties, no more than two or three years younger than she was. They looked like hard guys off the street, dressed in leather jackets and jeans. Attitude rolled off them in waves. An old woman carrying a bag of groceries crossed the street to avoid them.

They weren't, Annja decided, the kind of guys who normally hung out in a small tourist town like Lozère. Metropolitan arenas seemed to be their more likely hunting grounds. They looked like the kind of men a single woman in a strange place would do better to avoid.

She wasn't afraid, though. At five feet ten inches, athletic and full-figured, and in shape from running, climbing, and martial arts, she knew she could take care of herself. Her chestnut-colored hair was tied back. Wraparound sunglasses hid her amber-green eyes.

However, she was worried about the young man with her.

Avery Moreau didn't look as if he'd had to fight thieves in his short lifetime.

What are you doing here? Annja wondered. Why would anyone be following me?

"What will you do with fishing gear?" Avery asked.

"If I get trapped in the mountains," Annja explained, "by a storm or by bears—" She looked at him. "You did say there were bears, didn't you?"

He shook his head. "Wolves. I said there were wolves."

Annja nodded. "Right. Wolves, then."

The two men weren't going away. They stood across the street and tried to look inconspicuous. It didn't work. They might as well have been standing there with fireworks going off and wearing Scottish kilts in a Marilyn Monroe pose.

Who are you? Annja wondered.

She'd been in France for two days. She was rooming at a bed and breakfast outside of Lozère. So far, no one had bothered her.

But that was before she'd come into town and started asking questions about La Bête. The creature was one of French legend and its mystery had never been solved. She'd come to Lozère in an attempt to solve it.

And to get paid by *Chasing History's Monsters*, the cable show she did occasional pieces for to subsidize legitimate work in her field. It was strange how archaeologists could get paid more for something that remained mysterious, riddled with myth, and might never have been factual at all than for an honest look at history.

During the past two days, however, the local populace had learned that "the insane American woman"—they didn't know how well she spoke French or how acute her hearing was—was seeking the legendary monster.

"Well?" Avery prompted. He acted surly, as if he had something else he'd rather be doing.

"What?" Annja asked.

"Did you want me to take you to your car?" Avery had arranged to rent a truck that Annja would drive up into the Cévennes Mountains.

"In a moment." Annja nodded toward the shop. "Let's go inside."

She led the way, opening the door and causing the little bell over it to tinkle. Avery followed glumly.

Inside, the shop had a wooden floor and a simple demeanor. Shelves built into the walls held lures, line, reels and other fishing gear. Racks in the center of the room held up waterproof pants, vests and shirts. Farther back, displays of rubber boots, waders, seines and other equipment filled the floor.

"May I help you, miss?" a tiny old man behind the scarred counter asked. He polished his glasses on his shirt, then blinked at her and waited.

"Yes," Annja replied in French. "I'm looking for a tent pole."

"You don't have a tent," Avery said.

The old man pointed to one of the back corners.

Annja spotted a bin containing wooden dowels an inch in diameter and four feet long. They were treated and varnished, improving their strength against wear and the elements.

Retreating to the back of the shop, Annja took one of the rods from the bin. She spun it experimentally for a moment, moving it from one hand to the other, and found the dowel acceptable.

She returned to the counter. "This is great. I'll take it."

The old man rang up the price.

Annja paid and thanked him, then asked, "Is there a back way out of here?"

"Mademoiselle?" The old man's gaze told her he didn't think he'd heard her right.

"A back way." Annja pointed to the rear of the store. "A way out into the alley?"

"Yes, but why would you want to—?"

Annja laid a hundred euros on the counter. "Please," she said.

The old man pointed with one hand and picked up the money with the other.

Annja grabbed Avery by the arm, guiding her guide for the moment.

"What are you doing?" he protested, pushing her hand away.

"Trying to keep you from getting hurt," she answered.

"Hurt?" Avery brushed at his hoodie, smoothing the lines.

"Didn't you see the two guys across the street?" Annja threaded her way through the displays at the back of the shop.

A small metal door let out into the alley. She opened the door and went through.

"No," Avery said defensively.

Gazing back, Annja saw that the two men were in motion, heading for the shop. "The two guys who were following us?" she persisted.

Avery shook his head.

He's just a kid, Annja reminded herself. He's probably never seen a mugging in his life. She took a quick breath.

"Okay," she said, "there were two guys following us for the last three blocks." It might have been longer than that. She wasn't sure. She was still jetlagged from the long trip from New York.

"Oh," Avery said, sounding confused.

The alley was narrow and the walls of the two adjacent buildings were crooked. Stones jutted out in a random pattern.

"I want you to go to the car," Annja said.

"Aren't you coming?" Avery looked worried.

"In a second." Annja slid her backpack from her shoulders and handed it to him.

The bag carried her cameras, journals, maps and pocket PC. Replacing those items would cost a few thousand dollars, but she figured they were safer in Avery's hands than hers for the next few minutes.

"Take this to the car. I'll be there shortly." Annja put a hand on his thin shoulder and gave him a gentle push. "Please, I want you to be safe."

Clasping the backpack to his chest, Avery looked uncertain.

"I'll be there," Annja told him. "In a minute. Now go."

Reluctantly, the young man left. In a handful of steps he was out of sight behind the twisting alley walls.

Threading her tent pole through her belt, Annja turned toward the back wall of the fishing shop. An accomplished rock climber, she skillfully scaled the wall and came to a rest atop the doorway. Turning around so that she faced the alley was difficult, but she managed.

She took the tent pole in both hands and waited.

HENRI FOULARD GAZED around the fishing shop. He didn't see the American woman anywhere. Growing anxious, he trotted to the back of the shop and looked through the displays.

"She's not here," Jean said.

"I see that," Foulard snapped. At that moment, the cell phone in his pocket rang. He answered it at once. "Yes."

"Do you have the woman?" Corvin Lesauvage's tone was calm and controlled. He always sounded that way. But to the trained ear, his words held a dangerous edge.

"Not yet," Foulard answered. His head swiveled, searching desperately for the woman.

"I want to talk to her."

"I know. You will." Foulard pushed through a rack of jackets.

"If she knows something about La Bête that I do not know, I must be made aware of it."

"Soon," Foulard promised.

"Do not disappoint me."

Foulard could not imagine anything in the world that he would want to do less. Lesauvage was a violent man with an unforgiving nature. People who crossed him died. Foulard had helped bury some of them in shallow graves. Others he had chopped into pieces and fed to the fish in the Seine.

The phone clicked dead.

Replacing the device in his pocket, Foulard turned to the old man whose owlish eyes were narrow with disapproval. Foulard knew the old man was not as annoyed as he was.

"Where's the woman?" Foulard demanded.

The old man gripped the lapels of his vest. "You need to leave my shop."

Foulard crossed to the man in three angry steps.

Reaching beneath the counter, the old man took out a phone. "I will call the police."

Without pause, Foulard slapped the phone from the old man's hand, then grabbed a fistful of his vest and yanked him close. Effortlessly, Foulard slipped the 9 mm pistol from beneath his windbreaker and put the muzzle against the old man's forehead.

"The woman," Foulard repeated in a deadly voice.

Trembling, the old man pointed to the rear of the shop.

Rounding the counter, Foulard stomped the phone to pieces. "Don't call the police. I'm cutting you a break by letting you live. Understand?"

The old man nodded.

Foulard shoved him back against the shelves. The old man stayed there.

"She spotted us," Jean said.

"You think?" Foulard shook his head and started for the back door. He kept his pistol in his hands.

"It's hard to stay hidden in a town this small," Jean said as he drew his own pistol. He held it like a familiar pet, with love and confidence.

"Lesauvage wants the woman alive," Foulard reminded him, knowing how his cohort loved to kill.

"Maybe he won't want to keep her that way for long," Jean said hopefully.

"She's just a television person," Foulard said. "A historian. She won't be any trouble. Don't break her."

Jean grinned cruelly. "Maybe we can just scare her a little."

Foulard grinned at the thought. "Maybe."

Together, they passed through the back door.

Foulard stood at the doorway.

Two paths lay before him. He didn't know which direction the woman went. Avery Moreau should have left him a clue. The boy knew what he was supposed to do.

"Should we split up?" Jean asked.

Foulard didn't want to do that. He didn't like the possibilities that existed when Jean was out of his sight.

Then a cell phone chirped.

At first, Foulard believed that his employer was calling back. Lesauvage could be an impatient man and a demanding taskmaster. Then, his hand on the phone in his pocket, he discovered that the device wasn't ringing and didn't even sound like his phone.

The noise came from above.

He looked up and his pistol followed his eyes.

AVERY PRESSED HIMSELF against the alley wall. Even though he hadn't been running, his lungs constricted and his own breathing sounded loud to his ears. His heartbeat was a snare drum in his heaving chest.

He felt bad at having left the woman. Of course he had known the two men were there. He had contacted them to let them know she was seeking to uncover the mysteries of La Bête.

Corvin Lesauvage, the man Avery had gone to with his own problems only weeks ago, was interested in La Bête. Everyone in Lozère knew that. In fact, most who lived around the Cévennes Mountains knew of Lesauvage's interests.

When he'd first offered his services to Annja Creed, Avery had mentioned that she should meet Lesauvage, that he was something of an authority on the subject. She had declined, saying she wanted to form her own opinions before she talked to anyone who might influence her views.

Avery grew afraid for the woman. He knew the kind of men who followed her. Lesauvage maintained two kinds of businesses. The two men on the woman's trail were of the dangerous kind.

Squeezing his eyes shut, willing himself not to cry, Avery thought of his father. Surely his father was cold in his grave now. The funeral had been two—no, three—weeks ago. He'd lost all sense of time. It was June now.

Pressing tight against the wall, Avery waited. He concentrated on the fact that what he was doing would help him get revenge for his father's murder. The policeman who had killed Gerard Moreau would not bask in his glory much longer. He would freeze in a grave during winter. Avery had sworn that.

A cell phone chirped down the alley. It was her phone. He breathed a sigh of relief to know she was still there. He'd been worried she'd figured out he'd led the men to her. More than anything, he couldn't fail Lesauvage.

Then a gunshot shattered the quiet locked in the narrow alley.

OKAY, ANNJA THOUGHT grimly as she listened to the strident ring of her cell phone in her pocket, the element of surprise is surprisingly gone.

The two men whirled to look up at her. Both of them held pistols and looked ready to use them.

With the tent pole in both hands, Annja leaped, propelling herself upward and out.

One of the men fired, and the bullet tore through the space she would have occupied if she'd thrown herself directly at them. The steel-jacketed round fragmented against the stone wall and left a white scar.

Annja flipped through the air and landed gracefully in the alley, now to the men's backs.

"No shooting!" one of the men bellowed.

With her feet spread apart, knees bent to remain low, Annja swiveled her makeshift *bo* stick from her left hand to the right and hit the shooter in the side of the face. His sunglasses shattered and blood sprayed from the impact. He squealed in pain.

Moving quickly to her left, using the stumbling man as a barrier to prevent his companion from aiming at her, Annja gripped the stick in both hands again. This was so not a good idea, she told herself.

She wasn't by nature a violent person, but she immediately resented anyone who tried to take advantage of or intimidate her. That was one of the reasons she'd taken every martial-arts class she could in New Orleans as she'd grown up.

Plus, Sister Mary Annabelle at the orphanage—eighty years old and still spry—was a firm believer in a sound mind and a sound body. Sister Mary Annabelle had never missed a single tai chi class. She was an embarrassment to the other nuns, but she didn't care and Annja had loved the old woman for it.

Annja went on the attack at once. Outrunning a pistol in the twisting confines of the alley was out of the question.

Her phone rang again, sounding inordinately loud in the alley even after the thunderous peal of the gunshot. She wondered if anyone had called the police.

She stepped forward, her mind working rapidly as it always did. She wasn't scared. During her experiences as an archaeologist working in countries far from home, she'd encountered a number of potentially threatening situations caused by weather, ancient traps, geology and men.

Being scared wouldn't help anything.

Striding forward, her left hand over the top of the stick and her right hand under it, Annja slid her right hand down, leaving her right knuckle over the top of the stick as it came over and down, and struck.

The stick slammed against the man's forearm. Something cracked. He released his pistol and screamed. Annja cut off the scream with her next blow, an up strike that caught him under the jaw and dropped him to his knees.

Whirling, knowing the first man she'd attacked was regaining his balance, Annja took another grip on the stick. Stepping forward, she slammed the blunt end of the stick into the man's stomach, doubling him over.

Unbelievably, he brought his pistol up and squeezed the trigger. Two shots ricocheted from the wall behind Annja, missing her by inches.

Dodging again to the left, Annja spun the stick and swung at his gun hand, aiming for the thumb and wrist. Bones broke like dry branches cracking in a campfire.

Staying on the attack, Annja whirled again. She hit the man across the back, aiming for his kidneys. Then she struck him across the backs of his knees, dropping him to the ground.

Even then, doubtless blossoming with pain, he tried to face her. Annja drove the blunt end of the stick against his forehead. He was unconscious before he sprawled on the ground. Blood dripped from the half-moon wound on his forehead.

The other man reached for his dropped pistol.

Annja drove the end of the stick forward, catching the man in the side of the neck and knocking him aside. She kicked the pistol away.

Over the past few years, she'd learned how to use pistols, but she didn't want to touch either of theirs. There was no telling how many crimes were attached to them, and she didn't want to confuse the issue with her fingerprints in case they were all taken into custody.

Before the man could get up again, Annja pinned him to the ground with the stick against the base of his throat. "No," she said.

The man grabbed the stick in both hands and wrenched it away. She kicked him in the face with her hiking boot. The black La Sportiva with Gore-Tex lining had plenty of tread. For hiking slippery slopes and kicking butt, Annja thought, they just can't be beat.

The tread ripped at the man's face, opening a cut over his right eye. Annja put the end of the stick against his throat again, almost making him gag.

"Do that again," Annja said in an even voice, "and you'll regret it."

The man held his hands up beside his head in surrender. Blood trickled into his eye, forcing him to squint.

Holding the stick in place, Annja carefully stretched to search the unconscious man. She found money, two clips for the pistol, but no identification.

"Who are you?" Annja asked the pinned man.

The man growled a curse at her.

Annja pressed the stick against his throat and made him retch. She let him up enough to turn over and vomit.

"Bad mistake," she said.

A siren wailed in the distance, growing closer.

Annja decided she didn't want to be around to answer questions from the Lozère police. As an American, even one with a proper passport, things could become tense. She wasn't on a dig site with administration backing her.

She tapped the man hard on the back of the head with the pole. "Don't let me see you again."

The man cursed at her again, but he remained on the ground.

Annja held on to her stick and jogged down the alley. Her mind whirled and the adrenaline rush started to fade and leave her with the quaking aftermath. Her legs felt rubbery.

This wasn't supposed to happen. She was in Lozère hunting an old monster story. According to plan, she'd be in and out with a few details that would satisfy the young crowd who watched *Chasing History's Monsters*, and a paycheck would soon—she hoped—follow.

Was this a mugging? She wondered. Maybe the two men had heard about her or simply were intrigued enough about the backpack to come after her.

But she got the feeling something more was going on. She just didn't know what.

Get out of town, she told herself. Get to the mountains and see if you can find enough to do the story. Once you finish, you can get back to Brooklyn and edit it, get paid and maybe get to North Africa for Poulson's dig.

Poulson's dig site was interesting to her. The team was looking for one of Hannibal's campsites when he marched across with his elephants. Annja had never been to Africa. She'd always wanted to go. But Poulson's team was privately funded and he didn't have the budget to pay her way.

Still, he'd invited her. If she could make it on her own.

That was why she was here in Lozère chasing after a monster she didn't truly believe existed.

She kept running, telling herself that another day or two and she would be clear of France, and whatever problems the two men had brought with them.

2

The rental Avery had arranged turned out to be an old Renault pickup truck. If Annja had been a layman, maybe she'd have mistakenly called it ancient. But she was a trained archaeologist and she knew what *ancient* meant.

The man who'd rented it to her had seemed somewhat reluctant, but that had lifted once she'd put the money in his hand and promised to get the vehicle back in one piece.

For the money she'd handed over, Annja thought perhaps the man would replace the truck with a better one. But there weren't many vehicles to be had in town that the owners would allow to be driven where she was going.

At least the old truck looked high enough to clear the rough terrain.

After thanking Avery for his help and a final goodbye, Annja climbed behind the steering wheel, stepped on the starter and engaged the transmission with a clank. She headed toward the Cévennes Mountains.

Once out of town, following the dirt road leading up into

the mountains, Annja took out her cell phone. It was equipped with a satellite receiver, offering her a link in most parts of the world. Still, the service was expensive and she didn't use it any more than she had to.

Caller ID showed the number that had called her while she'd been in the alley. She recognized the number at once.

Steering one-handed, trying to avoid most of the rough spots, Annja punched the speed-dial function and pulled up the number.

The phone rang three times before it was answered.

"Doug Morrell." His voice was crisp and cheerful. He sounded every bit of his twenty-two years of age.

"Hello, Doug," she said. "It's Annja. I'm returning your call."

Doug Morrell was a friend and one of her favorite production people at *Chasing History's Monsters*. He lived in Brooklyn, not far from her, and was a frequent guest and dining companion. He was young and trendy, never interested in going out into the field for stories as Annja did.

"I was just looking over the piece you're working on," Doug said. He affected a very bad French accent. "The Beast of Gévaudan."

"What about it?"

"French werewolf thing, right?"

"They don't know what it was," Annja countered.

"Looking over it today, after Kristie did the werewolf of Cologne, I'm thinking maybe this isn't the story we want to pursue. I mean, two stories set in France about werewolves might not be where our viewers want to go."

Annja sighed and avoided an angry response. Evidently lycanthropy wasn't as popular as vampirism because *Chasing History's Monsters* had done a weeklong series on those.

And neither history nor geography was something Doug had an interest in.

"Peter Stubb, the so-called Werewolf of Cologne, was German, not French," Annja said.

"French, German—" Doug's tone suggested an uncaring shrug "—I'm not seeing a whole lot of difference here," he admitted. "Europe tends to blur together for me. I think it does for most of our fans."

That was the difference between a big-name show and one that was syndicated, Annja supposed. The networks had audiences. Cable programs had fans. But she could live with that. This check was going to get her to North Africa.

"Europe shouldn't blur together," Annja said. "The histories of each country are hugely different."

"If you say so." Doug didn't sound at all convinced. "My problem is I don't especially feel good about sticking two hairy guys on as my leads so close together."

"Then save the La Bête piece," Annja said as she became aware of the sound of high-pitched engines. Her wraparound sunglasses barely blunted the hot glare of the early-afternoon sun. *Just let me do my job and give me my airfare*, she almost said aloud.

"If I save the La Bête piece, I've got a hole I need to fill," Doug said.

"The pieces *are* different," Annja said. "Peter Stubb was more than likely a serial killer. He claimed victims for twenty-five years between 1564 and 1589. Supposedly he had a magic belt given to him by the devil that allowed him to change into a wolf."

Doug was no longer surprised by the amount of knowledge and esoteric facts Annja had at her command. He partnered with her at the sports bars to play trivia games on the closed-circuit televisions. He knew all the pop-culture references and sports, and she had the history and science. They split the literature category. Together, they seldom lost and in most of Brooklyn's pubs no one would wager against them.

"There's no mention of a magic belt in Kristie's story," Doug said.

Annja wasn't surprised. Kristie Chatham wasn't noted for research, just a killer bod and scanty clothing while prowling for legends. For her, history never went past her last drink and her last lover.

"There was a magic belt," Annja said.

"I believe you," Doug said. "But at this point we'll probably have to roll without it. Should send some of the audience members into a proper outrage and juice up the Internet activity regarding the show again."

Annja counted to ten. "The show's integrity is important to me. To the work I do." Archaeology was what she lived for. Nothing had ever drawn her like that.

"Don't worry about it," Doug said. "When the viewers start trashing Kristie's validity, I'll just have George rerelease video clips of her outtakes in Cancun while she was pursuing the legend of the flesh-eating college students turned zombies during the 1977 spring break. Her bikini top fell off three times during that show. It's not the same when we mask that here in the States, but a lot of guys download the European versions of the show."

Annja tried not to think about Kristie's top falling off. The woman grated on her nerves. What was even more grating was that Kristie Chatham was the fan-favorite of all the hosts of *Chasing History's Monsters*.

"The ratings really rise during those episodes," Doug continued. "Not to say that ratings don't rise whenever you're on. They do. You're one hot babe yourself, Annja."

"Thanks loads," Annja said dryly.

"I mean, chestnut hair and those amber eyes—"

"They're green."

"*You* think they're green," Doug amended. "I'll split it with you. We'll call them hazel. Anyway, you've got all that professorial-speak that Kristie doesn't have."

"It's called a college education."

"Whatever."

"She still has the breakaway bikini."

Doug hesitated for a moment. "Do you want to try that?"

"No," Annja said forcefully.

"I didn't think so. Anyway, I think we'll be okay. Maybe I can sandwich a reedited version of the zombie piece between the German werewolf and your French one."

"La Bête was never proved to be a werewolf," Annja said, skewing the conversation back to her field of expertise. "Between 1764 and 1767, the Beast of Gévaudan killed sixty-eight children, fifteen women and six men."

"Good. Really." Doug sounded excited. "That's a great body count. Works out to an average of thirty-three people a year. People love the number thirty-three. Always something mystical about it."

Annja ignored his comment because they were friends. She didn't bother to correct his math, either. Counting 1764, La Bête had killed for *four* years. "The creature was also reputed to be intelligent. It was an ambush predator and often avoided capture by leading horsemen into bogs around here. It also outran hunting dogs."

"This wasn't included in your outline."

"You said you don't like to read."

"Well, I don't," Doug admitted grudgingly. "But maybe you could put interesting details like this into your proposal."

"There's only so much you can do with half a page," Annja pointed out. "Double-spaced."

"Yeah, but you need to learn the right things to include. Body count. That's always a biggie."

When I get back, Annja promised herself, I'm going to finish that résumé. There has to be another cable show out there that's interested in archaeology. She knew she'd miss Doug, though.

"At any rate," Annja said, "no one ever found out what the creature was. It was supposed to be six feet tall at the shoulder."

"Is that big?"

"For a wolf, yes."

"I thought you said it wasn't a wolf."

"I said no one knew what it was."

"So it's not a wolf, not a *were*wolf. What the hell is it?"

"Exactly," Annja agreed.

"A mystery," Doug said with forced enthusiasm. "Mysteries are good. But only if you have answers for them. Do you?"

"Not yet. That's why I'm headed into the Cévennes Mountains right now."

"This creature was supposed to be up in those mountains?" Doug asked.

"Yes. According to some people, La Bête is still around. Every now and again a hiker goes missing and is never seen or heard from again."

"Cool. Sounds better already. How soon are you going to have this together?"

"Soon," Annja promised, hoping that some kind of breakthrough would take place. At the moment, she had a lot of interesting research but nothing fresh.

And she didn't have Kristie Chatham's breakaway top. Nor the desire to stoop so low. She said goodbye, then closed the phone and concentrated on her driving.

Glancing up at the mountains, Annja couldn't help thinking it would be better for her ratings if she actually ran into La Bête. Probably not better for her, though.

"THE WOMAN GOT away." Foulard sat in a small café across from the fishing shop. He held his beer against his aching jaw. The swelling made it hard to talk.

"How?" Lesauvage wasn't happy.

"She ambushed us." Foulard still couldn't believe the woman had leaped from above the door and taken them down so easily. It was embarrassing.

Lesauvage cursed. "Do you know where she's going?"

Foulard looked across the table at Avery Moreau. The young man was scowling. He sat with arms folded over his chest and blew out an angry breath now and again.

Foulard just barely resisted the impulse to reach over and slap the young man. It would have been a mistake. The police were still canvassing the neighborhood.

"The boy—" Foulard called Avery that on purpose, watching the young man tighten his jaw angrily "—says she is headed up into the mountains."

"Why?"

"That's where La Bête was known to roam." Foulard didn't believe in the great beast. But he believed in Lesauvage and the magic the man possessed. Foulard had seen it, had felt its power, and had seen men die because of it.

Lesauvage was quiet for a moment. "She knows something," he mused quietly, "something that I do not."

"The boy insists that she didn't."

"Then why go up into the mountains?"

Foulard cursed silently. He knew what was coming. "I don't know."

"Then," Lesauvage replied, "I suggest that you find out. Quickly. Take Jean—"

"Jean is out of it," Foulard said. "The police have him."

"How?"

"The woman knocked him out. I couldn't wake him before I had to flee. I was fortunate they didn't get me." Foulard rolled his beer over his aching jaw. "She fights very well. You didn't tell us that." He meant it almost as an accusation, suggesting that Lesauvage hadn't known, either. But he wasn't that brave.

"I didn't think she could fight better than you," Lesauvage said. "And I heard there were shots fired."

Wisely, Foulard refrained from speaking. He'd already failed. Lesauvage appeared willing to let him live. That was good.

"Find her," Lesauvage ordered. "Go up into the mountains and find her. I want to know what she knows."

"All right."

"Can you get someone to help you?"

"Yes."

Lesauvage hung up.

Pocketing the phone, Foulard leaned back and sipped the beer. Then he reached into his jacket and took out a vial of pain pills. They were one of the benefits of working for Lesauvage.

He shook out two, chewed them up and ignored the bitter

taste. His tongue numbed immediately and he knew the relief from the pounding in his head would come soon.

Turning his attention to Avery Moreau, Foulard asked, "Do you know which campsite she'll be using?"

Arrogantly, Avery replied, "I helped her choose it."

"Then you know." Foulard stood. He felt as if the floor moved under him. Pain cascaded through this throbbing head. He stoked his anger at the woman. She would pay. "Come with me."

"What about Richelieu?"

It took Foulard a moment to realize whom the boy was talking about. "The policeman?"

Avery's blue eyes looked watery with unshed tears. "My father's murderer," he said.

Waving the statement away, Foulard said, "Richelieu will be dealt with."

"When?"

"In time. When the time is right." Foulard finished the beer and set it aside. "Now come on."

"Lesauvage promised—"

Reaching down, Foulard cupped the boy's soft face in his big, callused hand. "Do not trifle with me, boy. And do not say his name in public so carelessly. I've seen him bury men for less."

Fear squirmed through the watery blue eyes.

"He keeps his promises," Foulard said. "In his own time. He has promised that your father's killer will pay for his crimes. The man will." He paused. "In time. Now, you and I have other business to tend to. Let's be about it."

Avery jerked his head out of Foulard's grip and reluctantly got to his feet.

Across the street, the Lozère police were loading Jean's

unconscious body into the back of an ambulance. The old shopkeeper waved his arms as he told his story. Foulard thought briefly that he should have killed the man. Perhaps he might come back and do that.

For the moment, though, his attention was directed solely at the woman.

A SNAKE LAY SUNNING on the narrow ledge that Annja had spent the past hour climbing up to. She had been hoping to take a moment to relax there. Climbing freestyle was demanding. Her fingers and toes ached with effort.

The snake pushed itself back, poised to strike.

Great, Annja thought. Climbing back down was possible, but she was tired. Risking a poisonous snake bite was about the same as trying to negotiate the seventy-foot descent without taking a break.

She decided to deal with the snake.

Moving slowly, she pulled herself almost eye to eye with the snake. It drew back a little farther, almost out of room. Freezing, not wanting to startle the creature any more than she already had, she hung by her fingertips.

Easy, she told herself, breathing out softly through her mouth and inhaling through her nose.

The snake coiled tightly, its head low and its jaws distended to deliver a strike that would send poison through her system.

At a little over twenty inches long, it was full-grown. A string of black splotches from its flared head to the tip of its tail mottled the grayish-green scales and told Annja what kind of venomous adder she faced.

Ursini's vipers were known to have an irritable nature, to be very territorial and struck quickly when approached.

Their venom was hemotoxic, designed to break down the blood of their prey. Few human deaths were attributed to Ursini's vipers in the area, but Annja felt certain a lone climber miles from help in the mountains would be a probable candidate.

The ledge Annja clung to extended six feet to her left.

Okay, she mentally projected at the snake, not wanting to speak because the vibrations of her voice might spook the nervous viper, there's enough room for both of us.

Moving slowly, she shuffled her left hand over a few inches. The snake tightened its coil. She stopped, clinging by her fingertips. If she'd been wearing gloves she might have felt more comfortable taking the risk of movement. But at present only a thin layer of climbing chalk covered her hands.

She stared at the snake, feeling angry as it kept her at bay. She didn't like being afraid of anything. She was, of course, but she didn't like it. That something so small could impede her was irritating. If she'd worn a harness and had belayed herself to a cam, getting around the snake would have been a piece of cake.

But she hadn't.

"Bonjour," a voice suddenly called from above.

Gazing upward briefly, Annja spotted an old man hunkered down in a squatting position thirty feet up and to the right of her position.

He was in his sixties or seventies, leathery with age. Sweat-stained khaki hiking shorts and a gray T-shirt hung from his skinny frame. His white hair hung past his thin shoulders and his beard was too long to be neat and too short to be intended. He looked as if he hadn't taken care of himself lately. He held a long walking staff in his right hand.

"*Bonjour*," Annja responded quietly.

"Not a good spot to be in," the old man observed.

"For me or the snake?" Annja asked.

The man's face creased as he laughed. "Clinging by your fingernails and you've still got wit." He shook his head. "You seldom find that in a woman."

"You aren't exactly enlightened, are you?" Annja shifted her grip slightly, trying to find a degree of comfort. There wasn't one.

"No," the old man agreed. He paused. "You could, of course, climb back down."

"I hate retreating."

"So does the snake."

"I suppose asking for help is out of the question?"

The old man spread his hands. "How? If I try to traverse the distance, should I be that skilled, I would doubtless send debris down. It might be enough to trigger a strike."

Annja knew that was true.

"It is poisonous, you know. It's not just the sting of a bite you'll have to contend with."

"I know." Back and shoulders aching, Annja watched the snake. "I have a satellite phone. If I fall or get bitten, maybe you could call for help."

"I'd be happy to."

Annja held up a hand, letting go of her fear and focusing on the snake. Its wedge-shaped head followed her hand. Then, getting the reptile's rhythm, she flicked her hand.

The viper launched itself like an arrow from a bow.

Without thinking, Annja let go the ledge with her left elbow and swung from her right, crunching her fingers up tightly to grip and hoping that it was enough to keep her from falling.

The snake missed her but its effort had caused it to hang over the ledge. Before the viper could recover, Annja swung back toward it.

Trying not to think of what would happen if she missed or her right hand slipped from the ledge, she gripped the snake just behind its head. The cool, slickly alien feel of the scales slid against her palm.

Move! she told herself as she felt the snake writhing in her grip. Skidding across the rough cliff surface, feeling her fingers give just a fraction of an inch, she whip-cracked the snake away from the mountain.

Airborne, the snake twisted and knotted itself as it plummeted toward the verdant growth of the forest far below.

Flailing with her left hand, Annja managed to secure a fresh grip just as her right hand pulled free of the ledge. She recovered quickly and let her body go limp against the cliff side. Her flesh pressed against the uneven surface and helped distribute her weight.

"Well done," the old man called. He applauded. "That took real nerve. I'm impressed."

"That's me," Annja agreed. She blew out a tense breath. "Impressive."

She hoisted herself up with her arms, hoping the viper had been alone and hadn't been among friends. Even with the ledge, she tucked herself into a roll and luxuriated on her back.

The old man peered down at her. "Are you all right?"

"I'm fine. Just resting. I'll be up in a minute."

Taking out a pipe, the old man lit up. The breeze pulled the smoke away. "Take your time," he invited. "Take your time."

Annja lay back and waited for her breathing to calm and

the lactic acid buildup in her limbs to ease. You should go home, she told herself. Just pack up and go. Things are getting way too weird.

For some reason, though, she knew she couldn't turn and go back any more than she could have retreated from the snake. As she'd begun her ascent on the mountain, she'd felt a compulsion to continue her quest.

That was dumb, she'd thought. There was no way she was going to uncover the secret of La Bête after three hundred years when no one else had been able to.

But something was drawing her up the mountain.

3

A dull roaring sounded in the distance.

Recognizing the noise, Annja sat up on the cliff's edge and peered out into the forest that broke across the foothills of the mountains like an ocean of leaves.

Six Enduro motorcycles bobbed and slid through the forest. The riders wore brightly colored leathers and gleaming helmets.

"Are you expecting company?" the old man asked from the ledge above.

"No."

"Perhaps they just came out here for the view," the old man suggested. "Or maybe they brought their own entertainment."

Meaning booze or drugs? Annja thought that was possible. But she didn't mean to get caught standing on a ledge if that wasn't the truth.

"Are you coming on up, then?" he asked politely.

"Yes."

"Good." The old man took a handkerchief from his pocket

and wiped his face. "It's rather warmer up here than I'd thought it would be."

Annja stood, balancing precariously on the narrow ledge. She reached into her pack and took out a bottle of water. After drinking as much as she could, she replaced the bottle in her pack and started climbing again.

"There's a rock to your left." The old man pointed to the outcropping with his staff.

She curled her hand around the rock and heaved.

"There you go," he congratulated.

Listening to his speech, Annja wondered at his accent. He spoke English, but she believed that was because he knew she was American. But his French accent wasn't something she was familiar with.

Moments later, Annja gained the top of the ridgeline. The motorcycle engines had died and the silence seemed heavy.

"Thanks," Annja said.

The old man shrugged. "It was nothing. You climb well," he said.

"Thank you."

"But you shouldn't climb alone."

Looking around innocently, Annja asked, "Where's your partner?"

He shrugged. "I'm an old man. No one will miss me if I fall off the mountainside." He started up the ridgeline.

Having no other destination in mind at the moment, Annja followed. The compulsion that she only halfway believed in seemed to be pulling her in that direction anyway.

"What brings you up here?" the old man asked.

"La Bête," Annja answered.

Halting, he peered over his shoulder. "Surely you're joking."

"No."

"La Bête is a myth," the old man stated. "Probably a story made up by a serial killer."

"You would know about serial killers?"

"I would." He didn't elaborate. Instead, he turned and continued up the ridgeline.

"What are you doing up here?" she asked.

"Searching for something that was lost."

"You lost something up here?"

"No." The old man swung around a boulder and kept going up. "It was lost a long time ago. Hundreds of years ago."

"What was it?"

"Nothing you'd be interested in, my dear."

"I'm an archaeologist. I like old things." Annja instantly regretted her words when the old man turned around. If he was an old pervert, she'd just given him the perfect opportunity for an off-color remark.

"You?" he asked as if in disbelief. "An archaeologist?"

"Yes," Annja declared. "Me."

The old man blew a raspberry. "You're a child. What would you know about anything of antiquity?"

"I know that old men who think they know everything *don't* know everything," she said. "Otherwise *children* like me wouldn't be discovering new things."

"Learning about them from a book is one thing," the old man said. "But to truly appreciate them, you have to live among them."

"I try," Annja said. "I've been on several dig sites."

"Good for you. In another forty or fifty years, provided you don't die of a snakebite or a long fall, perhaps you will have learned something."

A tremor passed through the ground.

Annja froze at once, not certain if she'd truly felt it.

The old man turned around to face her. His face knitted in concern. Irritably, he tapped his staff against the ground. "Did you feel that?" he asked.

"Yes," Annja said. "It's probably nothing to worry about."

"It felt like an earthquake. This isn't earthquake country."

"Earthquakes take place around the world all the time. Humans just aren't sensitive enough to feel all of them," Annja said.

The ground quivered again, more vigorously this time.

"Well," the old man said, "I certainly felt that." He kept walking forward. "Maybe we should think about getting down."

Annja stayed where she was. Whatever was pulling at her was stronger than ever. It lay in the direction opposite the way the old man had chosen. Before she knew it, she was headed toward the pull.

"Where are you going?" the old man asked.

"I want to check something out." Annja walked along the ridgeline, climbing again. A small trail she hadn't noticed before ran between bushes and small trees.

A game trail.

Despite the tremors, Annja went on.

FOULARD'S MOOD HADN'T lifted. A burning need for some kind of revenge filled him. The woman, Annja Creed, had to be delivered alive to Lesauvage, but she didn't have to be unbroken.

He parked his motorcycle beside a new SUV. The five men with him parked nearby.

They dismounted as one, used to working together. Jean had been one of them, one of Lesauvage's chosen few.

Drawing his 9 mm handgun, Foulard took the lead. The other men fell in behind.

They went quickly. Over the past few years, they had learned the Cévennes Mountains. Lesauvage had sent them all into the area at one time or another. Foulard had been several times.

None of them had ever found anything.

Foulard truly didn't believe the woman had found anything, either. He hoped she hadn't. Once Lesauvage saw that she knew nothing, he would quickly give her to them.

Eagerly, Foulard jogged up the trail. His face and arms still hurt, but the pain pills had taken off the edge.

When the first tremor passed through him, Foulard thought it was the drugs in his system. Then a cascade of rocks rushed from farther up the grade and nearly knocked him from his feet.

"What the hell is that?" one of the men behind him yelled.

"Earthquake," another said.

"We don't want to be on top of this mountain if it's about to come down."

Foulard spun toward them. "We were sent here to get the woman," he said. "I won't go back to Lesauvage without her."

The men just stared at him.

The ground quivered again.

"I'll kill any man who leaves me," Foulard promised.

They all looked at him. They knew he would.

Another tremor passed through the earth, unleashing more debris that sledded down the mountainside.

"All right," Croteau said. He was the oldest and largest of them. "We'll go with you. But make it quick."

Turning, Foulard kept his balance through another jarring session, then started to run.

THE GAME TRAIL LOOKED old and, judging from the bits and pieces of it Annja saw along the mountainside, it went all the way to the top.

The ground heaved this time, actually rising up and slamming back down beneath Annja's feet. She dropped to all fours, afraid of being flung from the mountainside.

"This way," the old man shouted. "Come back from there before you get yourself killed."

This is insane, Annja thought. She felt the earth quivering beneath her like a frightened animal.

"Don't be foolish," the old man said.

Frustrated, Annja took out her Global Positioning System device. She took a reading.

Twenty-four satellites bracketed the earth. Every reading taken by the device acquired signals from at least twelve of them. When she returned to the mountains, she'd be within inches of the exact spot where she now stood.

Returning the GPS locater to her pack, she turned and started back down the mountain. The compulsion within her surged to a fever pitch with a suddenness and intensity that drove her to her knees in an intense attack of vertigo.

"Are you all right?" the old man asked.

She wasn't. But she couldn't speak to tell him that.

Without warning, she was no longer on the mountaintop. She stood in the middle of a blazing fire. Pain threatened to consume her.

Her whole life she'd suffered from nightmares about fire but, for the first time, it was happening while she was awake.

"Girl!" the old man bellowed.

"Girl!" he roared again. Panic strained his features. Some other look was there, as well. Perhaps it was understanding.

Annja didn't know. The nightmare abated. She focused on the old man.

Forced to use his staff to aid with his balance across the

heaving earth, he came toward her. He held out his hand. "Come to me. Come to me now!"

Feeling drained and totally mystified, Annja tried to walk toward him. Then the ground opened up at her feet. In a heartbeat, the earth shifted and yawned till a chasm twenty feet across formed. Rocks and grass and debris disappeared into the earthen maw.

Barely staying on her feet, Annja backed away. She didn't want to try leaping down into the crevasse. During a quake, the earth could close back together just as quickly as it opened up. If the earth caught her, it would crush her.

"I can't reach you," she said.

The old man pointed, leaning on his staff as another quake shuddered through the earth. "There's a trail. Back that way. Just head down."

Turning, Annja gazed down the other side of the mountain. Here and there, just glimpses, she thought she saw a trail.

"Do you see it?" the old man called.

The earth heaved again, shifting violently enough that Annja almost lost her footing. "Yes!"

"Go!" the old man called. "Not much farther down, you'll find a campsite. I have a truck there. I will meet you." With more agility and speed than Annja would have believed possible, he started down the crest where he stood.

Annja didn't know what the old man was doing in the mountains. There were a number of hiking trails. Even famed author Robert Louis Stevenson, though in ill health, had been compelled by his curiosity about the Beast of Gévaudan to try his luck at solving the mystery in the mountains. The trail Stevenson had taken was clearly marked for tourists interested in the countryside, the legend or the author of *Dr. Jekyll and Mr. Hyde*.

The mountain shook again and Annja started running. Never in her research had she heard of any earthquakes in the area.

She followed the narrow path across worn stone that led through boulders and cracks along the mountainside. As she ran, the ground trembled and heaved. Several times she tripped and fell against the rock walls. Her backpack and the pouch containing the climbing chalk thudded against her.

"There she is!" The young male voice ripped across the sound of falling rock.

Going to ground immediately, Annja peered around.

Farther down the slope, one of the motorcycle riders, still wearing his riding leathers, peered up at her. For a moment she thought perhaps he was coming to help her.

Then she saw the small, black semiautomatic pistol in his hand and the bruises on his face. It was the man from the alley.

She turned and fled, racing back up the mountain.

The earth shook even more violently than before. A horrendous crack sounded nearby. Nearly knocked from her feet, aware that hundreds of pounds of rock and debris were skidding toward her, she pulled up short and tried to alter her course.

The ground opened up and swallowed her.

4

Out of control, Annja threw her hands out instinctively in an effort to catch hold of the sides of the fissure. Stone whipped by her fingertips, but she managed to somewhat slow her descent from a fall to a slide something short of maximum velocity.

Not a fissure, she told herself, her brain buzzing at furious speed the way it always did when she was in trouble. This is a sinkhole.

She felt the roughly circular contours of the shaft around her as she stretched to fill it. A sinkhole was a natural formation of a cave that finally hollowed out to the point it nearly reached the surface. As a nation, France was probably more honeycombed with caves and cave systems than any other country in the world.

The Cévennes Mountains held many volcanic caves, created by lava after it had cooled and the volcanoes had subsided. Along the coast, sea caves formed by waves had provided hidden harbors in the golden age of piracy. Limestone caves in the interior were made by erosion. There were even many caves made by the passage of glaciers across the land millions of years ago. Cro-Magnons had lived in caves at Pech-Merle and Lascaux, leaving behind cave paintings millions of years old.

Annja wasn't surprised to find a new cave in the mountains. In fact, in scaling the cliff she'd been hoping to find some sign of one. Le Bête had taken up refuge somewhere all those years ago.

However, she hadn't expected to *plummet* into her discovery.

In a hail of flying stones, she hit the ground hard. The impact drove the breath from her lungs. Blackness ate at the edge of her conscious mind, but she struggled through it and remained alert.

It's not the fall that kills you, she reminded herself. It's the sudden stop at the end.

She covered her head with her arms as more debris rained down around her. Several pieces of stone hammered her back and legs hard enough to promise bruises for a few days.

Then everything was quiet.

You're alive, she told herself. Get moving.

She pushed herself up. Nothing felt broken. That was always a good sign.

When her lungs finally started working again, dust coated her tongue. Reaching into her backpack, knowing by touch and years of experience where the contents were, she took out a bandanna, wet it with the water bottle and tied the material around her nose and mouth. The water-soaked cloth would keep her from suffering respiratory problems caused by inhaling too much dust.

Wet cloth won't protect you from carbon dioxide buildup

or poison gas, she reminded herself. Carbon dioxide wasn't a natural byproduct of a cave the way coal gas was, but if humans or animals had frequented it, the gas could have filled the chamber. She hoped the opening created by the sinkhole would help.

Echoes sounded around her, indicating that the cave was large or long.

Fishing out one of the two halogen flashlights she habitually carried, she turned it on. Then she took off her sunglasses and stored them in the backpack, marveling that they hadn't broken during the fall.

The flashlight beam cut through the darkness but was obscured by the swirling dust that filled the cave. The chamber was at least thirty feet across and almost that high.

The sinkhole was at the back of the cave. At least, it was in the area she decided to refer to as the back of the cave. Almost four feet across, it snaked up but the twists and turns were so severe that no outside light penetrated the chamber.

Going back up is going to be a problem, Annja realized. If it's possible at all. She carried rope in her backpack. Over the years spent at dig sites, she'd learned that rope was an indispensable tool. She never went anywhere without it. But she wasn't sure it could help her now.

Bats fluttered from the stalactites. She swept the flashlight beam after them.

Okay, Annja thought, if you guys are in here, there's got to be another entrance.

Unless the sinkhole that had opened up had originally been some small holes that had allowed the bats to enter and exit. She didn't want to think about that possibility.

The air was thick and stank from being closed up. More than that, it smelled like an animal's den. That was good news and bad news. If the cave did provide a home to an animal, the chances were good that another entrance was large enough to allow her passage. The bad news was that wolves were in the area, as well as bears. Large predators weren't going to be welcome. Especially not in their den.

A swift examination of the chamber revealed a passage. She went to it, finding she had to hunch down to pass through and that the floor was canted. At least the structure looked sound. No cracks or fissures showed in the strata. If there was another tremor, she felt reasonably certain the rock would stay intact and not come down on top of her.

The passage went on for fifteen or twenty feet, then jogged left and opened into another chamber nearly twice the size of the one she'd fallen into.

When she passed the flashlight beam over the wall to her right, drawings stood out against the stone. Seeing what they were, guessing that no one in hundreds or thousands or millions of years had seen them, all thoughts of anything else—the earth tremors, the motorcyclists, the old man—were gone.

Playing the flashlight beam over the rough rock surface, Annja made out mastodons, handprints, figures of people, fires, aurochs—ancestors of modern cattle—and other images of Cro-Magnon life.

Excitement flared through her. During her career, she'd seen cave paintings. She'd even seen similar paintings at Lascaux after the cave had been closed to the public.

But she had never found something like this.

Hypnotized by the images, she took a credit-card sized digital camera from her backpack. With the low light, she didn't know if the images would turn out, but whatever the camera captured would surely be enough to get funding for a dig site.

The Cro-Magnon painters had used animal fat and minerals to make colors. Black had been a favorite and easy to make. All that was required was charred bone ground into a fine powder mixed with animal fat.

She walked along the wall, taking image after image. Only a little farther on, the scenes on the wall were marred. Long, deep scratches ran through them, as if they'd been dug into the stone by great, dull claws. The claw marks were seven and eight feet high, so close together it looked as if an animal had been in a frenzy.

An animal marking its territory? she wondered. Or the desperation of an animal trapped inside this cave?

In that moment, Annja remembered she'd traveled to the Cévennes looking for La Bête. Then she tripped and nearly fell. Something furry brushed against her ankle.

For one moment she thought she felt it move. Stepping back quickly, she swung the flashlight around, prepared to use it as a weapon.

The light beam fell in a bright ellipse over a scene straight out of a nightmare. The half-eaten and mummified corpse of a sheep lay on the floor amid a pile of bones.

Tracking the bone debris, Annja shone her beam over the stack of skulls that had been arranged in an irregular notch in the chamber. At least seventy or eighty skulls filled the area.

Was this a place of worship? Annja wondered. Or an altar celebrating past triumphs?

She tried to imagine Cro-Magnon men sitting in the cave bragging about their success as fierce hunters. Except that the sheep's body was anachronistic. None of the sheep's forebears had looked like that in Cro-Magnon times. This sheep was small and compact, bred for meat and wool, not far removed from the sheep Annja had seen on farms she'd passed on her way to the mountain range.

Looking closely, she noticed that several of the skulls were human.

Used to handling human remains on dig sites, she had no fear of the dead. She set down the flashlight to illuminate the scene.

Upon further inspection, she discovered that several of the ribs, and arm and leg bones were likely human, as well. Shreds of clothing that looked hundreds of years old clung to some of the bones. Boots stood and lay amid the clutter.

A cold chill ran down her spine. Whatever had lived in the cave had preyed on humans.

Shifting the light, heart beating a little faster, Annja spotted the great body stretched out on the floor. For a very tense moment, she'd thought the animal was lying there waiting to pounce. She froze.

The light played over the mummified lips pulled back in a savage snarl that exposed huge yellow teeth. The eye sockets were hollow, long empty and dry. In that moment, the animal musk she'd smelled seemed even more intense.

Death had stripped the fantastic creature of much of its bulk, but it was still easy to see how huge it had been in life. The head was as big as a buffalo's but more bearlike in shape. Its body was thick and broad and the limbs were huge. It was unlike anything Annja had ever seen before.

Making herself move despite the fear and astonishment she felt, Annja took pictures of the creature with the digital camera. Maybe she'd made two incredible discoveries in the same day.

Finished with the camera, she hurriedly took out a small drawing pad and a mechanical pencil from her backpack.

If the camera failed to capture images, she could at least draw them.

On closer inspection, Annja saw a broad-bladed spear shoved through the beast's chest. Beneath the corpse of the impossible animal was a human corpse.

Decomposition hadn't settled in. Locked in the steady climate of the cave environment, kept bug-free by depth and ecology, the dead man had mummified as the beast had. His hands, the flesh so dehydrated it was almost like onionskin over the bones, still held tightly to the spear. Man and beast, locked in savage combat, had killed each other.

Kneeling beside the dead man and beast, she reached out her empty hand.

Something gleamed at the dead man's throat.

Taking a surgical glove from her backpack, Annja plucked the gleaming object from the corpse. It had partially sunk into the dead man's chest. A leather thong tied the object around the corpse's neck.

After freeing the gleaming object, Annja held it up so her flashlight beam could easily illuminate it. A jagged piece of metal, no more than two inches to a side, dangled from the leather thong.

The piece looked like an ill-made coin, hammered out on some smith's anvil in a hurry. One side held an image of a wolf standing in front of a mountain. The wolf was disproportioned, though the oddities seemed intentional, and it appeared as though the wolf had been hanged. The obverse was stamped with a symbol she couldn't quite make out.

Annja remained kneeling. She was checking the image when a flashlight beam whipped across her face.

Instinctively, she dodged away, remembering the motorcyclists and the old man she'd seen outside. She tucked the drawing pad, pencils and charm into her backpack as she scooped up her flashlight and switched it off.

"Where the hell did she go?" someone demanded in French.

Shadows created by the glow of the flashlight trailed the beam into the chamber.

Annja stayed low as the light sprayed around the room. She barely escaped it before reaching the pile of skulls. Once there, she flattened herself against the wall.

Light played over leather-clad bodies that stepped into the chamber.

Evidently the motorcyclists had made their way down the sinkhole. They'd come along the passage Annja had found. She'd been so absorbed by her discoveries that she'd forgotten all about them and hadn't noticed them. Silently, she cursed herself.

"She can't have just vanished," another man said.

In the soft glow of the reflected light from the flashlight, all six of them stood revealed. All of them held pistols.

"If we lose her, Lesauvage is going to kill us." The speaker's voice was tight with fear.

"We haven't lost her," someone stated calmly. "We came in that hole after her. There's no other way out."

"You don't know that, Foulard."

Another man gave a startled curse. "What the hell's lying there?"

Foulard aimed his flashlight at the creature's huge mummified body.

"The Beast of Gévaudan!" someone said. "It must be! Look at it! My grandfather told me stories about this thing!" His voice dropped and took on a note of awe. "I never believed him. Thought it was all crap old men told kids to scare the hell out of them."

Hidden by the shadow of the skulls, Annja's mind raced. They came here looking for me.

"Forget about that damned thing," Foulard commanded. "Spread out. Find the woman. Lesauvage wants to speak with her. I don't want to go back and tell him we lost her."

He directed his flashlight at the cavern's ceiling, providing a weak cone of illumination from above.

Thankfully, the light didn't quite reach the cavern floor. Annja sank down low. Her free hand plucked up one of the human skulls. Her fingers slipped easily through the empty eyeholes to secure her hold. It wasn't much as weapons went, but she hoped to improve her standing.

5

Annja leaned forward, skull in one hand and flashlight in the other, hunkered down in a squatting position.

The six men spread out. Foulard took his own path, but the other five stayed close enough to take comfort in the presence of the light.

"Do you think that really is the Beast of Gévaudan?" one of them asked.

"I don't know, but I heard the creature was a werewolf," another said. "He was supposed to be a guy, Count Vargo, who got cursed by a band of gypsies after he raped one of their daughters."

That was not a werewolf, Annja thought fiercely as she remembered how the great beast looked. It's some kind of mutated species. She pressed against the wall, profiling herself into it.

One of the men came close to her. Annja waited as long as she could, knowing their eyes were adjusting to the darkness. His body language, that sudden shift to square up with her, gave away the fact that he had seen her.

She rose, uncoiling as the viper had done earlier, and swung the skull with all her strength. The aged bone shattered against the man's face, driving him backward.

"There!" one of the men yelled. "Over by Croteau!"

Foulard swung the flashlight in Annja's direction.

Scuttling quickly, flinging away the remnants of the skull, she slid low along the unconscious man. Her partially numbed fingers found the 9 mm pistol lying on the cave floor. She fumbled it into her grip as the flashlight splashed over her and blinded her.

"She has Croteau's gun!"

"Kill her!" Foulard yelled. His pistol barked and spit flame that lit up the angry terror on his face. She recognized the bruises on his face and knew he was the man from the alley.

The wind from the bullet cut the air by Annja's left cheek. If she hadn't already been moving to her right, it would have crashed through her head.

"Lesauvage wants her alive!" someone yelled. "Stop shooting!"

Firing on the fly, Annja put two rounds in Foulard's immediate vicinity. Someone yelped. She'd taken one man out of play.

Annja tried to get her bearings. Maybe they'd used a rope to get down through the sinkhole, and maybe that rope was still there, just waiting. All she had to do was reach it.

Instead, still suffering from partial blindness caused by the bright flashlight beam, she ran into one of the other men in the gloom, unaware that he'd been there. He caught her gun wrist and shoved his own pistol into her cheek below her left eye.

"Move and I'll kill you!" the man shouted.

Immediately, Annja drew her knee up into the man's groin, twisted her head to the left and snapped backward. The pistol barked and the superheated barrel painfully kissed her lips with bruising force.

The detonation temporarily robbed her of her hearing, rendering her partially deaf in addition to the blindness. The man also stripped her borrowed pistol from her fist.

Before her would-be captor recovered, she butted her forehead into his face, breaking his nose and splitting his lips, causing him to stagger back.

Foulard fired again. His bullets ripped into the man who'd held Annja. Crying out in pain, the man dropped to the floor.

Annja was in motion at once, knowing that the bullets had been meant for her. She bent, trying to find one of the lost pistols. Her backpack spilled and something metallic slid free, dropping onto the dust-covered floor.

She skidded to a halt and reached for the necklace. Before she could close her hand on it, Foulard fired three more shots.

Two of the rounds thudded into the dead man and the third struck the metal charm, sending it skidding across the cave floor.

As Annja spun to look at the man, to attempt to read his next move, another figure stepped into the light pool created by Foulard's flashlight.

Savagely, the old man with the walking stick rammed the bottom of his thick staff into the back of Foulard's skull. Crying out in pain, Foulard sagged to the cave floor.

Moving quickly, the old man surprised the remaining men and came out of the darkness. He swung the staff, taking each man's feet from beneath him, then driving the end of his weapon into each man's chest hard enough to take away his breath.

The old man looked at Annja. "Come on, then. It wouldn't do to stay around until they get a second wind."

Despite the fact that an earthquake had occurred and the men had pistols and didn't seem afraid to use them, the old man acted perfectly calm. As if this was something he did every day.

Fisting the charm, Annja stood. The metal caught the glow of the light for an instant, twirling in her grip.

"What is that?" the old man demanded. "What did you find?"

Foulard roared a foul curse and pointed the pistol at them.

"Which way?" Annja yelled. The old man hadn't come from the passageway that led to the sinkhole.

"Here." The old man turned and ran as bullets struck the cave walls.

Almost immediately, the earth quaked again.

Thrusting her arms out in front of her, not understanding how the old man appeared able to see so well in the darkness, Annja located the opening in the wall by feel just in time to keep her face from smashing into it.

For a moment, until they left the glow of the flashlight behind them, the old man was a dimly visible patch of gray ahead of her. Then they twisted around a bend in the tunnel and he vanished.

"Watch your head," he advised.

Annja put a hand over her head in time to ward off the passageway's low ceiling. The rough impact bruised her forearm. *How can he see down here?*

"Who are those men?" Annja asked.

"I don't know. They were after you."

"What are you doing here?"

"At present, saving you. Unless you want to go back there and get acquainted with those highwaymen."

Highwaymen was an odd description. Annja thought about that for a moment, but swiftly geared her mind back to self-preservation as a flashlight beam cut through the darkness behind them. Foulard and his companions had evidently rallied.

"Left," the old man called.

Annja didn't respond at once and crashed into the bend of the passageway.

"Aren't you listening?" the old man snapped.

"Yes." Annja recovered and flicked on her flashlight.

The old man stood around the bend. He didn't protect his eyes from the sudden light that sent painful splinters through Annja's.

Satisfied that she was intact, the old man turned and ran with improbable speed. He carried his staff close to his body as if it were an appendage.

Annja followed through the next turn, then the opening of another chamber dawned before them. Low-level light from outside filled the chamber, coming from an entrance in the mountainside.

"I have a truck," the old man said. "Farther down the mountain. Try to keep up."

Try to keep up? Annja couldn't believe he'd said that. Who is this guy? she wondered.

Then he was outside the cave, sprinting down the steep, trembling mountainside as surefootedly as a mountain goat. Annja was hard-pressed to keep up, but she knew despite his boasting that she could have outrun him. If she'd known which way to go.

They ran, crashing through brush and avoiding trees and boulders that were in their way. An elegant light blue Mercedes SUV sat parked beneath the heavy boughs of a towering Scotch pine only a short distance ahead.

"There," the old man said.

"I see it," Annja acknowledged. She ran to the passenger side as the old man headed to the driver's side.

The Mercedes's alarm system squawked as he pressed the keyless entry on the fob he'd fished from a pocket.

"Belt yourself in." The old man started the engine and pulled the SUV into gear. He didn't bother backing up, just pushed through the brush and came around in a tight circle to get back onto a narrow road that wound through the thick forest. Splashes of sunlight whipped across the dusty windshield.

Annja fumbled with the seat belt and got it strapped just as she heard motorcycle engines roar to life. As she glanced over her shoulder through the back window, the old man put his foot down harder on the accelerator.

"Did you manage to get one of their guns?" he asked.

"No."

"You had one," he accused.

"They took it back." Anger surged in Annja at his tone. Despite the fact that they were running for their lives, the old man's rudeness bothered her on some baseline level. Like fingernails on a chalkboard.

"You should have shot them," he said.

"I tried."

Shaking his head, barely navigating a sudden turn that sent them skidding out of control for a moment, he reached under his seat and pulled free a rack. Restraining straps held two pistols and a cut-down shotgun securely in place.

"Do you always go this well prepared while hiking?" Annja couldn't help asking.

"Yes. It usually saves me from embarrassing situations like running for my life down a mountainside."

Annja couldn't argue the point.

Behind them, two motorcycles roared in pursuit, quickly closing the distance. Bullets crashed through the back glass and broken shards ricocheted inside the SUV. The old man pulled fiercely on the steering wheel again.

"Can you shoot?" he demanded.

Without responding, Annja freed one of the pistols. It was a .40-caliber Heckler & Koch. She racked the slide.

"It's already loaded," the old man said.

A fat round spun through the air. Annja dropped the magazine from the pistol, and replaced the bullet. She popped the magazine back into place with her palm.

"It would be pretty foolish to carry around an unloaded weapon, now, wouldn't it?" he asked sarcastically.

Another fusillade of bullets hammered the SUV.

"Perhaps," the old man said in exasperation, "you could try shooting *back* at them."

"I was just listening to that last-minute pep talk," Annja replied.

Hunched over the steering wheel, holding on with both fists, the old man grinned at her. "You do have a certain amount of spunk. I like that."

Annja didn't care what he liked. Despite the fact that he'd helped save her life, the old man annoyed her in ways she'd never before encountered, at a level that she hadn't believed possible.

Twisting in the seat, Annja rested her right hand in her left and took aim with both eyes open. The British ex-SAS officer who had taught her to shoot had ground that into her on the indoor and outdoor firing ranges. A shooter was never supposed to limit vision, not even on a scoped weapon.

The motorcycles had closed to within thirty yards and

were coming closer, fishtailing and lunging as they pursued their prey. Annja couldn't help thinking of the hunters who had chased La Bête all those years ago. Surely they had pursued it through these same woods.

But they'd never found the lair, had they? Despite her concern over her present situation, Annja couldn't help feeling a little joyful triumph mixed in.

She squeezed the trigger, blasting through a 3-round salvo. One of the bullets hit the lead motorcycle's handlebars and jarred the wheel. The rider quickly recovered and opened fire again.

"You missed!" the old man roared.

"I see that," Annja replied. "I kind of got that when he didn't fall off the motorcycle."

Bullets bounced off the SUV's exterior again, sounding like hail.

"Hold steady," Annja instructed, taking aim again.

"On this pathetic excuse for a road? Ha!" The old man jerked hard left, following the twists and turns.

Annja fired again, deliberately aiming toward the center of the lead rider's chest. She kept up the rate of fire, hoping to get lucky or at least give their pursuers something to think about.

One of the bullets struck the motorcycle's front tire. Rubber shredded and the motorcycle went out of control, lunging suddenly into the forest and smashing against a boulder the size of an earthmover. The gas tank ignited and exploded, blowing the rider free.

Her weapon empty, Annja reached for the second pistol. More rounds hammered the Mercedes.

The old man cursed, but his words were in Latin. And very descriptive.

"Latin?" Annja asked in surprise.

"I find the language more native to my tongue," the old man said. He followed another turn and the road flared out straight for a hundred yards. "Hold on."

Annja didn't have time to brace herself on such short notice. The seat belt bit into her chest as it clamped down when the old man jammed his foot on the brakes. She whipped her head around, watching as the last motorcycle following them down the mountainside tried to stop.

The man's efforts only succeeded in locking up his brakes and sending him into an out-of-control skid. He hit the back of the SUV and flipped over the top, landing on the hood of the Mercedes. He lay there for a moment, then weakly, tried to bring up the pistol he'd somehow managed to hang on to.

Annja lifted her own weapon, but the old man shoved the transmission into reverse and spilled the man from the hood before she could fire. Then the old man shifted back into a forward gear, floored the accelerator and ran him down as he tried to get to his feet.

A dull thud sounded as the man struck the front of the SUV. A moment later the Mercedes rocked back and forth as it crunched over the man's body.

In disbelief, Annja whipped her head around and looked back. The man lay twisted and broken in the path.

"That was cruel," she said.

"You're right," the old man agreed. "Shooting him would have been much more merciful. After all, for reasons unknown to me, he was willing to kill me to get you. However, I didn't see that we were going to be successful in persuading him to stand still long enough for you to shoot him several times. He'd probably have preferred blowing up against the side of a boulder like his friend."

"I don't know who they were," Annja said. "We could go back and check for identification."

"Men like that, assassins, rarely carry identification," the old man said, continuing to gain speed. "Feel free to jump out and go back. I won't have hurt feelings. It wouldn't be the first time I've saved someone's life only to have them squander it foolishly against the very person or thing I saved them from. Do you know if the other men in the cave are dead?"

"No," Annja replied.

"Well, I suppose you might consider the possibility that they're still indisposed is worth the risk. I, however, don't."

"Your attitude leaves a lot to be desired." Annja settled back in the seat, loosening the belt.

The old man shook his head and laughed. "You're hardly the grateful sort yourself." He shoved out his hand.

She took it, surprised at the strength she felt in his grip. Then it felt as if she'd grabbed hold of a branding iron.

The old man took his hand back and the strange sensation ended.

"Are you all right?" Concern touched his blue eyes beneath the thick white eyebrows.

"Yes," Annja replied, annoyed that he would think she wasn't.

"Good." He paused and looked back at the road. "My name is Roux," he said, as if it would explain everything.

TWO HOURS LATER, Annja sat waiting quietly in the Lozère police station. She was pointedly ignored.

"I think you've disrupted their day," Roux said. "Now there will be paperwork generated, reports to file."

"This is ridiculous," Annja said.

"You're an American." Roux sat in a chair against the wall. He held a deck of cards and shuffled them one-handed. "They aren't particularly fond of Americans. Especially ones that claim to have been shot at."

"There are bullet holes in your vehicle."

Roux frowned and paused midshuffle. "Yes. That is regrettable. I don't get overly attached to vehicles, but I did like that one."

Annja shifted in the hard chair she'd been shown to. "Don't you want to know who was shooting at us?"

The old man grinned. "In my life, I've found that if someone truly wishes to harm you and you survive the attempt, you usually get a chance to get to know them again." He paused and looked at her. "You truly don't know who tried to kill you?"

"No."

"Pity."

"Back at the cave, one of the men mentioned someone named Lesauvage," Annja said.

Roux took a moment to reflect. Then he shook his head. "I don't know anyone named Lesauvage."

Working quickly, he shuffled, cut the deck and dealt out four hands on the chair between them. When he turned the cards over, she saw that he'd dealt out four royal flushes.

"Are you certain you won't play?" he asked.

"After seeing that?" Annja nodded. "I'm certain."

Smiling a little, like a small boy who has performed a good trick, Roux said, "Not even if I promise not to cheat?"

"No."

"You can trust me."

Annja looked at him.

"I believe in the game," Roux said. "Cheating…cheapens the sport."

"Sure."

Roux shrugged. "Let's play a couple hands. I'll put up a thousand dollars against the trinket you found in that cave."

"No."

"We could be here for hours." Roux shuffled the cards hopefully.

"Mademoiselle Creed."

Glancing up, Annja saw a handsome man in a black three-piece suit standing in front of her. His dark hair was combed carefully back and he had a boyish smile.

"I'm Annja Creed," she said.

The man looked around. No one else sat in the waiting room.

"I'd rather gathered that you were." He held out his hand. "I am Inspector Richelieu."

"Like the cardinal," Annja said, taking his hand and standing.

"In name only," the inspector said.

Since Cardinal Richelieu had been responsible for thousands of people being beheaded on the guillotine, Annja realized her faux pas.

"Sorry," she said. "I haven't met anyone with that name before. I meant no insult."

"I assure you, *mademoiselle,* no insult was taken." Richelieu pointed to the rear of the room. "If you would care to join me, I will take your statement in my office."

6

Brother Gaspar of the Brotherhood of the Silent Rain sat at his desk and contemplated his future. It was not a pleasant task. Thankfully, there was not much of it left. Surely no more than three or four more thousand mornings and as many evenings.

He wore a black robe against the chill that filled the room. The years had drawn him lean and spare. Beneath his cowl, his head was shaved and his skin was sallow from seldom seeing the light of day. He got out at night. All of his order did, but they couldn't be seen during the day because it raised too many questions among the townsfolk.

As leader of the Brotherhood of the Silent Rain, he did not truly have a future. His mission was to protect and unlock the past. If he succeeded in the first, no one would ever know the monstrous predations his order had allowed to take place three hundred years ago.

But if he succeeded in the second and unlocked the past, made everything right again, his whole life would change. He looked forward to that possibility.

Even at sixty-eight years old, he believed he had a few good years left. It wasn't that he looked forward to getting out into the world. He had renounced all of that when he took his vows. But he had read all the books and manuscripts in his small post.

He longed for the true manuscripts, the ones he had seen as a child in Rome, where he'd been trained in the secrets he had to keep. The documents that told of secret histories and covered holders of power who weren't known to the general masses.

He sighed and his gentle breath nearly extinguished the guttering candles that illuminated the stone cave. The monastery, hidden from sight, was located deep inside the Cévennes Mountains. It wasn't a true edifice built by the hand of men in service to the church. Rather, it was an aberration within the earth that earlier monks had discovered and elaborated on.

On good days, Brother Gaspar thought of the monastery as a gift from God, made expressly for his order. On bad days, he thought of it as a prison.

He sat at his desk and wrote his weekly letter to Bishop Taglio, who guided his moves and provided counsel when needed. Although written with handmade ink, in elegant calligraphy, on paper made by the order, the letter was merely perfunctory. It was merely a chore that occupied his head and his hands for a short time.

After thirty-seven years, since he had taken on the mantle of the leader of the order, Brother Gaspar had begun to have difficulty finding ways to express the situation. *Everything is fine and going according to plan. We are still searching for that which was lost.*

He kept the references deliberately vague. Enemies didn't quite abound these days as they had three hundred years ago, but they were still out there.

In fact, even a few treasure hunters had joined the pack.

Corvin Lesauvage had snooped around for years. Over the past few the man had become extremely aggressive in his search. He had killed two monks who had fallen into his hands, torturing them needlessly because they didn't know anything to assuage his curiosity.

Only Brother Gaspar knew that, and he shuddered to think about falling into Lesauvage's hands. Of course, he would not. He would die before that happened.

His fellow monks had orders to kill him the instant he fell into someone else's custody. Since he never went anywhere alone, and seldom ventured outside the monastery walls, he didn't think he would ever be at risk.

Only the imminent disclosure of the secrets he protected would bring him forth. God willing, he would find the truth of those secrets himself. But, as they had remained hidden for three hundred years, there was little chance of that.

"Master."

Startled, Brother Gaspar looked up from his broad table and the letter he had been writing. "Yes. Come forward that I may see you."

Brother Napier stepped from the shadows. He wore hiking clothes, tattoos and piercings, and looked like any young man who prowled the Parisian streets.

"Yes, Brother Napier," Brother Gaspar inquired.

"I did not mean to bother you while you were at your letter," the younger monk stated.

Brother Gaspar put his pen in the inkwell with slow deliberation. "But you have."

"For good reason, master."

"What is it?"

"The woman has found something."

"The American?"

"Yes, master. She found La Bête's cave."

Angry and frightened, Brother Gaspar surged to his feet. He leaned on the desk and his arms trembled. "It can't be."

Kneeling in supplication, Brother Napier held up his hands. Sheets of papers containing images rested on them. "It is true, master. I saw the cave myself. But only for a short time. The earth closed back over it." He looked at Brother Gaspar. "I saw it, master. I saw the Beast of Gévaudan. The stories were *true*."

Of course they were, the older monk thought. Otherwise we would not all be trapped here.

Rounding the desk, Brother Gaspar took the papers from the young monk's hands. He stared at the pictures. They showed the young American woman on the mountaintop and apparently running for her life. Other pictures showed motorcycles chasing an SUV.

"You saw La Bête?" Brother Gaspar asked.

"Yes."

"Was it—" he hesitated "—alive?"

"No. It was dead. Very dead. A warrior killed it."

"A warrior?" Excitement flared through Brother Gaspar. The old stories were true. The knowledge offered validation for all the years he had spent at the monastery. "How do you know a warrior killed it?"

"Because he was still there."

"The warrior?"

"Yes, master."

"He was dead, as well?" Brother Gaspar doubted the man could have been in any other shape, but just knowing the story was true and knowing all the arcane things connected with it, he felt compelled to ask.

"Yes, master. It looked as though he and La Bête had fought and killed each other."

Brother Gaspar felt the air in the cave grow thicker than normal. "Did you examine La Bête's body or that of the warrior?" he asked.

"I did. But only for a short time. The cavern was shaking. The earthquake was still going on. Luckily, I got out before the cavern closed."

"It closed?"

"Yes, master."

"You could find this place again?"

The young monk nodded. "But it would do no good, master. The earth has sealed the cave tightly." He paused. "Perhaps a quake another day will reveal it again."

"We will watch for this, then," Brother Gaspar said. His hand caressed his throat. "When you looked at the warrior, did you see anything?"

"You mean the necklace?"

Brother Gaspar's heart beat sped up. "Yes," he replied in a hoarse whisper.

The necklace was the greatest secret of them all.

"The American woman carried a necklace from the cave," the young monk said.

"You followed her?" Brother Gaspar asked.

"As far as I could," the young monk agreed. "She was pursued."

"By who?"

"Lesauvage's men."

That announcement poured ice water into the old monk's veins. "How did they get there?"

"They followed the woman. I only happened to be in the mountains when I saw her with the old man."

"What old man?" Brother Gaspar was alarmed.

"I do not know, master."

Brother Gaspar went through the sheets of pictures. "Is he in these?"

"Sadly, no. I thought I took his picture, but when I developed the images, I found I had not."

Brother Gaspar, whose life had been so carefully ordered for so very long, felt very unsettled. He didn't like the fact that Lesauvage's men had been so close to the discovery of La Bête or that his monks had merely been lucky.

When he had found out about the American television person, he had dismissed her at once. *Chasing History's Monsters* was pure entertainment and a complete waste of time. No one doing research for such a show presented any threat to uncovering his secrets. Or so he had believed.

"Who has the necklace now?" Brother Gaspar asked.

"The woman, I think." Brother Napier looked flustered. "Lesauvage's men gave pursuit, but the American woman and the old man shot back at them and escaped."

"Where is the American woman?"

"She was staying in Lozère. I don't know where."

Lamenting that he hadn't given more thought to the threat the woman might have posed, Brother Gaspar sighed. "Find her. Find out if she still has the necklace."

"And if she does, master?"

"Take it from her and bring it to me."

"Of course." Brother Napier bowed and backed out of the room.

Resentfully, Brother Gaspar glared at the table. His nearly completed letter sat there.

It would have to be rewritten, of course. And he would have to call the bishop. Perhaps, Brother Gaspar thought, he would soon be free of his prison.

7

Inspector Richelieu's office was neat and compact. Not the kind of office Annja expected of a working policeman. She'd seen cop's offices before. None of them were this pristine.

She wondered if maybe Richelieu was gay or lived with his mother. Or perhaps he was a control freak. A personality trait like that was a real relationship killer.

Not that Annja was looking for a relationship. But the inspector did have nice eyes and nice hands. Her mind wandered for a moment.

"Have a seat," Richelieu invited, waving to the chair across from his tiny metal desk.

Annja sat. In the too neat office, she felt dirty and grimy. Outside in the main office with the other policemen, she'd felt that she belonged. Now she wanted a hot bath and a change of clothing. And food. She suddenly realized she was starving.

"I gave a statement to one of the officers," Annja said.

"I know." Richelieu sat on the other side of the desk. "I read it. Both versions."

While waiting for something—anything—to happen, Annja had written up her statement herself in addition to the one the policeman had taken. She hadn't trusted his eye for detail. Or his ear.

"Your penmanship and your French are exquisite," Richelieu commented.

"Thanks," Annja said, "but I wasn't here for a grade."

Richelieu smiled. "I've also been investigating the supposed site of the chase down the mountain."

"Supposed?" Annja echoed.

"Yes." The inspector looked concerned for a moment. "Would you prefer to speak in English? I'm quite good at it and perhaps it would be easier."

"French is fine," Annja said.

"I thought perhaps you hadn't understood."

"I understood perfectly." Annja put an edge to her words. Getting dismissed out of hand in the field of archaeology because she was a woman was something she'd had to deal with often. She didn't take it lightly. "There was no 'supposed' chase site. It was there. Along with two or three dead men."

Richelieu waited a moment, then shook his head. "No dead men."

Annja thought about that. "Perhaps Lesauvage had the bodies picked up."

"Why would he do that?"

"I don't know," Annja replied. "I came here to you to find out why he would send men looking for me in the first place."

"Do you know that he sent the men?"

"I overheard one of the men say that they were working for Lesauvage."

"But you don't know that they, in fact, did."

"Why would they say they were if they weren't?"

The inspector looked amused and perplexed. "I'm quite sure I wouldn't know"

"I could ask Lesauvage," Annja said.

"I thought you didn't know him."

"Maybe you could introduce us," Annja suggested with a smile. The inspector wasn't the only one who could play games. He was just the only one at the moment with some reason to.

A sour smile pulled at Richelieu's lips. He pulled at his left ear. "You're intimating that I have some kind of personal relationship with Lesauvage?"

Returning his gaze full measure, Annja asked, "Are you sure speaking French works for you? Maybe English translates more plainly."

Richelieu scowled. "I didn't come here to listen to disparaging remarks directed at me, Miss Creed."

"I didn't come here to cool my heels for three hours, then get patted on the head and sent away."

Opening the slim notebook computer on his desk, Richelieu opened a file that displayed several pictures. "We investigated the site. I took these pictures. I found expended cartridges, bullets in the trees and scorch marks." He paused. "No bodies. No motorcycles."

"Then Lesauvage picked them up."

"Why?"

"So he wouldn't be implicated."

Closing the computer, Richelieu looked at her. "I was hoping to establish the veracity of your claim, Miss Creed. I did find damage done out in the forest—which is federally protected, I might add, and something you might be called upon to answer for—but nothing that you and your friend couldn't have done yourselves."

"We didn't intentionally damage the forest," Annja said. She was annoyed. Truthfully, she hadn't expected much in the way of help from the police. This man, Lesauvage, appeared to have a large organization at his beck and call. Assuming he had inroads with the local police was no great leap of imagination.

"So you say," the inspector said.

"I *do* say."

"I will note your disavowal in my reports."

"Why would we do something like that?" Annja asked, exasperated.

Richelieu spread his hands. "You're a television personality, Miss Creed. Here in Lozère chasing a monster that's three hundred years old. Perhaps you thought tales of a running gun battle through the forest would, perhaps, *spice up* your tale. For your viewers. I am told that you people in television will do anything to improve your ratings."

"I wouldn't do that," Annja said angrily.

"Perhaps not. But there were no bodies out there. Nor was there a giant crevasse leading to an underground cave containing the remains of La Bête."

"The earthquake must have closed it back up."

Richelieu nodded. "Amazing, isn't it, that nature herself would align against you?"

"What about the bullet holes in the old man's SUV?"

"A lover's quarrel?"

Frowning, Annja said, "Me? And that old man? Please."

Richelieu laughed. "Perhaps it was over business. Perhaps you were both shooting at game and hit the truck instead."

"No."

"Your report here could be just to falsify an insurance claim."

"That's not what happened."

"But you are on the show with the woman with the... *problematic* apparel."

Terrific, Annja thought. Maybe poltergeists could get chased away from historic manors, but she'd be haunted by Kristie Chatham's bodacious ta-tas forever.

"I have never had a problem with my apparel," Annja pointed out.

"I have made a note of that, as well."

Annja reached into her pack and took out her digital camera. She switched it on and brought up the pictures she'd shot inside the cave. In spite of the darkness, the images had turned out well.

"This is La Bête," Annja said.

Taking the camera, Richelieu consulted the images, punching through them one by one. He handed the camera back. "Anyone with Photoshop could make these."

"And take the time to put them on a camera?" Annja couldn't believe it.

"It would," the inspector said as inoffensively as he could, "make your story seem more legitimate. When *The Blair Witch Project* appeared in theaters, many people believed the video footage was part of an actual paranormal investigation. And Orson Welles anchoring *The War of the Worlds* in news reports on the radio in 1938 was also deliberate, causing mass hysteria throughout your country. Media people know best how to present anything they wish to."

"Those are real pictures," Annja stated.

"If you insist."

Angrily, Annja put the camera away. "Who is Lesauvage?"

"A figment of your overactive imagination," Richelieu said.

Without a word, Annja got up to leave.

"Or…" Richelieu let the word dangle like a fishing lure.

Annja waited. Mysteries always kept her hanging well past the point she should leave.

"Or he's a man named Corvin Lesauvage," Richelieu said. "If it is this man, he's very dangerous. He's a known criminal, though that's never been successfully proved. Witnesses have a tendency to…disappear. Likewise, so do past business associates."

"Can you help me with him?"

"Can you offer me any proof that he's truly after you, Miss Creed?"

Annja thought for a moment. "There was a man who was knocked unconscious in an alley earlier this morning. In the downtown area."

More interested now, Richelieu leaned forward. "Do you know something about that?"

Ignoring the question, Annja asked, "Did he work for Corvin Lesauvage?"

"We don't know."

"Then I suggest you ask him."

Richelieu frowned. "We can't."

"Why not?"

"He was killed. Less than an hour after we took him into custody."

Annja thought about that. Evidently there was something at stake here that she didn't know about. "Did Lesauvage do it?"

"We don't know who did it."

Meaning you don't know if it was done by an inmate or a police officer, Annja thought.

"There was a local boy with me this morning," Annja said. "His name is Avery Moreau. I hired him to set up my trip, arrange for things."

Richelieu nodded. "I know Avery. He's a sad case."

"Why?"

"His father died quite suddenly a few weeks ago."

"I don't understand," Annja said.

"His father was shot to death."

"By Lesauvage?" Annja asked, thinking maybe the men had been after Avery more than her.

"No," Richelieu said. "By me."

Annja didn't know what to say to that, so she said nothing. She wondered if perhaps Richelieu was warning her.

"Gerard Moreau, Avery's father, was a small-time burglar," Richelieu said. "He'd been in and out of jail for years. That is a matter of record and was covered in the media. It was only a matter of time before we put him away for good or a homeowner shot him. As it happened, I shot him while investigating the report of a burglary. He hadn't made it out of the house and came at me with a weapon." The inspector leaned back in his chair. "Needless to say, Avery Moreau has been less than cooperative."

Thinking about things for a moment, Annja said, "Let's say for a moment that you believe me about the chase down the mountain."

Richelieu smiled. "Let's."

"Why would Lesauvage recover the bodies of the dead men?"

"To avoid being implicated."

"Which is what I said."

"You did. It's a conclusion that fits the facts as you present them. We're entertaining that for the moment."

"Why would Lesauvage risk sending men after me in the first place?"

"You know, Miss Creed," Richelieu said with a smile, "as

I read your reports and listened to you now, I have asked myself that several times. I'm open to your suggestion."

Annja had no idea what was going on. The weight of the charm rested heavily in her pocket. She hadn't told the inspector about it. If she had, he would have taken it away. Countries were funny about things that might be national treasures.

"I don't know," Annja finally said. "But I intend to find out."

OUT IN THE MAIN ROOM, Roux was playing poker with some policemen. He looked up as Annja stepped from the inspector's office.

Annja walked past him.

"Gentlemen, it's been a pleasure, but I'm afraid I have to go now," Roux said as he gathered the pile of money he'd won. He winked at the policemen and fell into step with Annja. "Are we going somewhere?"

"No."

"Humph," Roux said. "Our friend the inspector didn't believe your story?"

"Someone removed the bodies," she said. "The quake closed the cave again."

"Pity. It would have been an exciting episode for your show."

She whirled on him. "You know about *Chasing History's Monsters*?"

"I must confess," Roux admitted, "I'm something of a fan, I'm afraid. Not quite as stimulating as *Survivor*, but well worth the investment of time. I particularly like...I can't remember her name. The girl with the clothing problems." He smiled a little.

"You would," Annja said, disgusted.

Look at the fire in her, Roux thought. Simply amazing.

"I'm a man of simple pleasures," Roux said.

"Mr. Roux," Inspector Richelieu called out.

Roux turned to face the man. "Yes, Inspector?"

"Would you like to make a statement?"

Grinning, Roux shook his head. "No. Thank you." When he turned around, he discovered that Annja had left him. She was making her way out the door. He hurried to catch up.

Night had fallen while they were inside the police station. Shadows draped the streets.

"You'll have a hard time finding a cab at this time of night," Roux said.

She ignored him, arms folded over her breasts and facing the street.

"Probably," Roux went on, "walking back to wherever you're staying wouldn't be the wisest thing you could do."

She still didn't respond.

"I could give you a ride," Roux suggested. More than anything, he wanted a look at the metal charm she had found in the cave. If it was what he thought it was, his long search might at last be over. "I at least owe you that after what we've been through."

She looked at him then. "You didn't try to tell them about the men who chased us."

"No."

"Why?"

"I knew they wouldn't listen."

She continued to glare at him.

"Corvin Lesauvage," Roux said, "is a very connected man in this area. A very dangerous man."

"Tell me about him."

"Over dinner," Roux countered. "I know a little bistro not far from here that has some of the best wines you could hope for."

She looked at him askance.

"You won't regret it," Roux said.

8

The bistro did carry a very fine selection of wines. Roux insisted on their sampling a variety during dinner. The meal was superb. Annja devoured filet mignon, steamed vegetables, baked potatoes smothered in cheese, salads and rolls as big as her fist and so fresh from the oven they almost burned her fingers.

She hadn't eaten since breakfast, so she didn't strive for modesty. She ate with gusto, and Roux complimented her on her appetite.

As it turned out, Roux didn't know much about Corvin Lesauvage. All he had was a collection of vague rumors. Lesauvage was a murderer several times over. He ran drugs. He peddled archaeological forgeries. If an illegal dollar was made in the Lozère area, ten percent of it belonged to Corvin Lesauvage because he brokered the deal, allowed it to take place or kept quiet about it.

The bistro was quiet and dark. French love songs played softly in the background. A wall of trickling water backlit by aquamarine lights kept the shadows at bay. The wait staff proved almost undetectable.

Warmed by the wine, exhausted by her exertions, Annja found herself relaxing perhaps a little more than she should have. But her curiosity about Roux was rampant.

"Are you French?" she asked after they had finished discovering how little he knew about Lesauvage.

"As French as can be," Roux promised. He refilled her glass, then his own.

"Yet you speak Latin fluently."

Roux gestured magnanimously. "Doesn't everyone?"

"No. What do you do, Mr. Roux?"

"Please," he said, turning up a hand, "just call me Roux. It's a name that's suited me long enough."

"The question's still on the table," Annja pointed out.

"So it is." He sipped his wine. "Truthfully? I do whatever pleases me. If fortune smiles on me, there's a reason to get up in the morning. If I'm truly blessed, there are several reasons."

"Then you must be independently wealthy," Annja said, half in jest.

"Yes," he admitted. "Very. I've had plenty of time to amass a fortune. It's not hard if you live long enough and don't try to be greedy."

"Where do you live?"

"In Paris." Roux smiled. "I've always loved Paris. Even after it's gotten as gaudy and overpopulated and dirty as it has. You open the window in the morning there, you can almost feel the magic in the air."

"How did you make your fortune?"

"Slowly. Investments, mostly. I've been very lucky where investments are concerned. I've always been able to take the long view, I suppose."

Annja eyed him over her glass. "How old are you?"

"Far, far older than I look, I assure you." His blue eyes twinkled merrily.

Santa Claus should have eyes like that, Annja couldn't help thinking.

"You are quite aggressive in your investigative approach," he said gently.

"I've been accused of that before." Annja leaned forward, studying him. "I've made my peace with it. As an archaeologist, you're trained to ask questions. Of the situation. Of the people around you. Of yourself."

"I see."

"What were you doing up in the mountains this afternoon?"

"Taking a constitutional."

Annja smiled. Despite the abrasive nature the old man brought out in her, there was something about him that she liked. He was as openly secretive as the nuns at the orphanage where she'd grown up.

"I don't believe you," she told him.

"I take no offense," he told her. "I wouldn't believe me, either."

"You were looking for something."

Roux shrugged.

"But you're not going to tell me what it is," Annja said.

"Let me ask you something." Roux leaned in close to her and spoke conspiratorially. "You found something in that cave this afternoon, didn't you?"

Annja picked at a bit of leftover bread and used the time to think. "I found La Bête."

"A creature that you believe was once La Bête."

"I showed you the pictures."

"I saw it, too," Roux reminded her.

"You don't believe it was La Bête?" Annja asked.

"Perhaps." Roux lifted his shoulders and dropped them. "The light was uncertain. Things were happening very quickly in there."

"What do you think it was?"

"A fabrication, perhaps."

"It was real." Annja had no doubt about that.

"There's something else I'm interested in," the old man replied. "Something you haven't told me. I saw you in that cave. You had something in your hand."

"A human skull," she replied.

"That isn't all."

The charm was still in Annja's pocket. She'd had it out only once. That was back in the police station bathroom. She'd been afraid the police were going to take charm away from her so she'd made a rubbing of both sides in her journal.

"I saw you with something else in your hand," he said. "Something shiny. Something metallic. It looked old." He paused. "If you found it in the cave, I would think it was very old."

"Not when compared to the Mesozoic period."

Roux laughed. The sound was easy and pleasant.

Annja found herself laughing with him, but thought it was as much because of the wine as of the humor in the situation. She didn't trust him. She was certain his presence in the mountains was no accident.

"Touché," he replied. He sipped more wine. "Still, you have me intrigued, Miss Creed."

She looked at him. "I don't trust you. But don't take that personally. I don't trust most people."

"In your current state of affairs, with a criminal figure

pursuing you for some unknown, nefarious reason, I wouldn't be the trusting sort, either."

"I was taught by the best to be slightly paranoid."

Roux lifted his eyebrows. "The Central Intelligence Agency?"

"Worse than that," Annja said. "Catholic nuns."

Roux grinned. "Ah, that explains it."

"The paranoia?"

"The fact that you don't come bursting out of your shirts on the television program." Roux looked at her appraisingly. "You're certainly equipped."

Annja stared at him. "Are you coming on to me?"

"Would it be appropriate?"

"No."

Roux tapped the table with his hand. "Then that settles it. I was *not* coming on to you. It's the wine, the candlelight in your hair and the sparkle in those marvelous green eyes. A moment in a beautiful restaurant after a delightful repast."

"I think," Annja said, "that you probably hit on anything that has a heartbeat and stays in one place long enough."

Leaning back in his chair, Roux laughed uproariously. He drew the unwelcome attention of several other diners. Finally, he regained control of himself. "I do like you, Miss Creed. I find you…refreshing."

Annja sipped her wine and considered her options. So far, the origins of the charm had stumped her. She looked at the old man. "I'm going to trust you. A little."

"In what capacity?"

"Something professional."

Anticipation gleamed in his bright blue eyes. "Whatever you found in the cave?"

"Yes. How experienced are you in antiquities?"

Roux shrugged. "I've made more than a few fortunes dabbling in such luxuries. There are a great many forgeries out there, you know."

Annja did know. She had dealt with several of them. In addition to everything else she did, she also consulted on museum acquisitions and for private buyers. Her certificate of authenticity marked many of them.

"This isn't a forgery." She took the piece of metal from her pocket and placed it on the table between them.

A look of pleasant surprise filled Roux's face. "You didn't give it to the inspector?"

"No."

"Why?"

"He didn't possess an archaeologist's mind-set."

"I see." Roux gestured to the medallion. "May I?"

"As long as I can watch you, sure." Annja leaned in and watched carefully.

"You carried this unprotected in your pocket?" His voice carried recrimination.

"I wasn't able to properly store it."

"Perhaps something in your backpack."

"Perhaps the police could have gone through my things."

"Yes. Of course." Roux pushed the medallion around, studying the image stamped onto it.

As he touched the charm, the fiery vision that had filled Annja's head during the earthquake returned to her in full Technicolor.

"Are you all right?" He was looking at her.

"Yes," she said, though she didn't honestly know.

"Do you know what this is?" Roux asked.

"A talisman of some sort. Probably for good luck." Annja described how she had found it tied around the dead man's neck.

"Not very lucky," Roux said.

"He killed the Beast of Gévaudan."

"Even if this nameless warrior had received the glory due him, fame is a poor consolation prize."

"I don't think he was interested in prizes."

"You believe he was slaying a monster."

"Yes," Annja replied. Despite her experience disproving myths, she had always believed in slaying monsters.

"Do you know what this symbol is?" Roux asked.

Moving the flickering candle flame closer to the charm, Annja shook her head. "I've never seen it before."

"Nor have I." Roux reached into his pocket and took out a Leatherman Multitool. He held the charm in his fingers and aimed the point at the grimy buildup surrounding the image of the wolf and the mountain.

"Wait a minute," Annja said.

"Trust me. I'll be careful. I know what I'm doing."

Breathing slowly, Annja watched. She didn't think the old man could hurt the charm, but she didn't like having it out of her possession.

Roux worked gently. The grime fell away in tiny flakes. Beneath it, the metal proved as lustrous and shiny as the day it had been forged.

Given the conditions of the cave, Annja had expected a fair amount of preservation. Ships had spent hundreds of years in caves and were found remarkably intact, as if the pirates who had hidden there had only left days ago instead of centuries.

"Beautiful," Roux whispered when he had finished. He turned the piece of metal in his fingers, catching the candlelight again and again.

Annja silently agreed. "Have you ever seen anything like this?"

"A good-luck charm? Of course I have."

"Not just a good-luck charm," Annja said, "but one like this."

Roux shook his head. "It's a charm. I believe that. Since you found it around the dead man's neck, I'd say it was made to defend him—"

"—against the Beast of Gévaudan," Annja finished. "I got that. But the mark on the obverse looks like it was struck by a die. The wolf and the mountain appeared to have been carved."

"So you believe this to be a unique piece rather than one of many?" Roux asked.

"I do," Annja agreed. "You can see the die mark wasn't struck quite cleanly and two of the edges are slightly blunted."

Peering more closely at the charm, Roux said, "You have very good eyes." He studied the image for a moment. "And, you're exactly right." He looked up at her.

"Have you seen such a die mark before?" Annja asked.

"No."

Studying the old man, Annja tried to figure out if he was lying to her. If he was, she decided, he was very good at it. "I was hoping you had."

"Never. I would be very interested to learn what you find out about it." Roux studied her. "Tell me, in your archaeological travels, have you ever had cause to research the history of Joan of Arc?"

"I'm familiar with her stories, but I've spent no real time with them," Annja said.

"Pity. She was a very tragic figure."

For just a moment, Annja remembered the visions she had experienced. Joan of Arc had burned at the stake not far from where Annja now sat. Had her subconscious summoned that image during the quake?

"She was a very brave young woman," Roux said. "Foolish, certainly, but brave nonetheless. She should not be forgotten."

What are you trying to tell me? Annja wondered.

"One thing you should start doing immediately is taking better care of this charm." Roux said. "After all, it could prove to be a significant find if you discover its history." Roux took a handkerchief from his pocket and dropped the charm into the center of it. Picking up the ends of the handkerchief, he folded the charm inside. Then he handed the makeshift package to Annja with a smile. "There. That should better protect it until you can put it in a proper storage container."

Annja closed her hand over the handkerchief and felt the hard outline of the disk inside. She put the handkerchief into her shorts pocket and closed the Velcro tab.

"Thank you," she said.

Roux looked around, then tapped the table and said, "I'll be back in just a moment. Too much wine."

Comfortable and almost sleepy, Annja settled back in her chair and relaxed. Thoughts of the cozy bed at the bed-and-breakfast where she was staying danced in her head. She tried to marshal her thoughts and figure out her next course of action.

Identification of the charm was paramount. Doug Morrell would love the story and not hesitate at all over the digital pictures she had taken of La Bête. The television producer wasn't like some police inspectors Annja had met.

Thinking of Inspector Richelieu reminded Annja of Corvin Lesauvage. It didn't make sense to think that a well-organized crime figure would send a team after her for the camera equipment and whatever cash she carried.

But that wasn't what they were after, was it? The man had wanted her. Lesauvage had wanted to talk to her.

She started to feel frightened.

Suddenly she realized how much time had passed since Roux had quit the table. He had been gone a long time. Too long.

Glancing around the bistro, Annja discovered that the server and the manager were watching her. She stood and looked outside. Sure enough, the bullet-scarred SUV was no longer parked at the curb.

"Mademoiselle?"

Annja turned and found the young brunette server standing at the table.

"Is something the matter, *mademoiselle?*" the young woman asked.

"I don't suppose he paid the bill before he ducked out, did he?" Annja asked.

"No, *mademoiselle.*"

Annja sighed and took out the cash she carried. "How much is it?"

The server told her.

"That much?" Annja was surprised. She put her money back and reached for her credit card.

The waitress nodded contritely, obviously still hopeful of a large tip.

"He was supposed to be independently wealthy," Annja said. "Several times over."

"Yes, *mademoiselle.*" The server took Annja's credit card and retreated.

Then Annja remembered how Roux had effortlessly

shuffled and cut the deck of cards one-handed at the police station. A sick feeling twisted in her stomach.

She removed the folded handkerchief from her pocket. The disk shape was still there, but the panic within her grew as she opened the cloth package.

Inside the folds she found a two-euro coin. It was two-toned, brass and silvery, bright and shiny new.

Just the right size to make her think Roux had handed her the charm. Not only had he stuck her with the bistro tab, but he had also stolen her find.

Carefully, she folded the coin back in the handkerchief, noting that it was monogrammed with a crimson *R*. If she got lucky, he'd left her with more than he'd intended.

9

"You're getting back quite late, Mademoiselle Creed."

"I am, François. I'm sorry. I should have called." Annja
stood in the doorway of the bed-and-breakfast. She'd come
in feeling inept and foolish, and angry with the local police
because they didn't know Roux and hadn't even bothered to
ask his name. No one had even taken down his license plate.
She'd wasted an hour and a half discovering that.

She hated feeling guilty on top of it.

The clock on the mantel above the fireplace showed that
it was almost eleven p.m.

François Lambert was a retired carpenter who had thought
ahead. While building homes for others, François had also
built for his own retirement years. The bed-and-breakfast was
located a few miles north of Lozère, far enough out of the
town to afford privacy and a good view of the Cévennes
Mountains.

One of the things that Annja loved most about her
vocation was the endless possibility of meeting people. They

hailed from all walks of life, and were driven by all kinds of dreams and desires.

Over seventy years old, François was long and lanky, a whipcord man used to a life filled with hard work. He had a headful of white hair brushed back and touching his collar. His white mustache looked elegant and aristocratic. He wore slacks and a white shirt.

François waved away her apology. "I was worried about you, that's all. Lozère can be dangerous sometimes when it is dark." He studied her. "But you are all right, yes?"

"I am. Thank you."

He took a pack of cigarettes from his pocket and shook one out. He lit up with a lighter. "I heard the police were involved."

Small towns, Annja thought, you have to love them. She did, too. They were usually quaint and exotic and moved to their own rhythm.

But gossip spread as aggressively as running bamboo.

"I was attacked," Annja said. "Up in the mountains."

François shook his leonine head. "A beautiful woman such as yourself shouldn't be out alone. I told you that."

"I know. I promise I'll be more careful in the future." Annja started up the stairs.

"Were you injured?"

"No. I was lucky."

"I heard Corvin Lesauvage was involved."

Annja froze halfway up the stairs. "Do you know anything about him?"

A pensive frown tightened her host's lined face. "Very little. I'm told that is the best thing to know about him. Lesauvage is a bad man."

"Inspector Richelieu told me that, as well."

"You went to him for help?" François looked concerned.

"He was assigned to the investigation."

"He is not a good man, either, that one. He tends to take care of things his way."

Annja hesitated a moment. "I was told he shot Avery Moreau's father."

"Yes." François looked sad. "It is a bad way for a boy to lose his father. Avery, he struggles with right and wrong, you see. At least when his father was around, knowing that his father was a thief, he had an idea of what he didn't want to be when he grew up."

"You didn't mention this when I hired him to help me," Annja said.

François's face colored a little. "If I had, would you have hired him?"

Annja answered honestly. "I don't know."

"I was only looking out for the boy. Someone needs to. But I should have told you."

"This," she said, wanting to let the old man off the hook, "had nothing to do with that."

"I hope not."

"I'm sure it doesn't."

François nodded. "Camille wanted to know if you would be joining us for breakfast."

"Yes," Annja said. "I've got a lot to do tomorrow. There is one thing you could help me with."

"If I may," he agreed.

She asked for some rosin from his violin kit and was quickly supplied with a small portion in a coffee cup. After thanking François, Annja said good night and went up to the room she'd rented.

She had a lot to do tonight. She didn't intend to let Roux get away with what he'd done.

ANNJA'S RENTED ROOM WAS small and cozy. Camille Lambert had filled it with sensible curtains and linens. But the bed, desk, chair and trunk all spoke of François's knowing hands.

She opened the windows and stood for just a moment as the night breeze filled the room. She took a deep breath and let go of the anger and frustration she felt. Those emotions were good motivators, but they wouldn't sustain her during a project.

No, for that she'd always relied on curiosity.

This time, there were a number of things to be curious about. Why was a man like Lesauvage interested in her? Why had Roux stolen the charm she'd found in La Bête's lair? Could the hidden cave in the Cévennes Mountains be found again? What did the designs on the charm mean?

And who was Roux?

Annja started with that.

Although the house was wired with electricity, power outages sometimes occurred. The Lamberts had shown her where the candles were kept for emergencies.

She took one of the candles, placed it in a holder on the desk and lit it. Then she held one of her metal notebooks a few inches over the flame. In a short time, a considerable amount of lampblack covered the metal surface.

Using a thin-bladed knife she generally used on dig sites, Annja scraped most of the lampblack into the coffee cup with the rosin. When she was satisfied she had enough of the black residue, she used the knife handle to grind the lampblack into the rosin. The mixture quickly turned dark gray.

She spread Roux's handkerchief on the desk. Using one of the fine brushes from her kit, she dumped some powder onto the euro coin.

Gently, she blew away the powder. When she could remove no more in this manner, she employed the brush, using deft strokes like those she would use on a fragile piece of pottery to reveal the images she was after.

A fingerprint stood out on the coin.

Annja smiled. Roux hadn't been as clever as he'd believed.

Working with meticulous care, which was a necessary skill in archaeology, she trapped the fingerprint on clear tape. She mounted her discovery on a plain white index card.

Taking a brief respite from the backbreaking labor, Annja straightened and placed her notebook computer on the desk. She hooked it to her satellite phone, then used the Web service to log on to the Internet.

Moving mechanically, she brought up alt.archaeology and alt.archaeology.esoterica, her favorite Usenet newsgroups. The former was a format for archaeology and history professors, students and enthusiasts to meet and share ideas. The latter held discourse on more inventive matters.

If she needed hard information, Annja resorted to alt.archaeology. But if she needed something more along the lines for guesswork, she would generally post to alt.archaeology.esoterica.

Since she had no idea where to begin with the images of the charm, she elected to post to both.

Taking her digital camera from her backpack, she changed lenses and switched the function over to manual instead of automatic. She also used a flash separate from the camera rather than mounted on it.

Working quickly, confidently, she took pictures of the rubbings of the charm she'd made in her journal. Then she took pictures of the fingerprint from the coin.

Opening a new topic on the alt.archaeology newsgroup, Annja quickly wrote a short note.

I'm seeking information about the following images found on a charm/talisman/coin? Not sure which. I saw it in France recently, at a small town called Lozère. It caught my attention and now I can't get it out of my mind. Can anyone help? Is it just a tourist geegaw?

She framed her request like that to detract immediate attention. She knew if she sounded like a newbie other wannabe experts wouldn't leave her alone and would try to impress her. Hopefully only someone who knew something about the images would bother to respond.

She attached the images of the charm's rubbings and sent the postings to both newsgroups.

Going to her e-mail service, she opened her account, ignored the latest rash of spam and picked a name from her address book.

Bart McGilley was a Brooklyn cop she occasionally dated when she was home. He was a nice guy, on his way to making detective at the precinct. They had a good time whenever they were together. Thankfully, he shared an interest in some of the city's more historical settings and museums.

She typed a quick note.

Hey Bart,
I'm in France doing a workup on a piece for *Monsters*. I'm keeping my blouse together, so I'm having to make this good. Points of interest, rather than interesting points.

I ran into a guy who swiped something from me. Nothing big. But I thought if I could give the police his name, it might help.

I know it's a big favor to ask, but could you run this print?
Best,
Annja

She attached the image of the fingerprint and sent it. She also took a moment to send the pictures of La Bête and the cave to Doug Morrell. Then she retreated to her bathroom.

One of the finest things François Lambert had done in creating his retirement business was to add a soaker tub to each guest bathroom. It wasn't something that many bed-and-breakfasts in the area had. But it was one of the selling points that had caught Annja's attention.

Once the tub was filled, she eased in and turned on the jets. In seconds, the heat and the turbulence worked to wash away the stress and tension of the day.

CONTROLLING THE EXCITEMENT that filled him, Roux drove toward the iron gates of his estate outside Paris. The land was wooded and hilly. The large stone manor house and outbuildings couldn't easily be seen even by helicopter.

At a touch of a button on the steering wheel, the iron gates separated and rolled back quietly. An armed guard stepped out from the gatehouse holding an assault rifle.

"Mr. Roux," the man said.

Roux knew another man waited for confirmation inside the bulletproof and bombproof gatehouse. Not only was his landscape well tended, but so was his security. He paid dearly for it and never begrudged the price.

"Yes," Roux said, turning his head so he could be clearly illuminated by the guard's flashlight.

The guard swept the SUV with his beam. "Ran into some trouble?"

"A little," Roux admitted. There was no way to conceal the bullet holes from a trained eye.

"Anything we should know about?"

The guard was American. He was direct and thorough. Those were qualities that Roux loved about the Americans. Of course, they balanced that with obstinacy and contrariness.

"I don't think this will follow me home," Roux said. "But it wouldn't hurt to be a trifle more vigilant for a few days."

"Yes, sir."

Roux drove through. The gates closed behind him. For the first time since he'd left Lozère, he felt safe.

His headlights carved through the night as he followed the winding road to the main house, which butted up against a tall hillside. The location helped hide the house, but also allowed a greater depth than anyone knew of. Another electronic device opened the long door of the five-car garage bay.

He pulled the SUV inside and parked next to a new metallic-red-and-silver Jaguar XKE and a baby-blue vintage Shelby Cobra. He loved cars. That was one of his weaknesses.

Poker and women were others. Of course, he never bothered to make a list.

Henshaw, his majordomo and a British-trained butler, met him at the door to the house.

"Good evening, sir." Henshaw was tall and thin, thirty-eight but acting at least forty years older.

"Good evening, Henshaw."

Roux's good-natured greeting must have taken the man by surprise. Henshaw's eyebrows climbed.

"There's been a problem with the SUV?" Henshaw asked. In his capacity during the past six years, he was well aware of some of the problems Roux dealt with.

"Yes." Roux tossed the man the keys. "Take it. Dispose of it. Destroy all of the paperwork that ever tied me to such a vehicle."

Henshaw caught the keys effortlessly. He wasn't surprised by the request. He'd done it before. "Of course, sir. Will there be anything else?"

"A drink. Cognac, I think. The Napoleon."

"A celebration, sir?"

"Yes. In the study, if you please."

"Of course, sir."

Roux walked through the house, across the marble floor of the great room with its sweeping staircase and private elevator, to his personal study.

The study was huge, very nearly the largest room in the house. It was two stories tall, filled with shelves of books and artifacts, scrolls and pottery, statues and paintings. Even a sarcophagus, canopic jars and the stuffed and mounted corpse of an American West gunslinger that had been so gaudy he just hadn't been able to resist acquiring it.

At the back of the room, Roux took out his key chain and pressed a sequence of buttons on the fob.

Immediately, the back wall separated into sections and slid back to reveal a huge vault. It was built into the hillside. The only access was through the heavy vault door.

As Roux pressed more buttons, the vault's door tumblers clacked and turned. When it finished, the door slid open on great hinges.

Lights flared on. Shelves held money and gems and bearer's bonds. Roux didn't care much for banks. He'd found them greedy and unscrupulous, and entirely too curious about where his wealth had come from.

He had other such hiding places around the globe. When he'd told the young American woman he was independently wealthy, he hadn't been lying.

A sealed case five feet long occupied a pedestal at the back of the vault. He pressed his hand against the handprint scanner. Ten seconds later, the locks clicked open.

The excitement thrummed within him as he flipped open the lid. He gazed down at the weapon protected within the case.

The hilt was plain and unadorned. The blade, when it had been whole, had been nearly four feet long. Now it lay in pieces but appeared almost intact.

Over the years, Roux had scoured the world in search of the fragments. He couldn't believe how far and wide the pieces had been scattered.

Or how quickly. After the sword was shattered, they had seemed to disappear overnight.

Only a small piece, no bigger than a large coin, remained to be found.

Surprised at the way his fingers trembled, Roux took from his pocket the charm the young American woman had found in the cave. He still wondered about the way she had found it. In all the times he had visited the Cévennes Mountains, he had never known an earthquake to take place.

Hesitantly, almost reverently, Roux held the charm in his fingers and positioned it the best way to fit with the sword. He dropped it onto the velvet bedding.

Nothing happened.

Roux noticed he wasn't breathing and thought it might be better if he were. He frowned.

Looking at the piece, he had no doubt that it was the one he'd been seeking. But why wasn't anything happening?

"Bollocks," Roux snarled. "After five-hundred-plus years, *something* should bloody well happen."

Steeling himself, he nudged the missing piece in closer to its mates.

Still, nothing happened.

"Oh, *bollocks!*" Roux roared, unable to restrain himself. He glared at the broken sword and wondered what the hell was wrong.

"Sir."

Turning, Roux stared at Henshaw standing in the study. He held the brandy and a snifter.

Angrily, Roux stormed out of the vault. He thumbed the remote control and heard the vault hiss shut behind him. A heartbeat later, the wall reassembled.

"Something wrong?" Henshaw inquired politely.

"Yes," Roux growled as he snatched the brandy and snifter from Henshaw's hands.

He dropped into the large leather chair behind the ornate mahogany desk and poured a copious amount of brandy into the snifter. Then he drank it like water. It wasn't the most refined way to enjoy two-hundred-year-old brandy.

"Will you need anything else, sir?" Henshaw asked.

"A miracle, obviously," Roux grumbled. He filled the snifter again.

"I'm afraid I'm short of miracles, sir."

"I know," Roux stated sourly. "But once, I tell you, the world was fairly littered with them." He shook his head, thinking of the twisting flames that had consumed the young woman to whom he'd promised fealty. "So many people believed in them. And died because of them." He sighed. "I was stupid to believe. It's my own fault. I'm just lucky it hasn't gotten *me* killed."

10

The strident ring of Garin Braden's cell phone woke him from a narcotic-and-sex-induced slumber. It was something he'd almost grown used to. He peeled the arms and legs of two young women off him and reached for the bed's remote control.

Fumbling, Garin pressed buttons from memory and caused the bed to swivel around to the nightstand that held his cell phone. Cupping the tiny device in one of his huge, scarred hands, Garin stared blearily at the buttons and hoped for the best.

"Hello?" He didn't know who would call him at—he looked at the clock across the room and couldn't make out the hand placement—at whatever time it was.

"Are you awake?" the scurrilous voice at the other end of the connection demanded.

Garin was now. He knew the voice immediately. It belonged to a man he'd hoped would never contact him again.

Instantly, feeling as if deluged by ice water, the narcotic haze enveloping Garin's thinking and senses evaporated. He shoved himself up from the bed and looked back at the twisted and intertwined limbs of the women he'd convinced to share his bed last night.

He stood to his full six feet four inches, shook his long black hair and blinked his magnetic black eyes. He gazed at his reflection in the mirror. A goatee framed his mouth and he knew he looked like his father.

Scars covered his body from fights he'd had over the years. One of the scars was over his heart and had nearly killed him in Los Angeles. He'd stayed there too long and had almost been staked as a vampire.

It was amusing to him now, but at the time it caused quite an uproar. He gazed at the women again. At the moment, he couldn't even recall where he'd met them. The occurrence wasn't too uncommon.

"I'm awake," Garin finally said.

"You don't sound awake," Roux argued.

Stealthily, Garin crossed the room and checked the elaborate panel that relayed all the information about his security system. Everything was intact. No one had breached the perimeters.

No one was caught, Garin reminded himself. Even in this age of marvels, nothing was infallible.

The bedroom was large, filled with electronic entertainment equipment. The pedestal under the bed contained several items for adult entertainment. And a large supply of batteries and lotions.

"I'm awake," Garin said again. He slapped a hand against a section of the wall near the bed.

A panel flipped around and exposed a dozen handguns—

revolvers and semiautomatics—and three assault rifles. There was even an assortment of grenades. He picked up a Smith & Wesson revolver and quietly rolled the hammer back with his thumb.

One of the women turned over on the round bed, and Garin was so startled he nearly shot her through the head.

"Why are you calling me, Roux?" Garin asked. "The last time we talked, you swore that you'd kill me."

"I was angry with you."

Garin prowled around the room. If Roux wanted to invade his penthouse, Garin was certain the old man could do it. When they were partners all those years ago, Garin had seen Roux do some amazing things.

Shortly after that, the friendship was lost. Only a few years passed before the old man swore to kill him. That had been over four hundred years ago.

"Aren't you still angry with me?" Garin walked to the brocaded curtains covering the floor-to-ceiling windows that peered out over downtown Munich.

It was late. Or early morning. Colorful neon lit up the city. A jet roared through the night, the red-and-white lights blinking slowly.

"I am," Roux admitted. "But not enough to kill you. At the moment."

Garin stayed behind the curtains. It wouldn't have been hard to set up with a sniper rifle on one of the other buildings and shoot him.

"That's good," Garin said. "How did you get this number?"

"I read it in tea leaves."

Garin said nothing. He didn't believe it, but he supposed if that were possible, Roux was the one who could do it. Remaining as calm as he could, he fumbled in the dark for the pants he'd worn earlier, then pulled them on.

"Are you all right?" Garin asked. It felt strange asking that. On several occasions, some of them not so long ago, he'd hoped the old man would die.

In fact, he'd even sent two assassination teams after Roux to accomplish that very thing. Garin had never heard again from the mercenaries he'd hired.

"I'm fine," Roux said.

"You're drinking," Garin accused.

"A little." Roux slurred his words slightly.

"Not just a little. You're drunk."

"Not drunk enough." His voice somehow managed to carry the scowl over the phone connection. "I don't think I'll ever be drunk enough."

Garin paced the room with the pistol in his hand. Talking to Roux was impossible.

"What's happened?" Garin asked. He was surprised that he still wanted to know. But then, Roux was the only man in the world who really knew him.

"I found the *sword*, Garin. All of it. All the pieces. Every last one of them."

"You're sure?" Garin asked, not wanting to believe it.

"It's taken me over five hundred years to find them all."

A sinking feeling filled Garin's stomach. He tried to detect something different in his physical well-being, then felt comfortable that nothing had changed. But that wasn't true. Something had changed. The sword—her sword—had been found.

"You found the sword?" Garin sat in one of the overstuffed chairs in front of the floor-to-ceiling window. He edged the curtain open with the pistol barrel.

"I said I did, didn't I?"

"Yes." Garin didn't have to ask why Roux had called him with the news. Even though they were enemies these days, there was no one else in the world Roux could tell about the sword. "What happened?"

Roux paused, then whispered hoarsely, "Nothing. Nothing at all."

"Something was supposed to happen, right?" Garin asked.

"I don't know."

"Have we *changed?*"

"Nothing happened, Garin. The sword is just lying there. Still in pieces."

"Maybe you've missed one."

"No."

Garin stood and walked into the next room where the wet bar was. Chrome-and-glass furniture, looking somehow fragile and dangerous at the same time, filled the room. He put the pistol on the bar and fixed himself a tall drink. Roux's announcement had taken the edge off his buzz.

"Maybe the sword can never be put back together," Garin suggested.

"I know it can be."

Garin didn't argue with that. He had always been sure of it himself. "You're missing something," Garin said.

"Don't you think I bloody well know that?" Roux snapped.

"Yes." Garin sighed and took a long drink.

"That's why I called you."

That would be the only reason the old man called, Garin thought. "Tell me what happened."

He listened as Roux told him of the discovery of the last piece of the sword.

"The woman—the American—she was the one who found the last piece of the sword?" Garin asked when he'd finished.

"It was by accident," Roux insisted.

"Roux," Garin said in exasperation, "the earth *opened* up for her. Don't you find something significant about that?"

"I was there, too."

Garin sighed. He'd forgotten about the old man's ego.

"Who's to say the earth didn't open up for *me?*" Roux demanded.

"The sword didn't fix itself," Garin pointed out.

"Maybe it's not supposed to," Roux said suddenly. "Maybe *I'm* supposed to fix it. It's possible that it simply has to be forged once again."

Before Garin could suggest that perhaps being around a forge after drinking as much as Roux had wasn't a good idea, the old man hung up.

Garin's immediate impulse was to call back. He checked the caller ID. It was blocked. He left the phone on the bar.

He sat and drank. By dawn he'd thought up and discarded a hundred plans. But he knew he really had only two options.

One involved killing Roux, which would not have been the most intelligent thing he could do, given that the pieces of the sword had all been found and he didn't know what would happen next.

The other involved finding the American woman.

Neither option appealed to him. Both included the possibility that his life would change. At present, he was worth millions, owned companies and parts of corporations and did whatever he pleased.

He'd come a long way for a German knight's bastard son who had once been apprenticed to an old man who claimed to be a wizard.

It had taken all of five hundred years.

He finished his drink, picked up the gun again and went to take a shower.

Shortly after dawn, Garin was in his car and flying down the autobahn. He just hoped Roux wasn't setting a trap. The old man had never seemed to take any of the assassination attempts personally, but a person never truly knew.

11

Annja woke feeling refreshed but sore. A quick check of her e-mail and the newsgroups showed that Bart McGilley hadn't responded but there were twenty-seven hits on alt.archaeology.esoterica.

Nineteen of them asked for personal information, as if her age, sex and location had anything to do with the charm's images. Four solicited further information, but Annja didn't have any and suspected the authors just wanted to open a dialogue. Sometimes it felt as if alt.archaeology.esoterica were a lonely-hearts club for geeks. Two offered to do further research—for a price.

But Zoodio@stuffyourmomdidnttellyou.net wrote:

Don't know about the image of the wolf and mountain, but the other side—the stylized rain—

Curious, Annja looked at the images of the charm. She hadn't thought of the die mark as rain. She'd thought of braille at first, but the coin had been too old to use braille. That language for the blind hadn't even been invented at the time the charm disappeared in La Bête's cave.

Looking at it again, she decided it could be rain. She wished she still had the charm itself, and she faulted herself for getting taken in by the old man.

Annja returned to the Web site posting.

—the stylized rain—looks like something from one of the monasteries in that area. I'm fairly familiar with the Catholic orders here. Do you know the time period?

Annja sighed. She hadn't expected to have all the answers overnight, but it would have been nice. She dashed off a quick reply.

Zoodio,
Thanks for the help. No, I'm afraid I don't know the time period. At least four-hundred-plus years. The disk was worn as a charm. To ward off evil, I think. Kind of fits with the religious motif. If that gives you a clue, please let me know. I'm stumped.

After a quick shower, she dressed and packed the notebook computer in her research backpack. She decided to take the field pack with her, but doubted she'd get up into the mountains again.

Then she went downstairs to see if François could give her a lift into town. Otherwise she was in for a long walk.

"NO, ANNJA, I got the pictures," Doug Morrell said. "They were great. I just need more."

Annja made her way through the dusty shelves of the old bookstore she'd discovered on her first day in Lozère. When dealing with fairly recent history, it was amazing what finds were often made in old bookstores, pawnshops and at garage sales. If the city, town or village was large enough to support such enterprises.

People wrote books, journals and papers that were often shuffled around, loaned, borrowed or sold at estate auctions that ended up in those businesses. Colleges and students sold off old books that somehow stayed in circulation for a hundred years or more.

Over the past decade, though, many of those finds ended up on Amazon.com or eBay. Genealogy centers took up a lot of old documents, as well.

"There are no more pictures," Annja said. She ran a forefinger over multicolored spines that were more than four and five times her age.

Roland's Bookstore was a treasure trove. She'd already purchased seventeen books and shipped them back to her apartment in Brooklyn. Where she was going to put them in the overflowing mass that she laughingly called her library, she had no clue.

"There have to be more pictures," Doug whined.

"Nope."

"If you're holding out for more money—"

"That's not it."

Doug was silent for a moment. "You don't want more money?"

"More money would be nice," Annja said, "but it won't get you more pictures."

"You should have taken more pictures."

"Did you read my e-mail?"

"Yes."

"The part about how I was chased out of the cave by guys with guns?"

"Maybe."

"You didn't."

"I think I did, Annja," Doug said defensively. "I mean, I remember it now. I was just blown away by these pictures."

"I was nearly blown away by the guys."

"Why?"

"I don't know." Annja turned the corner and went down the next aisle. She usually read books written by religious groups. Amid the doctrine and self-righteousness and finger-pointing, nuggets of history and details about people's lives resided.

"Were you somewhere you weren't supposed to be?"

"I was in the Cévennes Mountains. They're open to the public."

"Those guys just didn't want you there?" Doug asked.

"I don't know."

Doug let out a low breath. "Generally when people chase you, there's a reason."

Annja smiled at that. "Have you been chased before, Doug?"

"I'm just saying."

"Maybe they wanted the gear I was carrying."

"You said the ground opened up and dropped you into this cave."

"Yes."

"Then it closed after you left."

"Right." Annja found a blue clothbound book placed backward on the shelf. When she extracted the volume and turned it around, she found the book had a Latin title. She translated it as if she were reading English.

The Destruction of the Brotherhood of the Silent Rain.

She flipped the book open and stared at the plate inset on the first page. It was a match to the image on the back of the charm.

"Do you think if you packed a few explosives back up into those mountains," Doug began, "that you could ?"

"Doug!" she interrupted.

He paused.

"No," Annja said.

"No?" The producer sounded as petulant as a child.

"No explosives. No more pictures. That's what we have. It's more than anyone else has *ever* had."

"You don't understand, Annja. You've got the makings of a great story here. A body count. An unidentified monster. Thugs chasing you. An earthquake."

And a mysterious missing charm, Annja thought. She hadn't told him about that.

Quickly, she flipped through the book. It appeared to be a history of a monastery that had fallen onto hard times and been disbanded. She knew the chances were good that it wouldn't help her, but gathering information meant taking in more than she needed in hopes of getting what she needed.

"How much longer do you think you'll need for the piece?" Doug asked.

"A few more days."

"The deadline looms."

"I know." Annja understood deadlines. Even in archaeology there were deadlines. Teams had to be in and out of dig sites during their agreed-upon times.

"If you need anything else, let me know."

"Sure."

"Maybe Kyle and the art department can touch up these pictures—"

Annja counted to ten, slowly. "Doug."

"Yes," he said contritely.

"If you touch those pictures—"

"They need to be enhanced."

"If anyone touches those pictures—"

"Just a little tweaking. I promise. You won't even know we did anything."

"Doug!"

Doug sighed in surrender.

"I'm going to call your mother and tell her about Amy Zuckerman," Annja threatened.

"You wouldn't."

"Do you remember the lagoon-creature piece I did a few months ago?"

Doug was silent.

"You took a perfectly interesting piece about a legendary swamp monster—"

"The mangrove coast of Florida isn't that interesting," Doug argued. "I had to switch the location to Barbados."

"You turned it into a freak fest. You stood me up in front of a digitally created, shambling pile of muck with eight-inch fangs—"

"The fangs were too much, weren't they? I told Kyle that the fangs were too big. I mean, who's going to believe a seven-foot-tall mud monster with eight-inch fangs? I wouldn't. I'll tell you that," Doug said.

"You told people the footage was shot somewhere it wasn't." Annja hadn't seen the finished piece until it aired.

Then the phone calls started coming in. She still hadn't lived down the fallout from that. If it weren't for the big checks that *Chasing History's Monsters* cut, or the fact that she couldn't get them anywhere else, she wouldn't continue her association with them.

"We got a lot of favorable comments about that show," Doug said defensively.

"I'm a respected archaeologist," Annja said. "I work hard at that. I'm not some wannabe video-game heroine."

"You'll always be respectable to me," Doug promised.

"Not when you stand me up in front of digital monsters that don't have shadows."

"That was an oversight. All the monsters we do now have shadows."

"Amy Zuckerman," Annja stated. "You burn me, that's the price tag for the damage."

"That's low, Annja. Truly low." Doug took in a deep breath. "Amy was a mistake. A tragic mistake."

"Your mother would never forgive you," Annja agreed.

"You know, it's conversations like this that remind me I should never drink with friends."

"At least friends put you in cabs and send you home," Annja said. "They don't roll you and leave you lying with your pants around your ankles in a rain-filled alley."

Doug sighed. "Okay. We'll do it your way. I have to tell you, I think you're making a mistake, but—"

"Bye, Doug. I'll talk to you later." Annja broke the connection and zipped the phone into her jacket pocket. She continued scanning the shelves.

The small bell above the entrance rang as someone opened the door.

"Ah," Roland greeted from the front counter, "Good morning, Mr. Lesauvage."

Cautiously, Annja peered around the bookshelf and tried to stay in the shadows.

12

Corvin Lesauvage was around six feet tall. He was broad and blocky, and looked like he could easily handle himself in a physical confrontation. Sandy-colored hair, cut short, framed his face. He looked freshly shaved, his jaw gleaming. Dark green eyes that held a reptilian cast gazed around the shop. His pearl-gray suit was Italian. So were the black loafers.

"Good morning, Roland," Lesauvage said. His voice was low and rumbling.

"I haven't any more books for you, sir." Roland was a gray ghost of a man. Life had pared him down to skin and bone long ago. But he was attentive, intelligent and quick. He barely topped five feet.

"I knew that," Lesauvage said. "If you'd found any, you'd have sent them along."

"Yes, sir. I would have."

"I came today only to browse." Lesauvage studied the stacks, but his cold eyes never found Annja in the shadows. "Is anyone else about?" he asked.

"A guest, Mr. Lesauvage." Roland never called the prospective buyers who entered his establishment customers. Always *guests*. "Just the one. Shouldn't be any bother to you," he assured Lesauvage.

"Who?"

"A young American woman."

Lesauvage smiled. "Good. I was hoping to catch her here."

Annja looked around the shop. There was no other way out. The bookshop butted up against a launderette in the back and was sandwiched between a cobbler and a candy store. The only door was at the front.

And at present, Lesauvage stood blocking the way.

"Have you met Miss Creed?" Roland asked. "She's a television celebrity."

"So I'm told. Unfortunately, I haven't had the pleasure," Lesauvage said. "Yet." He raised his voice. "Miss Creed?"

Annja debated calling the police. But after the report last night and their lack of interest, she doubted the effort would prove worthwhile.

She reached into her backpack and took out the spring-loaded stun baton she'd brought with her. The weapon was legal to carry as long as she packed it in luggage checked at the airport.

Sliding the baton into one of the deep pockets of her hiking shorts, Annja stepped around the bookcase so she could be seen. "Mr. Lesauvage," she said.

Roland blinked behind his thick glasses. "Do you know each other?" He looked at Lesauvage. "I thought you said—"

"We've got mutual acquaintances," Annja said.

Lesauvage smiled. "Yes. We did."

For just a moment, Annja thought about Avery Moreau

and worried that something had happened to the young man. Surely if something had, it would have been in the news.

"What can I do for you, Mr. Lesauvage?" Annja asked.

"Actually, I thought perhaps there might be something I could do for you."

"Nothing that I can think of."

Lesauvage flashed her a charming smile. If he hadn't sent men to kidnap her and possibly kill her, Annja thought he would have been a handsome man with intriguing potential. But now she knew he was as deadly as the Ursini's viper.

"I suggest that perhaps you haven't thought hard enough," Lesauvage said.

Roland, obviously unaware of the subtext that passed between them, said, "I hadn't mentioned Mr. Lesauvage as someone you might talk to, Miss Creed. Though maybe I should have. He's one of the more educated men in the area when it comes to history and mythology."

"Really." Annja tried to sound properly impressed. But she never took her eyes from the dangerous man.

"Oh, yes. He's interested in La Bête, too. And he's been researching the Wild Hunt—"

Lesauvage cut the old man off. "I think that's enough, Mr. Roland. There's no need to bore her with my idiosyncrasies."

Annja wondered why Lesauvage was interested in the Irish myth that had its roots in the days of the Vikings. She considered her own knowledge of the Wild Hunt.

According to Scandinavian myth, the leader of the Norse gods, Odin, was believed to ride his eight-legged horse, Sleipnir, across the sky in pursuit of quarry. Annja's quick mind juxtaposed the tale of the Wild Hunt and La Bête, finding similarities.

Except that she was in Lozère hunting La Bête, and

Lesauvage, who was keenly interested in the Wild Hunt according to Roland, was hunting her. As an archaeologist, Annja knew coincidences happened all the time. But she was sure this was no coincidence.

"I don't think your interests are boring," Annja said. "To the contrary, I find the idea of the Wild Hunt suddenly quite enlightening."

Lesauvage frowned. It was obvious he'd rather she not know of his obsession. "Perhaps we could talk elsewhere," he said.

"Do you have somewhere safe in mind?" Annja countered.

"There's a coffee shop across the street," Lesauvage suggested. "Or, if you're unwilling, I'm sure Mr. Roland would put us up for a brief conference."

Annja thought about the veiled threat in Lesauvage's words and hated the man for them. Roland would obviously be an immediate casualty.

"All right," she said.

DURING THE WALK across the street from Roland's bookstore, after she had paid for her purchase, Annja had been aware of the sleek gray Mercedes limousine that followed Lesauvage like a pet dog. Three men sat inside.

Annja wondered if Lesauvage had matched the color of his suit to the car.

The server guided Annja to a table in the rear. Lesauvage followed.

As she sat across from him, Annja took the baton from her pocket and placed it on the seat beside her, within quick, easy reach.

"You're being overly cautious," the man told her.

"After being shot at by your people yesterday?" Annja shook her head. "Overly cautious, in fact, sensible, would have been climbing onto the first plane out of France."

"But you couldn't do that."

"I can." Annja had no illusions about her courage. There was a fine line between bravery and stupidity. She knew what it looked like and made a habit of never crossing it.

"But you haven't."

Annja didn't say anything because there was nothing to say.

"You're here for a story," he said. "About La Bête."

"Yes."

"How did you find that cave yesterday?" he asked. "I've had men up in those mountains for years."

"There was an earthquake. I fell in."

"You're joking."

"No."

The server brought two steaming cups of espresso.

"I sent those men back up in the mountains last night and this morning," Lesauvage said. "During all the confusion—"

"During their attempts to kill me," Annja stated flatly.

"I ordered them only to restrain you and bring you to me."

"Kidnapping is a big crime," Annja pointed out. "Huge."

A feral gleam lit Lesauvage's eyes. "Let us cut to the chase, Miss Creed."

Annja waited.

"You have something I want. Something that you found in that cave."

"What do you think I found?" Annja countered.

"A coin," Lesauvage said. "About this big." He circled his forefinger and thumb, gapping them about the size of a euro.

"On one side is the image of a wolf hanging in front of a mountain. On the other is a die mark."

"The symbol of the Brotherhood of the Silent Rain," Annja said.

"Yes," Lesauvage admitted reluctantly. He pursed his lips unhappily. "You know more about this than I'd believed."

Elation filled Annja. She had confirmed a piece of the puzzle. She decided not to ask about the monastery. She'd consult her new book later.

"Knowledge, Miss Creed," Lesauvage said in a dead, still voice, "is not always a good thing."

But it's the things that you don't know about that kill you quickest, Annja thought. She chose to ignore the threat inherent in his words.

"Why do you have an interest in the Wild Hunt?" Annja asked.

"I want the coin you found," Lesauvage said. "I was told you found it around the dead warrior's neck. He wore it on a leather strap."

"Most people believe the Wild Hunt is an Irish myth," Annja said. "Or British. Depends on your bias. They're supposed to be a group of ghostly hunters who go galloping across the sky on their horses. They blow their hunting horns and their hounds bay." She grinned, noting the man's discomfort. "It's supposed to be a really spooky experience." She shrugged. "If you believe in that kind of thing."

Sitting back in his chair, Lesauvage regarded her from under hooded lids. "You don't believe in it?"

"No," Annja replied. "It's an old tale. A good one to scare kids when you want them inside the house after dark. According to the legend, if you witnessed the Wild Hunt, you would either become their prey or one of them."

"Yes."

"I hadn't thought about it until this morning," Annja said, "but the legend of La Bête might have something to do with the myth of the Wild Hunt."

Lesauvage remained silent.

"Did you know that several people in history claimed to have taken part in the Wild Hunt?" Annja asked. She remembered the drunken arguments Professor Sparhawk had had with an undergraduate during the Hadrian's Wall dig in England. It had continued over the three months of the dig a few summers ago.

Shifting uncomfortably, Lesauvage crossed his arms and glared at her as if she were merely an annoyance.

"Primitive peoples among the Gauls and Germans used it to combat the encroachment of civilization," Annja said. "The Harii warriors painted themselves black to attack their enemies in the night. They pretended they had special powers granted by the gods they worshiped. Whipped everyone there into a frenzy."

"You're wasting time," Lesauvage interrupted.

Annja ignored him. "Others took part in it, too. There are documented cases showing involvement by St. Guthlac and Hereward the Wake. In the twelfth century, one of the monks who wrote the *Peterborough Chronicle* gave a treatise on a gathering of warriors under the Wild Hunt banner during the appointment of an abbot. The monks and the local knights later disbanded the warriors."

"I want the coin," Lesauvage repeated. "Or things could get dire."

"I hadn't thought about La Bête being part of the Wild Hunt," Annja mused. "Not until you came calling this afternoon." She studied him. "Why are you so interested in the

Wild Hunt? And why did you send your men after me? Unless you figured La Bête was part of something you were interested in."

"You're playing with things that don't concern you, woman." Menace dripped in Lesauvage's words.

Annja closed her hand over the baton.

"Now I want that damned coin."

"I don't have it," Annja said. She didn't want to make herself a target. She had the rubbings. For the moment, they would have to serve to help unlock the mystery before her.

"You're lying," Lesauvage snarled. His face grew dark with suffused blood.

"No," Annja said, "I'm not. The old man I met in the mountains has it."

"What old man?"

"Didn't your men tell you about him?"

Lesauvage stared daggers at her.

"His name is Roux."

"What's the rest of his name?"

"That's all I know."

Lesauvage cursed, drawing the attention of nearby patrons. Even the English and German tourists who didn't speak French understood the potential for violence. They got up with their families and started to sidle away.

"We're done here." Annja said, grabbing her pack and sliding out of the booth.

Lesauvage reached for her with a big hand.

Pressing the button on the side of the baton, Annja released the extended length, giving her almost two feet of stainless steel to work with. She slapped Lesauvage's wrist away, causing him to yelp in surprised pain. Shoving the baton forward with an underhanded strike like she would deliver with an épée, Annja caught him with the end between the eyes and batted his head back. Before he could recover, she was on her feet.

With the baton still in her fist, her heart thumping rapidly, Annja strode toward the front door. Just before she reached it, two men dressed in black robes blocked the way.

They were young and hard-looking. When they lowered their cowls, she saw that their heads were shaved smooth. Tattoos at their throats repeated the same design that had been struck on the back of the charm.

"Miss Creed," one of them said in flawless English, "you must come with us." He reached for her.

Annja struck at the man with her baton. The other man shifted then, revealing what he hid beneath his robe. The short blade caught the light as it came up to intercept the baton.

Metal shrieked against metal.

Annja disengaged at once, stepping back to give herself more room. Glancing at the coffee shop's rear entrance, she saw that two more black-robed men were entering there. Outside the big windows that lined the side wall, four more black-robed men stood waiting.

Things did not look good. Annja hadn't been this outnumbered in a long time. Well, yesterday seemed like a long time ago.

She tightened her grip on her baton and looked at Lesauvage.

The man sat at the table cradling his hand. He grinned at her. "They're not after me."

The black-robed warriors closed in on her.

GARIN BRADEN WAITED in the black Mercedes while Avery Moreau dashed inside the bookstore to find out if the woman was still there.

After arriving in Lozère, Garin had experienced no trouble in picking up Annja Creed's trail. Within an hour, a private-investigations firm he owned had located the bed-and-breakfast where she was staying. Over the years, he'd found the investment in the detective agency had helped with a number of things, including blackmail and corporate espionage.

Camille Lambert had been glad to help Annja Creed's television producer find her. Apparently the old woman was quite taken with her guest.

She'd also given Avery Moreau's phone number to Garin and suggested hiring him to help track down the woman.

They'd already been to the museum and the library, two places the young man said the woman liked to haunt while she was in town. Now they were at Roland's Bookstore.

The cold air-conditioning cycled around Garin. A German industrial metal group played on the stereo, filling the big luxury car with sound.

He wondered what Roux was up to. If all the pieces of the sword were truly gathered, why had nothing changed?

The only conjecture Garin had come up with was that the woman was important to everything they were dealing with. After all, she was the one who had fallen into the bowels of the mountain and discovered the last piece of the sword.

Roux liked to look for hidden meanings and allegories and secrets. When serving as the old man's apprentice, Garin had discovered that not everything was filled with plots and portents. Sometimes things were as simple as they looked.

Like the fact that the woman was somehow mixed up with the sword.

Garin knew that Roux would take forever to get around to that line of logic. Roux's ego wouldn't let him arrive at that conclusion. Presumably, they both had forever to wait, but Garin didn't like waiting. Even after five hundred years, he was impatient.

If the sword—if *Joan's* sword, he corrected himself—was going to be a threat to him, he wanted to know now.

The young man ran back out of the bookstore.

Garin rolled the electric window down with a button.

"She's not inside," Avery said. "Roland said he thought she went over to the coffee shop." He pointed—and froze.

Following the direction of the boy's arm, Garin looked. He saw the men dressed in black robes surrounding the coffee shop and guessed at once that this wasn't a normal occurrence. Through the windows, he spotted Annja Creed backing away from the men closing in on her.

Without a word, Garin dropped the transmission into reverse. The powerful engine roared. Whipping the steering wheel and throwing an arm over the seat as he stared backward, he backed the Mercedes around in a tire-eating ninety-degree turn. He narrowly missed a farm truck and two small cars in the other lanes. Horns blared and angry voices followed him.

He reached under his jacket for the S&W .500 Magnum and backed into the coffee shop's parking lot, slamming into three of the black-robed warriors and sending them flying.

13

The chaos in the parking lot drew the attention of everyone inside the coffee shop.

Annja stared in disbelief as three men skidded across the concrete. One of them slammed into a parked car, setting off the alarm, and crumpled into a heap. Another slid under a car that had been backing out. The third man lay under the heavy luxury car.

A fourth man stayed on his feet. He pulled a semiautomatic pistol from somewhere inside his robe.

A huge man with the blackest hair Annja had ever seen—black as sin, she'd heard someone describe a color like that—pushed out on the driver's side. Dressed in black, from his gloves to his long coat to his wraparound sunglasses, he looked like the specter of death in a medieval painting. He held what looked like, and in the next split second, sounded like a small cannon.

The man pointed the pistol at the black-robed man without

even looking in his direction and pulled the trigger. The muzzle-flash ballooned from the barrel.

The black-robed man jerked backward, fell and lay still. His pistol skittered across the pavement.

Calmly the big man aimed the pistol at the coffee-shop windows. Everyone inside the shop hit the floor amid curses and cries for help.

Even Corvin Lesauvage was on the floor.

Guess this guy doesn't work for him, Annja thought. She crouched near one of the tables, but knew she couldn't stay there. The black-robed men at either entrance were duck-walking toward her.

The big man outside shot the large plate-glass window twice. The glass fell in sheets and shattered into thousands of pieces against the floor.

"Annja Creed!" he yelled in a deep voice. He spoke in English. "I've come to help you!"

Annja backed away from the nearest black-robed man. She stared at the livid tattoo on his neck. Without warning, he lunged at her.

She dodged back, falling to her left hand and sweeping the baton back with her right. The metal end caught her opponent along his jaw and broke his forward movement. She thought she broke his jaw, as well.

Then the man behind him pulled a pistol from his robe and aimed at her. "Come with us," the man demanded in accented English, "or I will kill you."

Annja believed him.

Before she could reply, before she could even figure out how she was going to react, the black-robed man's head emptied in a crimson rush and he pirouetted sideways. Then the massive boom of the big man's pistol filled the coffee shop again.

The lesser of two evils, Annja decided. These guys have promised to kill you, and getting kidnapped by them doesn't seem too appealing.

She pushed to her feet and ran for the broken window. The backpack's weight with the computer slowed her a little, but she gained a tabletop in one lithe leap. Shadows moved around her as she leaped through the broken window and cleared the hedges before the parking lot.

The big man took aim again.

For a moment, Annja feared she'd made the wrong choice. But when he fired, she wasn't the target.

"The door's unlocked," he said conversationally, as if he wasn't killing people and was only out for a walk. He broke open the massive handgun and spilled empty brass onto the ground with audible tinkling. Taking a speed-loader from his pocket, he refilled the cylinder and snapped the weapon closed.

Annja's hand found the car's door latch. She opened the door and clambered into the plush leather seat. Bullets hit the window as she tried to close the door, causing it to shiver under the impacts. She expected to feel shredded glass and metal tear through her.

That didn't happen.

When she looked back at the window, all she saw were faint hairline cracks.

"Bulletproof glass," the stranger said as he dropped into the driver's seat. He grinned at her and she saw her reflection in the black lenses of his wraparound sunglasses. "I never go anywhere without it."

Several other bullets caromed from the car without doing any appreciable damage.

The big man grinned at the men running out of the coffee shop toward them. "Idiots."

"They could shoot out the tires," Annja pointed out.

"Let them try," he growled. "They're run-flats. They would have to blow them off the car to get them to fail."

"If we wait, maybe they'll roll in a tank," Annja said, only half-joking.

He smiled at her. "You've got a sense of humor. I like that." Then he put the car into gear, shoved his foot down on the accelerator and sent them screaming out onto the street.

TWELVE ANXIOUS MINUTES later, with no sign of pursuit visible through the rear window, Annja turned to the driver. "Who are you?"

"Garin," he said, offering a hand. The pistol was tucked between his legs. "Garin Braden. At your service."

Caught off guard, Annja took his hand. Before she knew what he was doing, he folded her fingers inward and kissed the back of her hand.

"Enchanté," he said, then released her hand.

"Me, too," Annja whispered. She didn't know how to react. "Do you always go around rescuing people from—" she didn't know what to call the black-robed men "—other *strange* people who want to abduct or kill them for unknown reasons?"

"Not always." Garin drove confidently.

"How did you happen to be there?" she asked.

"Actually, I was looking for you."

Annja took a fresh grip on her baton. If Garin noticed he obviously didn't feel threatened. "Why?"

"Aren't you glad I was?"

"For the moment," she said.

He laughed then, and the noise was filled with savage glee. "I have no reason to wish you harm, Annja Creed."

"Then what do you wish?"

Looking at her, he asked, "Would you like to get back the charm Roux took from you?"

"Yes," she answered without hesitation.

"Then we'll go get it." Garin paused. "If that's what you want to do."

Annja considered her options briefly. She didn't want to remain in Lozère with Lesauvage and the black-robed warriors hunting her.

Getting to the airport and getting out of the country was out of the question. Inspector Richelieu probably had a warrant out for her arrest by now.

Leaving without understanding at least part of the reasons why everything was happening also didn't appeal to her.

"Well?" Garin asked.

"All right. Where are the old man and my charm?"

"In Paris. That's where he's lived practically forever." Garin kept his foot heavy on the accelerator.

THREE HOURS LATER they stopped for fuel at a truck stop.

Annja tried to open the door but it remained locked. When she looked for the door release, she saw that it had been removed. Feeling a little uneasy, she turned to Garin.

Without a word he pressed the release switch and the lock sprang free. He got out of the car with a lithe movement for such a tall man.

Outside the car, Annja looked around. Dozens of cars and trucks filled the service area. People milled about, making selections and chatting briefly. Most of them complained about the high price of fuel or confirmed directions to their destinations.

If she ran, Annja doubted Garin could stop her.

"They have a restaurant," Garin said as he opened the gas tank and shoved the nozzle inside. "If you're hungry."

Annja realized she was famished. She'd skipped the breakfast table Camille Lambert had laid out, then worked through lunch in Lozère searching for books.

For the first time she realized that most of her possessions, including most of her cash, was at the bed-and-breakfast. Using her credit cards meant leaving an electronic trail. She was sure it wasn't safe to do that.

"I'm hungry," Annja admitted. "Though I have to tell you, if you intend to walk away from the check on me, I'm coming after you."

"What?" Garin appeared confused.

"Nothing." Annja waved the question away. "How do you know the old man?"

"Roux?"

"Yes."

Garin shrugged as he settled back against the Mercedes and watched the digital readout on the gas pump flicker. "I knew him a long time ago."

"You don't look that old." Annja thought maybe he was in his early thirties.

"I'm older than I look. So is Roux."

Annja let the statement pass without comment. "Why did Roux take the charm?"

"He thought it belonged to something else he's been looking for."

The gas pump sounded as it shut off.

"Does it?" Annja asked.

Garin removed the nozzle from the gas tank. "I don't know. Maybe."

"What was he looking for?"

"You'll have to see." Garin hung up the hose and tossed her the keys. "Pull the car around to the restaurant side. I'll pay for the gas and join you there."

Keys in hand, Annja watched him walk away. There was nothing keeping her from taking the car and going. She had a full tank of gas. Paris was two and a half hours away. She could go to Paris and board a plane for New York.

If there's not a warrant out for your arrest, she told herself.

She didn't like the idea of running, though. And there was the matter of the charm and the black-robed men to consider. The book she'd found at Roland's had been quite helpful. She'd read most of it over the past three hours.

But it had also deepened the mystery. She knew what the Brotherhood of the Silent Rain had been, but not what had destroyed it.

Or driven it underground, she thought, remembering the tattoos at the throats of the black-garbed men.

In the end, she slid behind the wheel and started the engine. She drove to the parking lot by the restaurant and parked.

Garin Braden had never once turned around to check to see if she'd driven off. His confidence was almost insulting.

AFTER HE PAID for the fuel with cash, because he didn't want to be traced in case someone in Lozère had managed to identify the car, Garin purchased a phone card and retreated to the bank of pay phones in the back.

He consulted his PDA and retrieved the phone number he was looking for. Then he dialed.

The phone rang twice and was picked up by a man with a British accent. "Lord Roux's residence."

The announcement caught Garin by surprise. He hadn't talked to Roux in years before last night. "*Lord* Roux, is it? When did the old bastard get titled?" he asked.

"Excuse me?" The man at the other end of the connection sounded offended.

"Let me talk to Roux," Garin demanded.

"Lord Roux is not—"

"He'll talk to me," Garin growled. "Tell him Garin is on the line."

"Garin," the voice repeated. The way he said it told Garin that he had at least been briefed on the importance of the name if not why it was important. "Hold on, please."

Glancing up at the clock over the exit doors, Garin knew he didn't have long before the woman started getting suspicious about the length of time he'd been gone. Annja Creed was very alert, very much aware of things that were going on around her. She was no one's fool.

More than that, she was a beautiful woman. During the three-hour trip, while she'd evaded most of his attempts at conversation and kept her nose in her book, he'd wondered what she would be like in bed. Those thoughts had made the past three hours even more grueling because he didn't feel safe acting on impulses he normally didn't restrain. For the first time in a long time, Garin felt nervous.

"Garin," Roux said.

"Yes," Garin replied. He sighed, angry with all the troubling notions spinning around in his head. Here was the source of all his discontent.

"How did you get this number?"

"You gave it to me last night," Garin said because he'd always hated the old man's pomposity.

"I did not. Last night—"

"You were drunk," Garin interrupted.

"Not that drunk."

"We could argue the point." Garin had put his private detectives to work looking for the number upon his departure from Munich. It hadn't been easy to find.

"What do you want?" Roux demanded.

"Maybe, this time, I have something you want."

Roux was silent at the other end of the line. Then he said, "You have the woman."

Garin silently cursed. Of course Roux would figure out why he was calling. The man was keenly intelligent. "Yes."

"Is she alive?"

"For now."

"Why did you take her?"

"Because of the sword," Garin replied.

"It's not like you to be curious."

"I'm not. I'm scared."

Roux laughed. "I thought you had gone out and conquered the world, Garin. You with all your untold millions and women and fine living."

"I wouldn't say you've avoided wealth."

"No, but I live my life differently than you. I still enjoy taking risks. Throwing the dice and seeing what happens."

"I take risks, as well."

"Carefully calculated, carefully measured ones."

Garin knew it was true. Even the gunplay in Lozère was measured. He'd gone into it feeling supremely confident that he could get the woman. Or at the very least emerge from the encounter relatively unscathed.

The sword was another matter entirely.

"You have her with you now?" Roux asked.

"Yes."

"Where are you?"

"About two and a half hours from you."

"Good. Bring her here. I'll be waiting."

The phone clicked dead in Garin's ear. Trembling with anger and frustration, he cradled the handset. He took a deep breath. For those last few seconds of that phone call, he'd felt like that awkward nine-year-old child Roux had taken in trade for services rendered all those years ago.

I'm not that child anymore, Garin reminded himself. I'm my own man. A very dangerous man. If my father were to know me now, he would fear me.

But that hadn't been the case when he was a child. He'd been the son of a serving wench. Unacknowledged by his father. An object of scorn for his father's wife. An embarrassment to his blood mother. And a target for villainies perpetrated by his half brothers and half sisters.

Roux had taken Garin away from all that. But the old man had not done him a kindness by dragging him out across the harsh lands they traveled. He had used him as a vassal, to wait on him hand and foot.

Taking another breath, Garin calmed himself. Then he walked to the adjoining restaurant. Roux would see that he had changed. Even if Garin had to kill the old man to prove it.

14

Seated in a booth by the window overlooking the restaurant parking lot and the Mercedes, Annja glanced up at Garin's approach. She took in the man's dark mood at once and felt a little threatened.

"Something wrong?" she asked.

"No," he lied, then sat in the booth across from her.

"Oh," Annja said in a way that let him know she was fully aware that he was lying. She'd learned that from the nuns at the orphanage. The soft vocal carried a deadly punch of guilt that usually demolished the weaker kids. Annja had always continued stoically until she knew for certain she'd been caught. She'd been punished quite often for exploring New Orleans after lights-out.

"I've got a long history with the man we're going to see," Garin said.

Maybe he'd been raised on guilt, too, Annja thought. "What kind of history?" Annja asked.

"We don't exactly get on."

"I'm not surprised. He comes across as very arrogant and selfish."

"Those," Garin said with a grin, "are his redeeming qualities."

Annja decided she liked him a little then. Not enough to trust him, but enough to explore working together. Saving her life—or at least saving her from capture—back at the coffee shop in Lozère had been a mercenary action. She just didn't know what the price tag was yet.

"You called him?" Annja asked.

To his credit, Garin hesitated only a moment. "Yes. To let him know we're coming."

"He's okay with that?"

"Yes."

Annja leaned back in the booth and thought about Roux. "Going to his house doesn't exactly make me feel all warm and fuzzy."

Garin bared his white teeth in a predator's smile. "It's not exactly a trip to grandma's house. But you don't have a lot of choices, either."

"I think I do."

"Really?" Garin leaned back as well. "Do you know who is trying to kill you?"

"A man named Corvin Lesauvage and the monks of the Brotherhood of the Silent Rain."

Garin's eyes flicked to the book on the table. "You've been reading about them."

"You," Annja said distinctly, "can read Latin."

Garin shrugged. "One of several languages."

"You share that with Roux."

"I should. He taught me."

"What kind of work do you do, Mr. Braden?"

"Me?" Garin held a hand to his chest and smiled brilliantly. "Why, I am a criminal."

Somehow, Annja wasn't terribly surprised. From the way he'd moved back at the coffee shop, she might have guessed that he was in the military. She nodded.

"You knew that?" Garin asked in the silence that followed his declaration.

"I'd thought you were a soldier—"

"I've been a soldier many times," Garin said. "The tools change, but the practice and methodology remain much the same."

"But I realized a soldier would have stayed in Lozère and straightened things out with the law-enforcement people."

"The police and I, we're of a different…persuasion." Garin waved at a passing server. "Staying in Lozère was not an option. I could not protect you there."

"Or take me to Roux."

"Exactly."

The server took their order. Garin ordered for them both, which Annja found somewhat old-fashioned and pleasant. He was, she admitted upon reflection, an oddity. He had undoubtedly killed men only a short time ago and evidently gave no further thought to it.

Then she frowned at her own line of thinking. She'd more or less done the same thing herself yesterday. Or at least tried to. She didn't know if she'd actually killed anyone. Roux certainly had.

For a moment she felt stung by the guilt the sisters at the orphanage had worked so hard to foster in her. Then she pushed it out of her mind. If she'd learned one thing in those gray walls filled with rules and recriminations, it was to take care of herself. She'd learned the hard way that no one else would.

"Do the monks work for Lesauvage?" Garin asked when he'd finished speaking to the server.

"No." From Lesauvage's reaction to the situation, Annja was firmly convinced of that.

"Then they're working independently." Garin picked up a package of crackers, tore them open and started eating. "Who is Lesauvage?"

"A criminal."

"I've never heard of him. What does he want?"

"The charm your friend Roux stole from me."

Garin frowned. "Roux is not my friend." He shifted. "Why does Lesauvage want the charm?"

"I don't know. Does Roux?"

"If he does, he hasn't told me. What about the monks? What do they want?"

"During their attempt to abduct me, they didn't say."

Garin pointed at the book on the table. "Did that offer any clue?"

"No. According to the authors, who were monks, the brotherhood was a peaceful group. Big on vineyards and cheeses."

"Must have been very profitable being a monk back in those days. Or at least a good time."

The server returned with two glasses of wine and placed them on the table.

Garin hoisted his glass and offered a toast. *"Salut."*

"Salut," Annja said, meeting his glass with hers. "Why does Roux want the charm?"

Garin hesitated.

"If you start holding out on me, I'll have to reconsider my options," Annja said.

A look of seriousness darkened Garin's face. "Have you studied Joan of Arc?"

"Roux asked me that, too," Annja said.

"What did he say about her?"

"Nothing really. He moved the conversation on to the charm."

"Did he? Interesting. Obviously he didn't want you to know what he's working on."

"What are you talking about?" Annja asked.

"Roux believes the charm was part of Joan of Arc's sword."

Annja was stunned. She remembered the histories and the stories. The young woman had been burned at the stake, labeled a heretic by the church. Some tales claimed that her sword had magic powers, some that it had been shattered the day she was burned at the stake.

"Does Roux have other pieces of the sword?" she asked.

"With the acquisition of the piece you found, Roux thinks he has them all. That's why we're going to his house. That's why I'm risking my life taking you there and trusting that he will at least set aside our differences."

"Why?" Annja asked.

"Because I am convinced you have something to do with the sword."

"But I've never even had any real interest in Joan of Arc." The story was one Annja had read as a girl in the orphanage. She'd been fascinated by Joan's heroism and bravery, of course, but the whole "called by God" thing had left her skeptical.

"The earth," Garin stated, "opened up and let you find the final piece of the sword. Even after it had been hidden from sight for hundreds of years."

"That was an earthquake." Annja was beginning to feel that she was stepping into a side dimension and leaving the real world behind.

"It was a miracle," Garin said.

She looked at him, wondering if he was deliberately baiting her. "Do you really believe that?"

Pausing a moment, Garin shook his head. "I don't know. And I've got more reason to believe it than I'm willing to go into at this moment. For the rest of the story, we'll have to talk to Roux."

"Even if that charm was part of Joan of Arc's sword, that doesn't mean it was the last piece."

"Roux says it is."

"Do you believe him?"

"In this, of all things, I do."

"Then how do I fit in?"

"I don't know. I know only that you must. As ego deflating as it is for him, Roux has had to face that, as well. That doesn't mean he accepts it."

The server returned, carrying a massive tray piled high with food.

"Let's eat," Garin suggested. "At the moment, there's nothing more to tell."

Despite the confusion that spun within her, Annja hadn't lost her appetite. There was more to Garin's story. He was holding something back that he considered important. She was convinced of that. But she was also convinced that he wouldn't tell her any more of it at the moment.

As she ate, she kept watch outside the building. Part of her kept expecting to see local police roll up at any moment.

Night filtered the sky, turning the bright haze to ochre and finally black by the time they finished the meal. Then they were on the road again. The answers, at least some of them, lay only a few hours into the future.

15

"Put this on."

Avery Moreau accepted the robe fashioned from wolf pelts. It was heavy and itchy against his bare skin. He wrinkled his nose in ill-disguised disgust. And it smelled like wet dog even more this time than the last.

Without a word, he pulled the robe on and stood waiting in the small room lit by the single naked bulb. The air felt thin and tasted metallic. He struggled to catch his breath but couldn't quite seem to.

Where he had expected to feel only anticipation at this moment, he now felt dread. He hadn't succeeded in his assignment. Surely Lesauvage wasn't going to initiate him now.

But here he stood, clad in the furs of the Wild Hunt, called to one of the secret meetings.

Marcel stood before him, already wearing the wolf's-head helmet that masked his features. He was big and blocky, one of the older boys whom Avery had grown up in fear of.

Like most of Corvin Lesauvage's recruits, Marcel had been a bully all his life and had developed a taste for violence.

Avery had never truly felt that way. He'd been violent over the years. Growing up as the son of a known thief would do that to someone. If his father had been a successful bank robber or knocked over armored cars on a regular basis, perhaps things would have been different. There might even have been money in the house.

But Gerard Moreau hadn't done those things. He'd barely stolen enough to keep his family fed and a roof over their heads most of the time. He'd been too lazy to work at an hourly wage, which wouldn't have fed them, either, and too unskilled to find a job that would.

Gerard Moreau had been trapped by circumstance into the life that he had. Until the night Inspector Edouard Richelieu shot and killed him in cold blood. The act had been nothing less than premeditated murder.

That night, Avery had been with his father. Posted as a lookout, Avery had to keep watch and make sure no one approached from outside.

No one had approached from outside the house. The police inspector had been inside the house. Richelieu had been entertaining Etienne Pettit's wife that evening, unbeknownst to anyone in Lozère.

Pettit was a powerful man in the town, and not one who would have put up with being cuckolded in his own home by a police inspector who lived with his mother. If Pettit had found out about his wife's infidelities, the man would have divorced his wife and left her with nothing. And he would have broken Inspector Richelieu, had him tossed out of the police department onto the street.

That was why Richelieu had shot Gerard Moreau six

times. The police inspector loved his job because it validated him in ways that Avery didn't understand but knew existed.

When he closed his eyes, Avery could still see his father fleeing for his life through the window to the backyard. He'd slipped and fallen in dog feces, and tried to get back to his feet.

Then Richelieu, totally nude, stood in the window with his pistol in his fist and opened fire. The rolling thunder had driven Gerard Moreau to the ground and ripped the life from him in bloody handfuls.

Avery had hidden. He'd been too afraid to act, and too inexperienced to know what to do if he had tried. He'd held himself and cried silent tears. In the end, he'd had to clap a hand over his mouth in order to keep from crying out.

Later, Richelieu told everyone that he had been the first to respond to the burglar alarm at the Pettit house. After he'd dressed, he'd obviously told Isabelle Pettit to set off the alarm.

No one asked why Richelieu felt compelled to shoot a fleeing suspect six times in the back. The police inspector had simply stated that it had been dark, which was the truth, and he claimed not to have known who the burglar was.

Everyone knew that Gerard Moreau never carried a weapon. He'd always stolen what he could, laid out his time in jail, and lived a mostly quiet life.

Gerard Moreau had tried to stop his son from becoming a thief. In the end, though, there hadn't been any other way for Avery to get the kinds of clothes he needed to wear or any of a thousand things it took to be a teenager in today's world.

When he'd seen he couldn't curb his son's ways, Gerard

Moreau decided to properly train Avery in the ways of a burglar. He'd claimed that as his father, he could do no less than offer him the trade that he had employed to sustain his family.

That night at the Pettit house had been the first—and last—time father and son had worked a job together.

Knowing that his voice would never be heard—if it was, his tale would only land him in jail and would not bring his father's murderer any closer to justice—Avery ran that night. Later, when the policemen came calling at his door, he'd acted surprised about his father's death. Even if they'd suspected anything, his grief was real and they'd left him alone with it.

Three days after he'd been shot and killed, Gerard Moreau had been laid to rest in a pauper's grave in the church cemetery. And Avery had sworn revenge.

The only way he could conceive to get it, though, was through Corvin Lesauvage and his secret society. Avery had known about them through some of the other guys his age who had become part of Lesauvage's gang. Pack, they called themselves. They were part of what Lesauvage termed the Wild Hunt. And Lesauvage had a magic potion that could make men invincible.

"Are you ready?" Marcel asked.

Not trusting his voice, Avery nodded.

Turning, Marcel knocked on the wall of the basement beneath the big house Lesauvage owned. Gears ground within the wall, then a section of it pulled back and away to reveal a doorway.

"Praise be to the name of the Hunter," Marcel intoned as he stepped through the doorway.

"Praise be to the name of the Hunter," Avery echoed as he followed Marcel. He didn't know who the Hunter was.

But Lesauvage and his pack took their mysticism seriously.

Another young man dressed in wolfs' hides stood in the middle of the narrow, twisting flight of stairs that led down into the bedrock. He held two flaming torches. He passed one to Marcel.

In silence, they marched down the stairs. The wavering torchlight made footing tricky. Several times Avery made a misstep that could have sent him plunging down the stairs. He didn't think anyone waiting down there would have bothered to carry him back up.

The pack waited at the bottom. There were at least thirty of them standing together, each of them with a torch.

The first time Avery had come here, he'd been scared to death. There were caves all throughout the area, but he hadn't expected to walk around in one under a house near the center of town. According to the tales he'd heard, the cave had once served as a smuggler's den for pirate goods hauled up from the southern coast of France and bound for Paris.

Bats hung among the stalactites. Several of the corresponding stalagmites had been removed. Avery thought the cave smelled like death. It also smelled like wet dog and bat guano.

Marcel put a hand against Avery's chest and stopped him. Then Marcel and the other pack member went to join the group.

Avery felt the fear returning. Being set apart from peers had always been a bad thing. Either as punishment or as a reward, getting singled out nearly always resulted in negative consequences. He'd learned that in school. It was one of those lessons that stayed with a person the rest of his life.

"Avery Moreau." The deep voice echoed within the vast cavern.

"Yes." Avery had to try twice to get his voice to work. He raised a hand to shield his eyes from the light. Even squinting didn't help against the bright torchlight.

"You failed me."

Fear gripped Avery's heart then and he stood—barely— trembling. "I did everything I could. I led you to the woman. I told you where she would be in the mountains."

"Annja Creed escaped, and she took something that belonged to me." Lesauvage, dressed in hides and wearing a helmet that sported huge deer antlers, stepped forward from the pack. His helmet came complete with snarling deer features that were stained muddy scarlet. His light-colored eyes glittered.

"That wasn't my fault," Avery said. "I didn't do it."

"You bear the blame for this," Lesauvage accused. "You brought the outsider to the woman."

What about the other guys? Avery wanted to ask. What about those men dressed in black? It's not my fault they showed up!

"Look," he said desperately, "that wasn't my fault. I'll do anything you want me to."

Lesauvage stepped toward him.

Avery backed away.

"You failed us," Lesauvage said again. "But you can still serve us." He drew a long-bladed knife from the sleeve of the robe he wore under the wolf hides.

At a gesture from their leader, the pack descended upon Avery. Working quickly, as if they'd done this sort of thing countless times, they bound his hands and feet and draped him over a rounded stalagmite in the center of the cave.

One of them brought out a goat, yanking the poor creature savagely. Lesauvage stepped over to the goat and dragged his knife along its throat.

Blood spewed out. One of the pack members held a stainless-steel pot under the flow. But the dying creature fought and kicked, spattering the stone floor with its lifeblood. Finally, it grew still.

Chanting and cheering, two of the pack members seized the goat and heaved the animal into the shadowy crevasse. There was no thump of arrival. No one had ever measured the waiting fall.

Another pack member passed out tin cups and each person took a portion of the blood. Lesauvage passed among them, dropping powder into the steaming liquid. They stirred the brew with their fingers and drank it down.

Howling like madmen, their faces red with goat's blood, the pack danced with savage abandon as the drugs worked into their systems.

Avery had seen a sacrifice only once before. It had been two weeks ago, after his father had been murdered and before the American woman—Annja Creed—had arrived to search for La Bête. It had scared him then. Tied up as he was on the rock, potentially their next sacrifice, he was now even more frightened.

Lesauvage gestured to Avery.

Immediately four members, including Marcel, descended upon him like carrion feeders. They forced open his jaws and poured down a cup of goat's blood and drugs, howling in his ears the whole time.

At first, Avery thought he was going to drown. He tried not to drink, tried to turn his head away, but they held him firmly. He swallowed, gagging as he almost inhaled it. Once he'd drawn a full breath, they filled his mouth again.

Over and over, the salty taste of the blood coated the inside of his mouth. He thought he was going to be sick. I didn't want this! I only wanted justice for my father!

Finally they left him alone and returned to chanting and singing. They whirled and slammed into each other, laughing when they knocked each other down.

And the drugs hit Avery's system like surf smashing across a reef barrier, gliding through in a diffused spray that hit everything. The fear inside him evaporated. Energy filled him.

Lesauvage came and stood over Avery. The knife in the man's hand dripped blood.

"You can still serve us," Lesauvage told him.

Avery thought the way the man's voice echoed and rolled and changed timbres was amusing. So amusing, in fact, that he was laughing out loud before he knew it.

Then Lesauvage leaned in close to Avery. Light exploded all around, glinting from the crimson-streaked edge of the knife.

"Now!" Lesauvage shouted. "Now you will serve us!"

Avery watched as the blade rose and fell. He didn't know whether to laugh or to scream.

16

"Are you nervous?" Annja asked as Garin slowly approached the huge house built into the hillside.

"A little." Garin shrugged. "Roux and I never part on good terms. Not since—" He paused. "Not for a very long time."

"The last time I saw him, he walked out on a dinner tab on me." Annja gazed up at the house. She didn't know where they were. Garin had taken a number of turns after they'd left the highway. All she knew was that they were somewhere south of Paris.

"A dinner tab?" Garin chuckled.

"It was nothing to laugh about. My credit card took a serious hit over that."

"The last time I saw Roux," Garin said, "he tried to kill me."

Annja stared at him.

"I attempted to blow up his car first," Garin explained as if it was nothing. "With him in it. So I suppose he was entitled." He shrugged. "He was dazed at the time, or maybe he would have got me. I truly didn't expect him to survive."

"Then why isn't he meeting you at the gate with a rocket launcher?" Annja asked while wondering once again what rabbit hole she had fallen down.

"Because I've got you and he's interested in talking to you. Right now. Perhaps getting out of the house will be more…risky."

"Oh." Annja thought maybe she should have opted for the airport and a chance at escape.

But she would have left behind the mystery and she didn't like unfinished business.

"Maybe Roux has gotten over your attempt to kill him," Annja suggested.

"I doubt it. He can be rather unforgiving."

She thought about Lesauvage and the Brotherhood of the Silent Rain. She didn't feel very forgiving toward them.

Garin eased to a stop at the gatehouse. His gun rested in his lap. He dropped his right hand over it.

"How long has it been?" Annja asked. "Since you tried to blow him up, I mean?"

"Twenty years. In Rio de Janeiro."

"Twenty years ago?"

"Yes." Garin's attention was on the armed guard approaching the car.

Annja thought he had to be joking. But as he thumbed down the window, he was tense as piano wire. It wasn't a joke. *But twenty years?*

"You hold your age well," she commented dryly.

"You," Garin assured her, "have no idea." He raised his voice and spoke to the guard. "Stay back from the car."

The guard started to lift his assault rifle.

"If you raise that rifle," Garin said, showing the man the big pistol, "I'm going to kill you."

The guard froze. "Mr. Roux," he said in a calm voice.

"Yes," Roux's unmistakable voice came over the radio.

"Your guest is armed."

"Of course he is. I wouldn't expect him any other way. Let him pass. I'll deal with him."

"Yes, sir." The guard waved to his counterpart inside the gatehouse.

Garin smiled but never moved the pistol from the center of the man's chest. "Thank you." The gates separated and he rolled forward, following the ornate drive to the big house.

"A lot of testosterone in the air tonight," Annja commented. She had to work to make herself sound calm. She was anything but.

"There is a lot," Garin said, "that you don't know."

ROUX STOOD outside the house, defiant and confident, as if he were a general in control of a battlefield instead of a lion trapped in his den. He wore a dark suit that made him look like a wealthy businessman. His hair and beard were carefully combed.

A young man in butler's livery opened Annja's car door. He said, "Welcome, miss," in a British accent sharp as a paper cut.

Annja stepped out, still wearing the blouse and shorts she had worn for her research trip through Lozère that morning and afternoon. She felt extremely underdressed.

Garin's black clothes suited the night and the surroundings. He slipped the big pistol under his jacket.

"Miss Creed," Roux greeted her with a smile, as if they had just been introduced and none of the previous day's weirdness had occurred between them. "Welcome to my home."

Annja tried not to appear awestruck.

The home was huge. Palatially huge. Ivy clung to the stone walls and almost pulled the house into the trees that surrounded it, softening the straight lines and absorbing the colors. The effect was clearly deliberate.

The butler stood by Roux and his eyes never left Garin. In response, Garin bared his teeth in a shark's merciless grin.

"You have a new lapdog," Garin said.

"Do not," Roux growled in warning, "trifle with Henshaw. If you do, one of you will surely be dead. I will not suffer his loss willingly."

Roux even talked differently in his home, Annja realized. He's really buying into the whole lord-of-the-manor thing.

"An Englishman?" Garin snorted derisively. "After everything we've been through, you trust your life to an Englishman?"

"I do," Roux said. "I've found few others worth trusting."

Garin folded his arms and said nothing.

Roux turned his attention to Annja. "You must be tired."

"No," Annja replied.

"Hungry?"

"No," she said. She returned his bright blue gaze full measure. "Eating with you is too expensive."

Roux laughed in honest delight. "I did hope you had enough to cover the bill."

"Thanks," Annja said. "Tons." She held out her hand. "You owe me for your half of the bill."

Amused, Roux snaked a hand into his pocket and pulled out a thick sheaf of bills. He pressed several into her hand.

Annja counted out enough to cover his half of the bill, then gave the rest back.

He frowned a little. "I'm sure the tab was more than that."

"It was," Annja said. "I only took half. Plus half the tip."

"I would have paid for it all."

"No," she told him. "I don't want to owe you anything."

Roux put the money way. "There's still the bit about me saving your life in the cave."

"Really?" Annja smiled sweetly. She spoke without turning around, but she could see the man in her peripheral vision. "Garin?"

"Yes," he replied.

"Do you want to kill Mr. Roux right now?"

"Nothing," the big man said, "would make me happier."

"Please don't."

Garin's smile broadened. "If you insist."

"I do." Looking directly at Roux, Annja nodded. "We're even. I just saved your life."

A displeased look filled Roux's patrician features. "You're going to be trouble," he declared.

"I find I'm liking her more and more all the time," Garin said.

"If nothing else, this should be interesting," Roux announced.

"I want to see the charm," Annja said.

Roux ushered them into his house.

IF THE HOUSE HAD APPEARED wondrous and magical on the outside, it was even more so on the inside.

Annja gave up trying to act unimpressed. Paintings, ceramic works of art, stained glass, weapons, books and other pieces that should have been in museums instead of a man's home adorned the spacious rooms. Most of them had private lighting.

If Roux wasn't already wealthy, he would be if he sold

off his collections. And a crook besides. Several of the pieces Annja saw were on lists of stolen items or had been banned from being removed from their country of origin.

The trip back to his personal office took time. Garin—obviously no lover of antiquities—looked bored as he trailed along after them, but Roux took obvious delight in showing off his acquisitions. He even offered brief anecdotes or histories regarding them.

Annja didn't know how long it took to get to the sword, but she was convinced it was a trip she'd never forget.

"The sword, the sword," Garin said when he could no longer hold his tongue. "Come on, Roux. You and I have waited for over five hundred years. Let's not wait any longer."

Five hundred years? Annja thought, realizing only then what he'd said. She figured it was only an exaggeration meant to stress a point.

Roux's office offered an even more enticing obstacle course that cried out for Annja's attention. Evidently he kept his favorite—and unique—items from his collections there.

Finally, though, with much prodding from Garin, and a promise of physical violence that almost triggered an assault from Henshaw, they reached Roux's vault room.

The huge door swiveled open. Roux disappeared inside the vault and returned carrying a case. He placed the case on the huge mahogany desk and opened it.

Something deeply moving attracted Annja's attention even more strongly than all the priceless objects she'd passed to reach this point. She stared at the pieces that had once made up the sword blade. Some of them were only thin needles of steel. Others looked as if they'd burned black in a fire. None of them would ever fit together again.

Yet she knew they all belonged together.

Somehow, on a level that she truly didn't understand, Annja knew that all the pieces were there. And that they had at last come home.

Unbidden, she stepped forward and reached out her right hand. Heat radiated against her palm.

"The pieces are hot," she said.

Standing beside her, Roux stretched out a hand. "I don't feel anything," he said.

Annja shook her head. "These pieces are giving off heat. I can feel it." She studied the pieces, finding the charm she had discovered in La Bête's lair.

It lay with the wolf and mountain side up. Bending down, the switched on the desk light and peered at the image.

"What do you know about the charm, Roux?" she asked.

The old man shrugged. "Nothing. I only knew when I saw it that it was part of this sword."

"Joan of Arc's sword?"

Roux turned on Garin. "You told her?"

The younger man looked impassive. "Does it matter?"

"You're a fool," Roux snapped. "You've always been a fool."

"And it's taken you over five hundred years to find the pieces of this sword," Garin returned. "*If* you've found them. I'd say that's pretty ineffectual. Perhaps recruiting people to help would have moved things along more quickly."

Annja moved her hand slowly over the sword fragments.

Roux, Garin and Henshaw all drew closer.

"Is this really her sword?" Annja asked. She moved her hand faster. "Joan of Arc's?" The heat was back, more intense than before.

"Yes," Roux said hoarsely.

"How do you know?"

"Because I saw her carry it."

Annja looked at him. "That was more than five hundred years ago."

"Yes," Roux agreed seriously. "It was. I saw the soldiers break Joan's sword. I watched her burn at the stake." Sadness filled his face. "There was nothing I could do."

Numb with disbelief, but hearing the echo of truth in the old man's words, Annja tried to speak and couldn't. She tried again. "That's impossible," she whispered.

The old man shook his head. "No. There are things you don't know yet. Impossible things happen." He paused, studying the pieces. "I'm gazing at my latest reminder of that."

Annja held her hand still. The pieces seemed to quiver below her palm. Before she knew she was doing it, she shoved both hands closer.

Her fingers curled around the leather-wrapped hilt.

An explosion of rainbow-colored light filled the case and overflowed into Roux's den. The shadow of something flew overhead on wings of driven snow. A single musical note thrummed.

For one brief second, Annja lifted the sword from the case. In that second, she was amazed to see that the sword's blade was whole. The rainbow-colored light reflected on the highly polished metal.

Images of other lights were caught in the blade's surface. A hundred pinpoints of flaming arrows sailed into the sky. Small houses burned to the ground. Running men in armor and covered with flaming oil died in their tracks, their faces twisted by screams of agony that thankfully went unheard.

At that moment, more than anything, Annja wanted to protect the sword. She didn't want Roux or Garin to take it from her. She had the strangest thought that it had been away too long already.

The sword vanished. The weight dissipated from her hands. She was left holding air.

"Where did it go?" Roux roared in her ear. "What did you do with the sword?" He grabbed Annja roughly by the shoulders and spun her around to face him. "What the hell did you do?"

At first, Annja didn't even recognize he was speaking in Latin. She reacted instinctively, clasping her hands together and driving her single fist up between them to break his hold on her. Still moving, she swung her doubled fists into the side of his head.

Roux spilled onto the Persian rug under the ornate desk where the empty case now sat.

The sword was gone.

17

Garin and Henshaw froze. Annja knew if either of them had so much as flinched, someone—perhaps both—would have died.

Getting to his feet with as much aplomb and dignity as he could muster under the circumstances, Roux cursed and worked his jaw experimentally, a bad combination as it turned out.

Annja dropped into fighting stance, both hands held clenched in fists before her. "I didn't do anything to the sword," she told the old man. "It disappeared. I lifted it from the case—"

"The pieces disappeared as soon as you touched the hilt," Roux snarled. "I saw that happen."

"Pieces?" Annja echoed. "It wasn't pieces that disappeared. I drew the sword out of that case. It was whole."

Roux searched her face with his harsh, angry gaze. "Poppycock. The sword was still in pieces."

He's insane, Annja thought. *That's the only explanation.*

And Garin, too. Both of them as mad as hatters. And they've given you something—a chemical—something that soaks in through the skin. Or maybe the room has something in the air. You didn't see what you thought you saw. Something like that can't have happened.

She told herself that, but didn't completely believe it. She'd been under the influence of hallucinogens strong enough to give her waking dreams and walking nightmares before.

Once, in Italy, she'd come in contact with a leftover psychotropic drug used by one of Venice's Medici family members that had still been strong enough to send her to the hospital for two days.

In England, she'd been around Rastafarians who had helped with packing the supplies on a dig site who had smoked joints so strong she had a contact high that lasted for hours. She'd never used recreational drugs. But she knew what kinds of effects to look for.

There were none of those now.

"Think about it, Roux," Garin insisted. "If she took the sword pieces, where are they? She has no pockets large enough to store them. We were all watching her."

Roux cursed more as he searched the case and came up empty again.

"The sword wasn't in pieces when it disappeared," Annja told them. "Aren't you listening?"

"It was in pieces," Roux growled. "I saw them."

"I took the sword from the case—"

"Those pieces disappeared while they were still inside the case," Roux snapped. "I watched them."

"Then you didn't see what happened." Annja blew out her breath angrily. "The sword was whole."

Roux turned to Henshaw. "What did you see?"

"The sword was fragmented when it disappeared, Mr. Roux," Henshaw said. "Just as it was when you first showed it to me. Never in one piece."

"There you have it," Roux declared angrily. "All of us saw the sword in pieces."

"No," Annja said. "You didn't see it properly."

"You're imagining things." Roux sank into the huge chair behind the big desk. He regarded her intently. "Tell us what happened."

"I reached into the case for the sword—"

"Why?" Garin asked.

"Because I wanted to feel the weight of the haft," Annja answered. She didn't feel comfortable talking about the compulsion that had moved her to action. "As I touched the sword hilt, the pieces fit themselves together."

"By themselves?" Roux asked dubiously.

"I didn't move them."

"She didn't have time to fit the pieces together," Garin said. "You, on the other hand, have had time. And I'll bet nothing like this happened while you were trying to put those pieces together."

After a moment, Roux growled irritably, "No."

"*Something* happened to the sword fragments," Garin said.

"It was whole," Annja said again. She could still see the sword in her mind's eye. It felt as if she could almost touch it.

But neither of the men was listening to her.

"Five hundred years, Garin." Roux leaned forward and put his head in his hands. "*Over* five hundred years. I searched everywhere for that sword, for those pieces. Now they're all gone."

Garin's voice was gentle and kind. He didn't sound like someone who had tried to kill Roux.

Of course, Annja decided, he didn't sound insane, either, and he had to be. Both of them had to be.

Roux stared at the empty case.

"Once I had them all together, *something* should have happened," Roux complained bitterly.

"It disappeared," Garin said. He looked relieved.

"It wasn't supposed to do that," Roux argued.

"You said you didn't know what it would do."

"Wait." Annja held her hands up and stepped between them. "Time out."

They gave her their attention.

"*Who* told you to find the sword?" For the moment, Annja decided to go along with their delusion or outright lie that they had seen Joan of Arc carry the sword.

"I don't know," Roux said.

The old man shrugged. "Joan was one of God's chosen. A champion of light and good. It was my duty."

Annja breathed deeply and tried not to freak. The situation was getting even crazier.

An alarm erupted, dispelling the heavy silence that fell over the room.

Immediately, a section of the wall to the left of the computer desk split apart and revealed sixteen security monitors in four rows. Ghostly gray images sprinted across the landscaping outside the big house.

"Intruders," Roux said.

The intruders wore familiar black robes and carried swords that flashed in the pale moonlight. They also came armed with assault rifles and pistols.

A security guard took up a position beside the house and

fired at the monks. Almost immediately, a monk with an assault rifle chopped him down, then turned and came toward the house.

The new arrivals began targeting the security cameras. One by one, the monitors inside Roux's study went dark.

Galvanized into action, the old man ran for the vault. "Who the hell are they?" he shouted.

"Monks," Garin replied.

"Monks?" Roux took an H&K MP-5 submachine pistol from the vault, shoved a full magazine into it and released the receiver to set the first round under the firing pin.

Annja was familiar with the weapon from the training she'd received.

"Some kind of warrior monks from the looks of them," Garin added. "Like the Jesuits. With better firepower."

"What are monks doing attacking my home?" Roux asked.

"In Lozère, they were looking for the woman," Garin said. After a brief glance at Roux's armory, he took down a Mossberg semiautomatic shotgun with a pistol grip and smiled like a boy on Christmas morning. He shoved boxes of shells into his jacket pockets.

Roux turned his gaze on Annja, who stood panicked and confused.

"Do you prefer a short gun or long gun, Miss Creed?" Henshaw asked. He had two rifles slung over his shoulders and was buckling a pistol around his waist.

"Pistols," Annja said, thinking that they would be more useful in the closed-in areas of the big house.

Henshaw handed her a SIG-Sauer .40-caliber semiautomatic with a black matte finish.

"I thought I saw another one in there," Annja said.

For the first time that night, Henshaw smiled. "Bless your heart, dear lady." He handed her a second pistol, then outfitted her with a bulletproof vest with pockets for extra magazines.

Roux buckled himself into a Kevlar vest, as well. "I don't suppose they're here to negotiate?" he asked rhetorically.

The lights went out. For a moment blackness filled the room. Then emergency generators kicked to life and some light returned.

Roux clapped on a Kevlar helmet. "What the bloody hell do these monks want?"

"Their mark was on the back of the charm," Annja said. "What do you think the chances are?"

"I think I should have paid more attention to that damned charm. Giving it back to them before was merely out of the question. Now that option appears gone for good."

"This house is pretty well fortified," Garin said as he saw to his own protection.

"Thank you," Roux said. "I tried to see that it was well-appointed."

"Do you think they can get through the front door?"

A sudden explosion shuddered through the house with a deafening roar.

Roux touched a hidden button on his desk. The dark monitors, powered by generator, came back on. This time the views were from inside the house.

On one of the screens, a dozen monks poured through the shattered remains of the elegant front door. They opened fire at once.

"Yes," Roux declared. "I believe they can." He picked up the submachine pistol.

"Do you have an escape route?" Garin asked.

"I recall having escaped from your assassins on a number of occasions."

Garin scowled. "This isn't a good time to revisit past transgressions."

"Then you'll warn me before you transgress again?" Roux asked.

Garin remained silent.

"I didn't think so," Roux said. "Henshaw?"

"Yes, sir." The butler stood only a short distance away, always positioned so that Garin couldn't take him and his master out at one time with a single shotgun blast.

"You know what to do if this bastard shoots me," Roux said.

"He won't live to see the outcome, sir."

"Right." Roux smiled. He took the lead with Garin at his heels as if they'd done it for years.

At the wall beside the security monitors, the old man pushed against an inset decorative piece. A section of the wall yawned open and revealed a narrow stairwell lit by fluorescent tubes.

"Where does it go?" Garin asked.

"All the way up to the third floor. Once there, we can escape onto the hillside. I've got a jeep waiting there that should serve as an escape vehicle." Roux stepped into the stairwell and started up the steps.

Garin followed immediately, having to turn slightly because he was so broad.

Two monks dashed into the study and raised their rifles.

Calmly, Henshaw pulled the heavy British assault rifle to his shoulder and fired twice, seemingly without even taking the time to aim. Each round struck a monk in the head, splattering the priceless antiques behind them with gore.

Before the dead men could fall, Henshaw had a hand in the middle of Annja's back. "Off you go, Miss Creed. Step lively, if you please." He sounded as pleasant as if they were out for an evening stroll.

Annja went, stumbling over the first couple steps, then running for all she was worth. The door closed behind them. Her breath sounded loud in her ears as she rapidly caught up with Garin. Gunshots sounded behind her, muffled by the door, and she knew the Brotherhood of the Silent Rain was tearing up Roux's study.

All of this over a charm? Annja couldn't believe it. The charm was hiding something, but she had no clue what.

THE TUNNEL ENDED against the sloped side of the roof. Roux sprung some catches and shoved the hatch open.

Through the opening, Annja stood on the roof and gazed around. The pistols felt heavy in her hands. Cooled by the breeze skating along the trees behind the house, she surveyed the area. Shouts echoed from inside the tunnel as their pursuers followed.

"Here." Roux ran toward the tree line where the house butted into the hill. There, barely lit by the moon, a trail whip-sawed across the granite bones of the land. "Another two hundred yards and we'll reach the jeep."

At that moment, shadows separated from the trees and became black-robed monks.

Garin swore coarsely. "These guys are everywhere!" The shotgun came to his shoulder and he started firing at once, going forward after Roux all the same.

Annja fired, as well, but she didn't know if she hit anything or just added to the general confusion. Bullets pocked the rooftop, tearing shingles away at her feet.

Another round hit her, slamming into her high on the shoulder. The Kevlar vest did its job and didn't allow the bullet to penetrate, but the blunt trauma knocked her down all the same.

She fought her way back to her feet, stayed low and moved forward. When her second pistol fired dry, she whirled behind a tree, shoved the first one up under her arm to free her hand and reloaded the second. She was reloading the first when a monk leaped out of the shadows in front of her.

His face was dark and impassive. "We have come only for the charm," he said in a quiet, deadly voice. "That's all. You may live."

"I don't have it," Annja said as she brought the pistols up.

He leaped at her, his sword held high for a killing stroke.

Crossing the pistol barrels over her head, hoping she wasn't about to lose her fingers, Annja blocked the descending blade. When she was certain the sword had stopped short of splitting her skull and lopping her hands off, she snap-kicked the man in the groin, then again in the chest to knock him back from her.

Before Annja could get away, two more monks surrounded her. They didn't intend to use swords, though. They held pistols.

"Move and you die," one of them warned.

Annja froze.

"Drop the pistols."

She did, but her mind was flying, looking for any escape route.

One of the monks spun suddenly, his face coming apart in crimson ruin. The bark of the gunshot followed almost immediately.

The surviving monks turned to face the new threat. Muzzle-flashes ripped at the night and lit their hard-planed faces.

Garin fired the shotgun again, aiming at the nearest target. The monk moved just ahead of the lethal hail of pellets that tore bark from the tree behind him.

While the attention was off her, Annja stooped and scooped up the pistols. Just as she lifted them, a monk rushed Garin from the rear, following his sword.

"Behind you!" Annja pointed the pistols toward the monk, but Garin swung around into her line of fire.

The sword sliced through Garin's black leather jacket. Coins and the keys to his car glittered in the moonlight as they spilled out. Catching the man on the end of the shotgun's barrel, Garin loosed a savage yell and fired.

Trapped against the body with nowhere for the expanding gases to go, the shotgun recoil was magnified. Caught while turning on the soft loam, Garin went down under the monk's body. Carried by the forward momentum he'd built up, almost ripped in half by the shotgun blast, the dead man wrapped his arms around Garin's upper body.

Shouting curses, Garin rolled out from under the corpse and pushed himself to his feet. Gunshots slapped against his chest. Another cut the side of his face and blood wept freely. He pulled the shotgun to his shoulder and tried to fire, but it was empty.

He looked at Annja. "Run!" Then he sped up the mountainside as fast as he could go.

Annja tried to follow. Before she went more than ten feet, the arriving monks turned on her. The escape route was cut off. She didn't know if Garin was going to make it before he was overtaken.

Metal glinted on the ground only a few feet away. Even as she recognized what the object was, she was firing both pistols, chasing the monks back into hiding. It was a brief respite at best.

When both SIG-Sauers blasted empty, she dropped the pistol from her left hand and scooped up Garin's keys amid the scattered change lying on the ground. Then she turned and ran back down the mountain. Garin's car, almost as heavily armored as a tank, still sat out in front of the main house. If she could reach the car, she thought she had a chance.

18

"Stop her but do not kill her!"

As she ran, Annja knew the command gave her a slight edge over the monks pursuing her. She didn't try running back onto the roof of the house. Monks were already taking up perimeter positions atop it.

Instead, Annja ran for the side of the house. When she was past the house's edge, she put the car fob between her teeth, shifted the pistol to her left hand and used her right to drag against the house. Her fingers clutched and tore at ivy as she began the steep descent.

She ran faster and faster, gaining speed as gravity reached for her and she raced to keep up the pace by lengthening her stride. But in the end she didn't have a stride long enough to remain in control.

Somewhere past the second story, Annja's foot slipped on a rock, her hand tore through the clinging ivy and she grabbed a handful of air.

She fell.

Tumbling end over end, unable to control either her speed or her direction, Annja gathered a collection of bruises and scrapes. She landed with a force that left her breathless.

Get up! she willed herself. Somehow, her body obeyed, pushing, shoving, working even though she felt as if she'd been broken into pieces. Incredibly, her knees came up and she was driving her feet hard against the ground.

Bullets slammed into the house beside her and into the ground. A man stepped out of the darkness ahead of her. She brought her pistol up automatically and fired for the center of his body. The bullets hit him and drove him back.

She was around the house and running for all she was worth. Shadows closed in around her. She couldn't help wondering how many members belonged to the Silent Rain monastery.

She thought of the sword in her hand. The look and feel of it, the weight, it was almost there. As if she could reach out and touch it.

Everyone around her seemed to be moving in slow motion. But she moved at full speed.

Bullets thudded into the ground where she'd been. She moved more quickly than the monks could compensate. When she saw Garin's Mercedes, monks flanked it, standing at either end. One stood on the hood of the car and raised an assault rifle.

She didn't hesitate; there was nowhere else to go. Pointing the pistol, never breaking stride, she found she'd fired it dry. Knowing that if she turned away she would only be an easier target, she ran straight toward the monk and leaped, sliding across the car's hood and knocking her opponent from his feet as he fired over her head.

Landing on the other side of the car in a confusing tangle of arms and legs, she fought free and stood. The man standing at the rear of the car tried to turn but he was too slow. She swung the empty pistol at the base of his skull and knocked him out.

As the man fell, she stepped forward and delivered a roundhouse kick to the monk in front of the car. Her foot caught him in the chest and knocked him backward several feet.

Annja was too scared to be amazed. Adrenaline, she told herself. She'd never kicked anyone that hard in her life.

She slid behind the wheel, keyed the ignition and heard the powerful engine roar to life, and shoved it into gear. The rear wheels spun and caught traction, then she was hurtling forward.

The front gates were still locked. Annja mentally crossed her fingers and hoped that the armored car was sufficient for the task. As she drove into the gate, she ducked her head behind her arms and hung on to the steering wheel.

For a moment, it sounded as if the world were coming to an end. An ugly image of her trapped and burning in the car filled her head. Fire had always been one of her greatest fears.

The car shuddered and jerked. Then, miraculously, it powered through the broken, sagging tangle of gates. Sparks flared around her as the car rode roughshod over the gates. She was on the other side, fighting the sudden fishtailing as the car lunged briefly out of control.

She cut the wheels just short of the trees at the side of the road and managed to keep the Mercedes pointed in the right direction. One of the headlights was broken—she could tell that from the monocular view of the road—but she could see well enough with the other.

She hoped Garin, Roux and Henshaw had made it to safety, but she had no intention of trying to find them. She'd had enough craziness for now.

Switching on the car's GPS program, she quickly punched in directions to Paris. She was catching the first flight to New York she could find.

ANNJA BOUGHT a change of clothes—a pink I Love Paris sweatshirt and black sweatpants—a black cap she tucked her hair into and black wraparound sunglasses at a truck stop outside Paris. They were tourist clothes, overpriced and gaudy. It wasn't much of a disguise, but wearing her own clothes was out of the question. Somewhere along the way she'd gotten someone's blood on them. She left them in the trash in the bathroom.

She abandoned the car and caught a ride with a driver making a delivery to the airport, wanting to conserve her cash in case she had to run again.

As Europe's second-busiest airport, Charles de Gaulle International was busy even at one o'clock in the morning. The driver was kind enough to drop her at Terminal 1, where most of the international flights booked.

Annja cringed a little when she paid full price for the ticket, but went ahead and splurged for a first-class seat. After the events of the past two days, she didn't want people piled on top of her.

Especially not when the persons around her could be black-garbed monks in disguise.

You're being paranoid, she chided herself. But, after a moment's reflection, she decided she was all right with that. A temporary case of paranoia beat a permanent case of dead.

ANNJA DOZED fitfully on the plane. No matter what she did to relax, true sleep avoided her. Finally, she gave up and spent time with her journals and notebook computer. Thankfully she'd left them in Garin's car when they got to the mansion.

She didn't know if she'd ever again see the materials she'd left at the bed-and-breakfast.

She opened the computer and pulled up the jpegs she'd made of the sketches she'd done of the charm. She moved the images side by side and examined them.

"Would you like something to drink, miss?"

Startled, Annja looked up at the flight attendant. The question the man had asked slowly penetrated her fatigue and concentration.

"Yes, please," Annja replied. "Do you have any herbal tea?"

"I do. I'll get it for you."

The flight attendant returned a moment later with a cup filled with hot water and a single-serving packet of mint tea.

"Are you an artist?" the flight attendant asked.

"No," Annja answered, plopping the tea bag into the cup. "I'm an archaeologist."

"Oh. I thought maybe you were working on a video game."

"Why?"

The flight attendant shrugged. He was in his late thirties, calm and professional in appearance. "Because of the coin, I suppose. Seems like a lot of games kids today play have to do with coins. At least, that's the way it is with my kids. I've got three of them." He smiled. "I guess maybe I'm just used to looking for hidden clues in the coins."

"Hidden clues?"

"Sure. You know. Maybe it's a coin, but there are clues hidden in it. Secret messages, that sort of thing."

Annja's mind started working. She stared at the side of the charm that held the wolf and the mountain. Is there a clue embedded in here? Or is this just a charm? Why would that warrior wear it when he fought La Bête? Another thought suddenly struck her. Why was the warrior alone?

"I'll leave you alone with your work," the flight attendant said. "Have a good flight."

"Thank you," Annja said, but her mind was already hard at work, separating the image of the wolf and the mountain into their parts.

The obverse was the stylized sign of the Brotherhood of the Silent Rain. But she didn't know how stylized it was. Perhaps something had been added there, as well. She peered more closely, pumping up the magnification.

A moment later, she saw it. Behind three of the straight lines in the die mark of the Brotherhood of the Silent Rain, she saw a shadowy figure she hadn't seen before.

WHEN SHE REACHED New York City, the first thing Annja did was look to find out if she was going to be picked up by the police. Since the NYPD SWAT team wasn't waiting to cuff her when she stepped off the plane, she hoped that was a good sign.

Still, she didn't want to go home without knowing what to expect.

She hailed a cab in front of LaGuardia International and took it to Manhattan to an all-night cyber café. Since she lived in Brooklyn, she felt reasonably certain Manhattan would be safe.

Settled into a booth, her laptop plugged into the hard-line connection rather than the wireless so there would be no disruption of service—or less of it at any rate—she opened her e-mail. A brief glance showed she'd acquired a tremendous amount of spam, as usual, and had a few messages from friends and acquaintances, but nothing that couldn't keep.

There was a note from NYPD Detective Sergeant Bart McGilley that just read, Call me about those prints.

Annja didn't know if he was going to protest being asked to look them up or if he'd gotten a hit. Or maybe he was just the bait to bring her in. That gave her pause for a moment.

She decided to put off the call for a few minutes. At least until she had time to eat the food she'd ordered with the computer time.

She was surprised to find that once her mind started working she didn't feel the need for sleep. She didn't know where she was getting the extra energy from, but she was grateful.

She opened the alt.archaeology site and found a few comments expressing interest in the images she'd posted, but nothing helpful.

The alt.archaeology.esoterica board netted three replies to her question regarding the images.

The first was from kimer@thetreasuresinthepast.com.

Saw your pictures. Loved them. What you're looking at is some kind of coin minted for the Brotherhood of the Silent Rain. Wasn't used for money, but it's made of silver, Right?

If it is, then it's legitimate. There were also copper ones, and there are rumors of gold ones, too, though I've never talked to anyone who's seen one.

I've been researching European Monastic cults for my thesis. The brotherhood was disbanded three or four hundred years ago for some kind of sacrificial practice.

Sorry. Don't know any more than that. If you find out anything, I'd love to know more. Always curious.

The sandwich arrived, piled high with veggies and meat, with a bag of chips and a dill pickle spear on the side. A bottle of raspberry iced tea completed the meal.

As she ate one-handed, Annja worked through the other entries.

You've probably already found out that the stylized rain on the back of the coin represents the Brotherhood of the Silent Rain. They were one of the longest-lived monasteries in the Lozère/Mende area. Back when it was more commonly called Gévaudan.

That made the tie to La Bête more accessible, Annja thought. Since she didn't truly believe in coincidences, she looked for the connection.

Anyway, what you might not know is that it's still around. That coin you found was only minted for a few years. Maybe a dozen or twenty. Like everything else the monks did, they smithed the coins themselves. Had a forge and everything. What you've got there is a real find. I've got one of them myself. I've included pics.

Why would a basically self-supporting monastery mint its own coins? Annja asked herself.

Not only that, but the charm hadn't been minted of silver. Whoever forged it made it from the metal of the sword.

From Joan of Arc's sword. Annja still couldn't get around the thought of that.

Setting her sandwich to the side for a moment, Annja opened the attachments. The poster had done a great job with the pictures. They were clear and clean.

Judging from the pictures, the coin the poster owned was very similar to the one Annja had found in the cave. But that one looked like silver, even carried a dark patina that had never touched the one that Annja had found.

However, the coin in the pictures only had the image of the mountain, not the wolf. And there was no shadowy figure trapped behind three lines in the die mark.

She sighed and returned her attention to her sandwich. The mystery had deepened again. She loved archaeology for its challenges, stories and puzzles. But she hated the frustration that sometimes came with all of those.

The third message was from Zoodio, the original responder to her posting.

Hey. Hope you've had some luck with your enigma. I've had a bit, but it appears contradictory and confusing.

Welcome to archaeology, Annja thought wryly.

The coin you've got is different than the ones minted at the monastery. And minting for a monastery is weird anyway. I understand they took gold for the Vatican and all that. Had to fund the additional churches somehow. But they marked ingots with the papal seal. Most of the time, though, the church never bothered to melt down and recast anything that came through the offerings.

I noticed differences on your coin, though. I mean, the images I pulled up and got from friends are different. But I didn't find any that looked like the one you've got.

Taking a moment, Annja opened the images Zoodio had embedded in the message. Sifting through them, she found they were similar to the ones she'd gotten from the previous poster.

To start with, the coin you found doesn't appear to be made out of silver. Some other material?

Also, yours has differences. Did you notice the shadowy figure behind the stylized rain? I didn't at first. Had to look at it again, but I think it's there.

Excitement thrummed through Annja. She clicked on the embedded picture and it opened in a new window.

The image was one of those she had posted, but Zoodio had used a red marker to circle the shadowy figure, then colored it in yellow highlighter to make it stand out more.

This really caught my eye. I love stuff that doesn't make sense. I mean, eventually it will, but not at that precise moment, you know?

So I started looking. Turns out that the original Silent Rain monastery was attacked and burned down in 1767.

Shifting in her seat, noticing that it had started to rain outside, Annja felt another thrill of excitement. Zoodio hadn't been looking for a connection between the Brotherhood of the Silent Rain and La Bête, but she had suspected it was there because of Lesauvage's interests.

Of course, the monks showing up hadn't daunted that conclusion.

La Bête had claimed its final victim, at least according to most of the records, in 1767, over three hundred years ago.

And the monastery burned down that same year. Annja smiled at her rain-dappled image in the window. That can't be a coincidence, she thought. She was feeling energized. I do love secrets that have been hidden for hundreds of years.

She pondered the sword and how it had vanished. That was a whole other kind of secret.

During the flight back to the United States, she had come to the conclusion that Garin and Roux had somehow tricked her. She didn't know how, and she didn't know why, but there was no other explanation for the sword's disappearance that made any sense at all.

She shivered slightly and returned her focus to the computer.

Turns out that the monastery was self-contained. They didn't take just anyone who wanted in.

Not only that, these guys are supposed to be like the Jesuits. Warlike, you know? Trained in the sword and the pistol. Supposed to be masters of the blade and crack shots and all that rot.

Well…Annja thought, maybe they weren't as good as their reputation. Or maybe the latest generation has gotten rusty.

Then again, Roux, Garin and Henshaw weren't your average man on the street. The monks had walked into a hornet's nest.

The brotherhood wasn't well liked by the rest of the church. Too independent, too self-involved. Instead of reaching out to the community, the brotherhood sort of withdrew from it.

From the accounts I read, they didn't want to be contaminated by outsiders.

Then where did they get recruits? Annja wondered. She opened her journal and started making notes. As questions arose, she entered those, as well.

Later, she'd timeline it and start combing through the facts and suppositions she had and try to find the answers she needed. She'd learned to work through an outline, make certain the bones were there regarding an event she was researching, then flesh it out once she knew what she was looking for.

In a way they became the perfect prison.

Shortly before the monastery was destroyed, the pope or one of the high church members ordered a prisoner moved there. The Silent Rain monks were supposed to keep the prisoner until they were told to set him or her free. Rumor exists that the prisoner was a woman.

Annja found the possibility intriguing. Why would a woman be locked up in a monastery? Normally a woman would have been sent to an abbey. Or simply imprisoned.

But the story of Joan of Arc, how she'd been imprisoned and later killed at the hands of brutal men, echoed in Annja's head. Written history had a way of being more kind and gentle than what an archaeologist actually found broken and bashed at the bottom of a sacrificial well or buried in an unmarked shallow grave.

While working on dig sites throughout Europe, and even in the American Southwest, Annja had seen several murder victims. Those people had never been important enough in history's selective vision to rate even a footnote most of the time. People were lost throughout history. It was a sad truth, but it was a truth.

Whoever it was, the story goes that an armed force descended on the monastery to free the prisoner. During the battle, the monastery burned to the ground. The fields were sown with salt so nothing would grow there for years.

And, supposedly, everyone at the monastery was killed. No one knows what happened to the prisoner.

But there's also a story that a few local knights, unhappy with how the church was speaking out against their hunting parties, decided they'd had enough and razed the monastery for that reason.

Don't know.

But I found the shadowy image (if it's there and not just a figment of my imagination!) really interesting.

I hope you'll let me know what you find out.

Annja closed down the notebook computer and gazed out the window. There were so many unanswered questions.

A few minutes later, she flagged down a taxi and gave her address in Brooklyn. The sound of the tires splashing through the rain-filled streets lulled her. Her eyelids dropped. She laid her head back on the seat and let her mind roam. So many images were at war for her attention. The find at the cave. La Bête. Lesauvage, so smooth and so dangerous. Avery Moreau, whose father had been killed by Inspector Richelieu. The Brotherhood of the Silent Rain. Roux. Garin.

And the sword.

In her mind's eye, she pictured the sword as it had been, broken into fragments. She could clearly see the piece that had been stamped by the Silent Rain monastery.

In her memory, she reached for it again. Incredibly, the pieces all fit together and the sword was once more whole.

She reached for the sword, felt the rough leather wrapped around the hilt and the cold metal against her flesh.

When she closed her hand around the sword, she felt as if she was connected to it, as if it was part of her, as if she could pull it out of the case again.

She played the memory slowly, feeling the solid weight of the sword. Slowly, unable to stop herself from attempting the task even though she knew it was going to disrupt the memory, she withdrew the sword from the case.

It came, perfectly balanced for her grip.

"What the hell are you doing, lady?"

Annja's eyes snapped open. In disbelief, she saw the sword in her hand, stretched across the back of the taxi. It obstructed the driver's view through the back window. He looked terrified.

She was holding the sword!

19

Cursing loudly, the taxi driver cut across two lanes on Broadway. Thankfully traffic was light at the early-morning hour, but horns still blared in protest. His tires hit the curb in front of a closed electronics store.

Still under full steam, the driver leaped out of the taxi. He reached under the seat for an L-shaped tire tool that looked as if it could have been used on the kill floor in a slaughterhouse.

He jerked Annja's door open. "You!" he snarled, gesturing with the tire tool. "You get outta my cab!"

He was thin and anemic looking, with wild red hair tied back in a bun, wearing an ill-fitting green bowling shirt and khaki pants. He waved the tire tool menacingly.

For the moment, though, Annja ignored him. Somewhere during the confusion, the sword had disappeared. But it was here, she thought. I saw it. I felt it. *It was here.*

"C'mon!" the driver yelled. "Get outta there! What the hell do you think you were doin' waving that sword around like that? Like I wasn't gonna notice a sword!"

Dazed, Annja got out of the taxi. "You saw the sword?"

"Sure, I did!" the driver shouted. "Six feet long if it was an inch! And it—" He stopped suddenly. In disbelief, he stared at Annja, who stood there with her backpack slung over her shoulder. Then he motioned her away from the taxi. "Back up. Get outta there already."

Annja complied.

The driver's antics had drawn a small crowd.

The cabbie looked all over the back seat of the taxi. Then he dropped to his hands and knees and peered under the car. He even dragged his hands through the shadows as if doubting what his eyes revealed.

He clambered back to his feet. "All right," he demanded, "what did you do with it?"

"Nothing," Annja replied.

"You had a sword back there, lady. Biggest pig sticker I ever seen outside of *Braveheart*." The taxi driver glared at her.

"I don't have a sword," Annja said.

"I saw what I saw, lady."

Realizing the futility of the argument, Annja dropped twenty dollars on the seat, then turned and left, walking out into the street and hailing another cab immediately. She rode home quietly, trying not to think of anything, but wondering about everything.

TO THE CASUAL OBSERVER, Annja's neighborhood was run-down. She liked to think of it as lived-in, a piece of Brooklyn history.

Sandwiched amid the tall apartment buildings, the delis, the shops, the pizza parlors and the small grocery stores, her building was one of the oldest. Only four floors high, the top two floors were divided into lofts instead of apartments. An artist, a photographer, a sculptor and a yoga instructor lived there.

The ground floor was occupied by shops, including a small gallery that showcased local artists. A violin maker, a dentist, a private investigator, a fortune-teller and music teachers occupied offices on the second floor.

A freight elevator ran up all four stories, but Annja didn't take it. The residents had a tacit understanding that no one used the elevator at night because of the terrible noise it made. Annja had also found that she could generally just about pace the elevator as it rose.

She took the stairs in the dimly lit stairwell. In the years that she'd lived there, she'd never had any trouble. Vagrants and thieves tended to stay away from the building because so many people lived above the shops and kept watch.

Her door was plain, scarred wood under a thick varnish coat, marked only by the designation 4A. She liked to think of it as 4-Annja, and that was how she'd felt when she'd first seen the loft space.

She worked through the five locks securing the door, then went inside.

A feeling of safety like she'd never known descended upon her as soon as she closed the door. For a moment, she stood with her back to the door, as if she could hold out the rest of the world.

As far back as she could remember, she had shared her space. Though she'd been so young when her parents were killed that she couldn't really remember living with them. In the orphanage, there had been bunk beds stacked everywhere, and nuns constantly moving among them. Privacy had been nonexistent. As she'd grown older, her roommates had dropped down to four, but there was still no privacy.

In college, she'd shared a dorm room the first year, then settled into an apartment off campus with a revolving cast of roommates until graduation because none of them could afford to live on their own. The first few years after she'd graduated had been much the same. Only she'd been on digs—sharing campsites—ten months out of the year.

But then she'd sold her first book, a personal narrative detailing her experiences excavating a battlefield north of Hadrian's Wall in Britain. The rumor was that the legendary King Arthur had fought there. At least, the man the stories had been built on was believed to have fought there.

Professor Heinlein hadn't found any trace of King Arthur or his Knights of the Round Table, but he had discovered the murders of a band of Roman soldiers. In the official records, the unit had been lost while on maneuvers. From the evidence Annja had helped to unearth, the commander of the Roman centurions had killed them because they'd discovered his dealings with the Picts.

It appeared that the Roman commander had managed quite a thriving business in black market goods. Most wars inevitably produced such a trade, and there were always men ready to make a profit from it.

During the dig, though, Annja and the others reconstructed what had happened. The intrigue—digging for bones, then going through fragments of old Roman documents to re-create the circumstances—had captured her attention. Everyone on the dig team had been excited by what they were finding and by the murders.

She'd kept a journal simply to keep track of everything they were figuring out, detailing the dig with interconnected pieces on what must have happened during that action all those years ago, interspersing colorful bits of history and infusing the story with life. A British journalist had taken an interest in her writing, and read everything she'd written. He'd made a lot of suggestions and pointed out the possibility of a book.

Annja had worked on the journal, with an eye toward possible publication, at the site and when she'd returned to New York. Two years later, after the manuscript had found a publisher and come out as a book, it was enough of a success to allow Annja to make the down payment on the loft. Reviewers had said she'd made archaeology appealing for the masses and kicked in a bit of a murder mystery on the side.

After that, she'd continued getting dig site offers because the book served as a great introductory letter and résumé. She'd also made some appearances on the late-night talk-show circuit and had a chance to show that she was good in front of a camera.

She became a favorite of David Letterman, who worked hard to keep her off balance and flirt with her at the same time. Her minor celebrity status eventually landed her on *Chasing History's Monsters*.

Annja looked around the loft. The big room had a fourteen-foot ceiling. Shelves filled the walls and sagged under the weight of books, rocks, artifacts and other finds. Her desk sat overflowing with open books, sketchpads and faxes. File folders, although everything was in order about them, stood stacked in haphazard piles. A sea of technology washed up around the desk: scanners, digital cameras, audio equipment, GPS devices, projectors and other items that she found useful. Despite her love of history, she loved technology, too.

She'd had every intention of cracking the notebook

computer open and working on what she'd found out about the coin and the Brotherhood of the Silent Rain. But it felt so good to be home. Instead, she barely made it through a shower and into an oversize T-shirt before she collapsed into bed.

Her thoughts were of the sword. Had she really held it? Had the taxi driver really seen it? Was she losing her mind...?

THE ANNOYING SOUND of a ringing phone penetrated the haze of sleep.

"Good morning," Annja said. Without opening her eyes, she rolled over in bed and struggled to think clearly. She felt as if she'd been on cold medicine.

"Don't you mean 'Good afternoon'?" the caller asked. NYPD Homicide Detective Bart McGilley always sounded way too chipper, Annja thought grumpily as the words slowly registered.

She opened her eyes and looked at the skylight. From the hard, direct shadow on the varnished floor, she knew it had to be around noon.

Glancing over at the bedside clock, she saw the time was 12:03.

"Sorry." Annja pushed herself up from bed. She never slept this late. "You woke me. It's taking me a minute to catch up with myself."

"When did you get in yesterday?"

"You mean what time did I get in this morning?"

"Ouch. That's harsh. You must have slept hard."

Annja sat on the edge of the bed. "Why?"

"I called three times already."

"I didn't hear the phone ring."

"Lots of fun in France?" Bart sounded a little envious.

He'd told her more than once he could find his way around
New York City blindfolded. Seeing something new would
have been welcome.

"Hardly." Annja yawned and suddenly realized she was
ravenous. "Did you find out something about those prints
I sent you?"

"I did. We need to talk."

"We are talking." Annja heard the hesitation in his voice.
It wasn't something she usually heard in Bart McGilley.

"Face-to-face," he told her.

"Is it that bad?" Annja stood and walked to the window.
She moved the curtain aside and peered out. She loved the
view from the building. The streets were filled with pedes-
trians and cars.

"Are these fingerprints new?" he asked.

"Would that make a difference?"

"It would make it weird. Bad may follow. I've noticed that
with you. You archaeologists sometimes lead strange lives."

You, Annja thought, remembering the Brotherhood of
the Silent Rain and the disappearing sword, don't know the
half of it.

"Besides," Bart added, "I've missed talking to you."

"I need to get dressed," she told him.

"I could come over and help."

Annja smiled at that. The thought was a pleasant one that
she'd entertained before. Bart McGilley had great eyes and
great hands.

The problem was, he was the marrying kind. He couldn't
deal with a relationship where all things were equal. Getting
involved with him would mean a regular struggle choosing
between relationship and career.

And Annja couldn't leave archaeology. There were too

many wonders out there just waiting to be discovered. She could share her life, but she couldn't give it up. Finding a guy who could meet her halfway was going to be hard, and she wasn't even sure she wanted to look.

"I appreciate the offer," Annja said, "but I'm sure you have better things to do."

Bart sighed. "I don't know about better, but I know the captain's kicking tail for me to move some files off my desk."

"So we'll meet for lunch," Annja said. "I'll buy. Where to you want to meet?"

"Tito's?"

Tito's was one of their favorite Cuban restaurants. It also wasn't far from her loft.

"Tito's sounds great. Are you in the neighborhood?"

"If you hadn't answered the phone this time, the next thing you'd have heard was me knocking on the door."

"See you there in twenty minutes?"

"If you show up in twenty minutes, I'll be the guy with the surprised look."

ANNJA ARRIVED at the restaurant in twenty-seven minutes. She dressed in jeans, a fitted T-shirt, a leather jacket against the cool breeze and carried a backpack containing her computer and accessories.

She also turned the head of every male in the restaurant. After everything she'd been through the past few days, she indulged a moment of self-gratification.

Tito's carried the flavor of Cuba in the fare and the surroundings. The smoky scent of fajitas swirled in the air. Spices stung her nose. Lime-green seats and yellow tables filled the hardwood floor. The drinks came crowded with fruit and a little umbrella.

"Annja!" Standing behind the counter, Maria Ruiz waved excitedly. Plump and gray-haired, she was in her sixties, the mother of Tito, and the chef who made the kitchen turn on a dime. Nothing escaped Maria's sight. She wore a short-sleeved floral shirt under her apron.

"Maria," Annja said warmly, and stepped into the short woman's strong embrace.

"It has been too long since you've been with us," Maria said, releasing her and stepping back.

"I've been out of the country," Annja replied in Spanish.

"Then you should come and bring pictures," Maria said. "Show me where you have been. I always enjoy your adventures so much."

"Thank you. When I get everything ready, I'd love to."

Maria wiped her hands on her apron. "Let me know when. I'll make a special dessert."

Annja smiled. "I'll look forward to that." And I'll have to go to the gym for a week afterward. Still, she loved Maria's attentions, even if she had to pay for it in extra workouts.

"Do you need a table?" Maria asked.

"Actually, I'm meeting someone."

Maria's eyebrows climbed.

"I'm meeting Bart," Annja said, laughing.

"He's a good-looking man," Maria observed.

"Yes," Annja agreed, "but I think he already knows that."

Maria waved her comment away. "You could do much worse."

"I know."

Shaking her finger in warning, Maria added, "You're not getting any younger."

Chagrined, Annja smiled and shook her head. If Maria had her way, she'd already have her married off.

"He's here already. Come with me." Maria led the way through the packed restaurant, calling out instructions to the busboys, urging them to greater speed. She also dressed down a couple of waitresses who were lingering with male customers.

Bart sat at a table in the back that offered a view of the street. He was six feet two inches tall, with dark hair clipped short, a square jaw that was freshly shaved and wearing a dark blue suit with a gold tie firmly knotted at his neck. He stood as Maria guided Annja to the table.

"You look like a million bucks." Bart pulled out a chair.

"You see?" Maria pinched Bart's cheek. She spoke English so he could understand. "You see why I like this one? Always he knows the right thing to say."

Annja put her backpack on the chair next to her.

Embarrassed and off balance, Bart sat across from her.

"Have you ordered?" Maria asked.

Bart shook his head. "I was waiting for Annja."

Maria threw her hands up. "Don't you worry. I'll prepare your meals. I'll make sure you get plenty." She turned and walked away.

Bart shook his head and grinned. "This is a big city. How do you get to know these people so well?" he asked.

"I like them," Annja said.

"Then you like a lot of people. It seems like everywhere we go, you know somebody." Bart didn't sound jealous.

"I've met a lot of people."

"But you're an absentee resident. Gone as much as you're here."

"I grew up in an orphanage," Annja said. "I learned to meet people quickly. You never knew how long they were going to be around."

Bart leaned back in his chair. "I didn't know that."

Annja smiled. "It's not something I talk about."

"I mean, I figured you had a family somewhere."

"No."

He shook his head. "How long have I known you?"

"Two years."

Smiling, he said, "Two years, four months."

Annja was surprised he'd kept track. It made her feel a little uncomfortable. She didn't timeline her life other than when she was on a dig site. In her daily life, she just... flowed. Got from point A to point B, with an eye toward a multitude of possible point Cs.

"I'll take your word for it," she told him.

"It's been that long. And in all that time, I didn't know you were adopted."

"I was never adopted," Annja said. For just an instant, the old pain twitched in her heart. "I grew up at the orphanage, went to college and got on with my life."

Bart looked uncomfortable. "Hey, I'm sorry. I didn't mean to get into this."

"It's no big deal," Annja said. But she remembered that it used to be. She'd walled all that off a long time ago and simply got on with living. Just as the nuns had counseled her to do.

Gazing into her eyes, Bart said, "It's just that you have this way about you. Like with that woman—"

"You mean Maria?"

"See? I didn't even know her name."

"That's because she's never been a homicide suspect," Annja said.

Bart gave her a wry look. "No. That's not it. You're just...someone people are lucky to get to know."

"Thank you." Annja felt embarrassed and wondered if

the meeting was going to suddenly get sticky and if Bart wanted to explore the possibilities of a relationship.

"I was telling my girlfriend about you. That maybe we should try to fix you up with somebody we knew."

Annja didn't think she'd heard right. "Girlfriend?" She suddenly felt let down in ways she hadn't even imagined.

"Yeah. Girlfriend."

Hesitating, Annja said, "How long have you had a girl-friend?"

"We've dated off and on for the last few years," Bart said. "It's hard to maintain a steady relationship when you're a cop. But a week ago, we got engaged."

"You asked her to marry you?" Annja was reeling.

He grinned and looked a little embarrassed. "Actually, she asked me. In front of the guys at the gym."

"Gutsy."

"Yeah. She's some piece of work."

"So what did you say?"

Bart shrugged. "I told her I'd think about it."

"You did not."

"No," he agreed, "I didn't. I said I would." He shifted in his seat. "I'd like to ask you a favor if I could."

"You can. I seem to ask you for favors from time to time." Annja didn't like the little ember of jealousy inside her. She knew she didn't want commitment at this point in her life, but she'd liked the idea of having Bart kind of waiting in the wings. She didn't like how casually that had just been taken off the table. Or how she'd made the wrong assumptions about his feelings for her. She felt foolish.

"I'd like something special for a wedding ring," Bart said. "Something that has...a history to it. You know. Something that has—"

"Permanence," Annja said, understanding exactly what he was looking for.

Bart nodded and smiled happily. "Yeah. Permanence. I want to give her something that didn't just come off an assembly line."

"I can do that. How much time do I have?"

Spreading his hands, Bart shrugged. "A few months. A year. We haven't exactly set a date yet."

"What does she do?"

He gazed at her through suspicious, narrowed eyes. "Are you curious about the kind of woman that would go out with me? Or choose to marry me?"

"I figured I'd be checking a psych ward."

Bart snorted.

"Actually," Annja went on, "I was thinking it might be nice to get her something that might tie in to her profession. Give her a duality. A bonding of her life with you as well as the life she's chosen."

"I like that," Bart said seriously.

"Good. So what does she do?"

"She's a doctor. In Manhattan."

"A doctor is good," Annja said. "What kind of doctor?"

"She works in the ER. She patched me up three years ago when I was shot."

"You never told me you'd been shot," Annja said.

"I didn't die. Nothing to tell. But I got to know Ruth."

"Ruth. That's a good, strong name."

"She's a strong lady."

"So the offer you made earlier about coming up to my loft and helping me dress—"

"Whoa," Bart protested, throwing his hands up. "In the first place, I knew you would never say yes."

Feeling mischievous, Annja said, without cracking a smile, "And if I did?"

"You wouldn't."

She decided to let him off the hook. "You're right."

"So what about you?" he asked. "Do you have a special guy stashed someplace?"

"No."

"Then you should let Ruth and me fix you up."

"I'm not looking for a relationship," Annja said. "I have my work."

"And that's why I knew you wouldn't let me come up." Bart smiled. "Speaking of work, yours, as I might have mentioned, has taken on a decidedly weird twist."

"How?" Annja asked.

"Those fingerprints you asked me to run? They're connected to a homicide that took place sixty-three years ago."

Surprise stopped Annja in her tracks for a moment. "A homicide?"

"Yeah. They belong to the prime suspect."

20

"Sixty-three years ago," Bart McGilley went on, "a woman was found dead in a hotel room in Los Angeles. She worked for MGM studios. Bought set pieces. Stuff they used in the backgrounds to make a scene more real."

"Anyway, from the way everything looks, this woman, Doris Cooper, age twenty-eight and an L.A. resident, was murdered for one of the things she bought."

"What was it?" Annja felt a sudden chill.

Bart shrugged. "Nobody knows. Nobody knew what she'd bought that day. The detectives working the case didn't follow up all that well. During the heyday of the movies back then, the death of a set designer only got a splash of ink, not a river of it."

"She was a nobody," Annja said, knowing the sad truth of how things had gone.

"Right."

Annja wondered if Roux was the type to kill a woman in cold blood. It didn't take her long to reach the conclusion that he was—if he was properly motivated. She was doubly glad that she hadn't followed Roux and Garin. Their talking about having lived five hundred years was already weird enough without also thinking of them as murderers.

"Those fingerprints popped up on a computer search?" Annja asked.

"At Interpol," Bart replied. "They're called friction ridges in cop speak, by the way. Back in the day, so the story goes, the L.A. investigators thought maybe the guy was from out of the country. On account of how Doris Cooper bought a lot of things from overseas. So they sent the friction ridges over to Interpol. After you sent them to me, I sent them on, thinking maybe you were looking for an international guy."

"Interpol happened to have the fingerprints of a sixty-three-year-old murder suspect?"

Bart blew out his breath. "Interpol has a lot of information. That's why they're a clearinghouse for international crimes. They've gone almost totally digital. Searchable databases. You get a professional out there in the world doing bad stuff, they've got a way to catch them. This case was one of those they'd archived."

"There's no doubt about the prints?"

Bart shook his head. "I had one of our forensics guys match them up for me. When I saw what I saw, that these friction ridges belonged to the suspect on a sixty-three-year-old murder, I knew I wanted a professional pair of eyes on that ten-card."

"Was there a name attached to the friction ridges?"

"No."

Two of Maria's cooks arrived with steaming plates of food. They placed them on the table in quick order and departed.

Annja's curiosity didn't get in the way of her appetite.

Laying a tortilla on her plate, she quickly loaded it with meat, tomatoes, peppers, onions, lettuce and cheese.

"So this guy you printed," Bart said, "he was what? Eighty or ninety?"

He didn't look it, Annja thought. She would have guessed Roux was in his early sixties, but no more. During the shoot-out with the Brotherhood of the Silent Rain, he hadn't moved like even a sixtysomething-year-old man.

"I found the fingerprints on a coin," Annja said truthfully. She didn't want to mention that the coin was of recent vintage.

"So you thought you'd send them along to me?" Bart shook his head. "You had more reason than that."

Annja looked at her friend, thought about him getting married and realized that she truly hoped things didn't change between them. She knew one of the things that would change their relationship, though, was a lie.

"I was given the coin by a man in France," she told him. "He swapped it, while I wasn't looking, for a charm I'd found."

"Was the charm valuable?"

"Maybe. It was made out of hammered steel, not gold or silver. Not even copper. I haven't even found a historical significance yet." Annja couldn't tell him that it had been part of a sword that Roux had claimed once belonged to Joan of Arc.

Bart took a small notebook from inside his jacket. "Did you get his name?"

"Roux," she answered. "I'm not even sure of the spelling."

He wrote anyway. "No address?"

Annja thought of the big house butted up against the hill outside Paris. She'd never seen an address and Garin had never mentioned one.

"No," she said. "No address."

Bart sighed and closed the notebook. "I can ask Interpol to look up records on this guy. Maybe we'll get a hit on something."

"Sure," Annja said. Curiosity nagged at her. Roux was wanted in connection with a sixty-three-year-old murder. She wondered what other information the old man was hiding. She was glad that she was out of France and far away from him.

ANNJA SPENT the afternoon putting together the video on La Bête. She used the software on her desktop computer, loading up the video footage of Lozère, the books she'd cribbed for pictures and drawings of what the Beast of Gévaudan might have looked like, and the digital pictures she'd taken of the creature in the cave.

Using the green screen setup in one corner of the loft, she filmed different intros for the segment, a couple of closings, and completed the voice-overs. When she had it all together, it was late and she was tired.

She watched the completed video and timed it. *Chasing History's Monsters* generally only allowed nine to ten minutes per segment, allowing for setup by the host and the ensuing commercials.

So far, she was three minutes over but knew with work she could cut that down.

Okay, she told herself, all work and no play makes Annja a dull woman.

After grabbing a quick shower and a change of clothes, she packed her gym bag and headed out of the loft.

EDDIE'S GYM WAS an old-school workout place. Boxers exercised and trained there, smashing the heavy bag then each other in the ring. It had concrete floors, unfinished walls, and trendy exercise machines had never taken up residence there. Free weights clanked and thundered as lifters worked in rotation with their spotters.

It was a place where men went to sweat and burn out the anger and frustration of the day. Young fighters learned the intricacies of the fighting craft and the statesmanship necessary to sweep the ring and move up on a fight card. No one tanned there, and hot water in the showers was a random thing.

There really was an Eddie and he and another old ex-boxer had each been Golden Gloves and fought professionally for a time. They owned the place outright and didn't suffer poseurs or wannabes with no skill.

Training wasn't part of what a membership bought. That was given to those deserving few who caught the eye of Eddie and his cronies.

Occasionally, young men who had seen *Fight Club* too many times came into the club and tried to prove they were as tough as Brad Pitt or Edward Norton. The regulars, never very tolerant, quickly sent the newbies packing with split lips and black eyes.

Eddie's was all about survival of the fittest. Annja liked to go there because it felt real, not like one of the upscale fitness clubs that were more about the right kind of clothing and the favorite smoothie flavor of the week.

When she'd first started working out there, she'd had trouble with some of the men. Eddie hadn't wanted her around because he didn't want the complication.

But she'd stood her ground and won the old man over with her knowledge of boxing. The knowledge was a newly acquired thing because she'd liked the gym, had wanted to work out there and did her homework. She also worked out at a couple of martial-arts dojos, but she preferred the atmosphere at Eddie's. She was a regular now and had nothing to prove.

"Girl," Eddie said as he held the heavy bag for her, "you musta been eatin' your Wheaties. You're pounding the hell outta this bag more than ever before."

Annja hit the bag one last time, snapping and turning the punch as Eddie had taught her.

"You're just getting weak," Annja chided playfully.

"The hell I am!" Eddie roared.

Annja grinned at him and mopped sweat from her face with a towel hung over a nearby chair. She wore black sweatpants and a sleeveless red shirt that advertised Eddie's Gym across it in bold yellow letters. Boxing shoes and gloves completed her ensemble.

Eddie claimed he was sixty, but Annja knew he was lying away ten years. The ex-boxer was black as coal, skinny as a rake, but still carried the broad shoulders that had framed him as a light heavyweight. Gray stubble covered his jaw and upper lip. His dark eyes were warm and liquid. Boxing had gnarled his ears and left dark scars under his eyes. When he grinned, which was often, he showed a lot of gold caps. He wore gray sweatpants, one of his red shirts and a dark navy hoodie. He kept his head shaved.

"Don't tell me you just dissed me in my own place of business!" Eddie shouted.

"You're the one who said he was having trouble hanging on to the bag," Annja reminded him. He sounded mad, but she knew it was all an act. Eddie was loud and proud, but she liked him and knew that the feeling was reciprocated.

"Girl, you're hittin' harder than I ever seen you hit. What have you been doin'?"

"Archaeology." Annja shrugged.

Eddie waved that away. He looked at her. "You don't look no different."

"I'm not." Annja mopped her arms. "Maybe you're just having an off day."

"I told people I had an off day when I fought Cassius Clay. The truth of the matter was that man hit me so hard I couldn't count to two." Eddie picked up a towel and wiped down, as well. "But something's different about you."

Annja shrugged. "I just feel good, Eddie. That's all."

"Humph," he said, looking at her through narrowed eyes. "Usually when you come back from one of your trips, it takes you a little while to get back to peak conditioning."

"I do my roadwork and keep my legs strong wherever I go," she replied. But she knew what he was talking about. Tonight's workout had seemed almost...easy.

She'd done plenty of jump rope, the speed bag and the heavy bag, a serious weight rotation with more weight and more reps than she'd ever put up before. Something was different. Because even after all of that she felt as if she could do it all again.

EDDIE STOOD by his office with his arms folded and stared at the young black man in headgear beating on a guy who couldn't seem to hold his own against his opponent. Annja had noticed the guy, watching the sadistic way he'd beaten the other fighter.

"Who's the new fighter?" she asked.

Eddie shook his head. "Trouble."

"Does he have another name?" Annja watched as the fighter knocked his opponent down again.

Three men about the fighter's age all clapped and cheered the fighter's latest triumph.

"Name's Keshawn. He says he's a businessman." Eddie didn't sound ready to give the young man an endorsement.

Annja took in the tattoos marking the fighter's arms and legs. "He looks like a banger," she said.

"He is," Eddie agreed. "Knew him when he was little. Had a heart then. It all turned bad now. He keeps doin' what he's doin', he'll be dead or locked away in a couple years."

This time the other guy in the ring couldn't get to his feet. Keshawn's hangers-on cracked up, cheered and threw invective at the man.

Keshawn turned to Eddie and spit out his mouthpiece. "Hey, old man!" he yelled. "You sure you ain't got nobody that'll spar with me? Just a couple rounds? I promise I won't hurt 'em much." Arrogance and challenge radiated in him like an electric current.

The other boxers working the rotations didn't respond.

"Anybody?" Keshawn gazed around the club. "I got a thousand dollars says nobody here can put me outta this ring."

"It time for you to go, boy," Eddie said. "Your ring time is up."

Keshawn beat his chest with his gloves. "I'll fight anybody who wants this ring."

Eddie walked toward the ring. "That ain't my agreement with you, boy. You paid for time, you took your time. Now you haul your ass outta my place."

A cocky grin twisted Keshawn's lips. "You best stop callin' me 'boy,' old man. I might start takin' it personal."

Annja stepped behind Eddie, staying slightly to his right.

"Go on," Eddie growled. "Get outta here."

Releasing his hold on the ring ropes, Keshawn skipped out to the middle of the ring and took up a fighting stance. "You want this ring, old man?" He waved one of his gloves in invitation. "Come take it from me."

Eddie cursed the younger man soundly, not holding back in any way. "You best come on down outta there."

"You best not come up in here after me," Keshawn warned. He was over six feet, at least two hundred pounds and cut by steroids. His hair was blocked and he wore a pencil-thin mustache. He grinned and slammed his gloves together. "You'll get yourself hurt, old man."

Eddie started to climb up into the ring.

Annja caught the old man's arm. "Call the police. You don't need to go in there."

"This is my place, Annja," he told her fiercely. "I don't stand up for what's mine, I might as well pack up and go sit in an old folks' home." He shrugged out of her grip and slid between the ropes.

Keshawn smiled more broadly and started skipping, showing off his footwork. "You think you got somethin' for me, old man?"

Annja caught hold of the ropes and stood at the ring's edge. The confrontation had drawn the attention of the rest of the club's regulars. No one appeared ready to intercede, though. Annja hoped someone had called the police, but she didn't want to leave long enough to go to her locker for her cell phone.

Slowly, hands at his sides, Eddie walked toward the younger man. "I told you to get outta here, boy. I meant what I said."

Keshawn danced away from Eddie. "They say you used to be somethin' to see, old man. Were you really? Were you a good boxer?"

Eddie moved so fast that even Annja, who had been expecting it, almost didn't see it. He fired a jab straight into Keshawn's face, slipping past the headgear and popping the younger man in the nose.

Surprised, Keshawn staggered back. He cursed virulently. Holding a glove to his nose, he snorted bloody mucus onto the canvas. Crimson ran down his face. "You're gonna pay for that, old man."

"I told you to get out," Eddie said. Although his opponent was taller and bigger and at least forty years younger, there was no fear in the old boxer. "You best listen to your elders. Somethin' you shoulda learned at your granny's knee."

Without a word, Keshawn attacked. For a minute, no more, Eddie withstood the flurry of blows, tucking his elbows in and keeping his curled fists up beside his head to protect his face. He even managed a few punches of his own, but Keshawn blocked them or shook them off, in the full grip of rage.

In seconds, Keshawn had the old boxer penned in the corner and was beating and kicking him.

Annja used her teeth to unlace her gloves, then shook them off. Other gym members started to move in, but Keshawn's hangers-on held them back.

Annja rolled under the ropes and onto the canvas before anyone could stop her. Coming up behind Keshawn, she kicked the gangbanger's legs out from under him and pulled him away from Eddie.

"You shouldn't a done that," Eddie whispered, barely able to hang on to the ropes. "Should've stayed outta this, Annja."

Annja didn't say anything. There had been no choice. She turned as she sensed Keshawn moving behind her.

"Don't know who you are, white girl," the big man said, "but this sure ain't any business of yours."

"Somebody's called the cops by now," Annja said, lifting her hands to defend herself. "If you stay here, you're just going to get arrested."

Fear wriggled inside her. She felt it. She breathed in and out, concentrating on that, keeping herself ready. Reading his body language, she knew exactly when he was going to throw the first punch.

21

Keshawn threw a jab with his left hand.

Twisting, Annja dodged the blow, letting it fly past her head to the left. At the same time, she brought her right hand up and slammed the Y between her thumb and her forefinger into the base of her attacker's throat.

As he stumbled back. Annja rolled her hips, drew her right hand back and swiveled. She drove her left foot into Keshawn's face so hard that she forced him back several feet.

Stunned, he landed hard, off balance, and rolled over to his knees. He looked at her in shock and rage, blood dripping down his chin. Leaping to his feet, he launched himself at her.

Annja dodged away, planting both hands in the middle of his back and shoving him into the ropes. He was tangled for a moment, cursing loudly and promising her that she was going to die.

Annja believed he meant it. She saw that Keshawn's friends were still struggling with other gym members.

He stood again, then came at her more slowly, trying to keep his hands up and use his size and reach, getting more canny now that his confidence was eroding. He threw punch after punch. Annja easily dodged them or blocked them, giving ground and drawing him to the middle of the ring. He breathed like a bellows.

Incredibly, even after her workout, Annja still felt fast and strong. Her breathing was regular, her mind calm. Eddie had been right. She *had* changed. She didn't know where the extra energy was coming from. She guessed anger and adrenaline had kicked in powerfully.

Annja stopped giving ground. Keshawn came at her with another flurry of blows. She stood still, moving her arms just enough to block everything he threw at her. Then—when he was tiring, gasping for breath—she struck back.

The right fist swept forward. Her first two knuckles slid through his defense and between the slits of his headgear. More blood gushed from his nose.

She lifted a knee into his crotch hard enough to raise him from the mat. Before he could fall, she swept her leg out and knocked the unsteady man's feet out from under him. He hit the mat hard.

Sirens wailed just outside the gym.

"You're done," Annja said in a slow, controlled voice. She felt much cooler than she would ever have imagined.

ANNJA WATCHED as EMTs worked on Eddie Watts. Most of his injuries were superficial. He bled from his nose, split lips and a cut over his right eye. His left eye was swollen shut.

Uniformed police officers had taken Keshawn and his friends into custody. Detectives stood questioning witnesses.

"Are you sure you're okay?" Annja asked as she held Eddie's callused hand.

"I'll be fine, girl. When I came outta that fight with Cassius Clay, I looked worse than this." Eddie gave her a lopsided grin. "Don't know what you been doin', Annja, but what you just did?" He shook his head gingerly. "That was something special. Ain't ever seen nobody do that before."

Annja didn't know what to say. She couldn't believe everything that had happened. Over the years, she'd had to fight on occasion. Even in the past few days, she'd had to fight against the Brotherhood of the Silent Rain.

But this time *was* different. She had changed.

HOURS LATER, after the police had finally released her and she'd checked on Eddie in the hospital, finding that the old boxer's daughter was with him, Annja returned home.

She took a shower so hot that it steamed up the bathroom, leaving fog on the glass walls and the mirror. Scrubbed and feeling clean again, she sat on the floor in the center of the loft with the lights out. She pulled herself into a lotus position, back straight, and breathed deeply.

Working slowly, knowing it would take time, Annja gradually relaxed her body. She breathed in and out, slowing her heartbeat, centering herself the way she had been taught.

She stared at the dark wall, then imagined a single dot on it. She focused on the dot until the city ceased to exist around her.

Something had changed about her, and she sought it out. In Eddie's Gym, she'd moved with greater speed and more strength than she'd ever possessed. Where had that come from?

Something had unlocked the speed and strength inside her.

It wasn't just adrenaline. She'd been afraid before. She'd felt pumped from fear. But she'd never been that strong or that fast. The source was something else.

The image of the sword appeared in her mind.

Earlier that day, after she'd returned from lunch with Bart McGilley, she'd sat in her loft and tried to reach the sword the way she had in the back of the taxi. Nothing had happened.

Now she saw the sword perfectly. It was whole, resting once more in the case.

Slowly, Annja reached in for the sword, closed her hand around the hilt and drew it out. When she opened her eyes, the sword was in her hand.

It was real.

She stood slowly, afraid that it would disappear at any moment as it had in the taxi the night before.

Taking a two-handed grip, Annja started moving through one of the forms she'd been taught in martial arts. Her interest in swords had started early, before she was even a teenager. She'd learned forms for the blade in several disciplines.

In the quiet of the loft, in the darkness of the night with the moon angled in through the window, Annja danced with the blade. In no time at all, it felt as if she'd always known it, and that it was a part of her.

THE RINGING PHONE WOKE Annja. She blinked her eyes open and glanced at the clock beside the bed. It was 9:17 a.m. Caller ID showed it was Bart, calling from his personal cell phone.

"Hello?" she said, her voice thick.

"Sorry," Bart said. "I guess I woke you."

"Yeah, again." Annja sat up and reached for the sword. It was gone. She'd laid it beside the bed before succumbing to fatigue in the wee hours.

"I heard you had a late night and a little excitement," the policeman said. "I told you before that Eddie's Gym is a rough place."

"I like Eddie. He's a good guy," Annja replied.

"He is a good guy," Bart agreed. "But his place is in a bad neighborhood."

Annja pushed up out of bed and walked over to the window. She raised the blinds and peered out. The city was alive and moving. "I live in a bad neighborhood."

"I know. Anyway, I wasn't calling to gripe at you. I just wanted to know if you were okay."

"I am," she said. "Thanks for caring." *Where does the sword go?* she wondered, distracted.

"I heard Eddie's going to be okay."

"He will be."

"Good. Do you need anything?"

"No."

"So what are your plans?"

"I'm going to stay in all day and work on my segment for the show."

"Fantastic," Bart said. "The way your luck has been running lately, maybe it's in your better interests to keep a low profile for a while."

Annja smiled a little. "I resent that."

"Yeah, well, sue me. Right now, you seem to be quite accident prone."

"No more than normal," she said, laughing.

"Stay in, Annja," Bart said. "Stay safe. If you need any-thing, call me."

"I will. You, too." Annja broke the connection.

She put the phone away and looked for the sword again. It made no sense. She wondered again if she was losing her mind.

Had the sword really belonged to Joan of Arc? She had no way of knowing. But she wanted to make sure she wasn't hallucinating. She didn't believe in magic. But every culture she'd studied had very deep and abiding beliefs in the supernatural and incredible powers.

Taking a deep breath, she visualized the sword hanging in the air before her. She reached for it. When she closed her hand around the hilt, she felt it. It was real.

Walking over to the bed, she put the sword down and drew her hand back. The sword remained where it was. She sat down in the floor and watched it. Twenty minutes later, it was still there.

Deciding to experiment, she closed her eyes and wished the sword was not there, that it would return to where it came from.

When she opened her eyes, the sword was gone. Panic swelled within her. She couldn't help wondering if she'd wished it away and broken whatever mysterious force bound them.

Stay calm, she advised herself. Breathing easily, shaping the sword in her mind, she reached for it.

She held it in her hand once again.

It was the most frightening yet wonderful thing she had ever seen.

FRUSTRATED, her back aching, Annja straightened up from her desk. Judging from the darkness outside her windows, it was evening—or night.

She'd worked without stopping since that morning, except

for phone calls to different museums and libraries to gain access to information that wasn't open to the general public. Instead of working on the La Bête piece, she'd researched Joan of Arc.

Surprisingly, she didn't really find much more than what she'd remembered from childhood. There was little mention of the sword other than it was commonly believed at the time that it held magical powers. And there were stories that it had been shattered. But as far as she could tell, no fragments from the warrior maid's weapon had ever been authenticated.

Giving up for the time being, totally stumped as to what to do next, she went to the bed and picked up the sword. She was ready to experiment some more.

Annja dropped the sword back onto the bed.

Leaving the loft, she made her way up to the rooftop. Lightning ran thick veins across the sky, heated yellow blazing against the indigo of swirling clouds. The wind rushed through her hair and cooled her. She breathed in, wondering if what she proposed would work.

Closing her eyes, she imagined the sword and reached for it. She felt the cool of the metal and the roughness of the leather in her hand. When she opened her eyes again, she held the sword.

Thunder rolled, pealing all around her and echoing between the buildings. A light rain started, cooling the city and washing the air free of dust and pollution for the moment.

Filled with childish glee, still not quite believing what she had proved over and over again, Annja whirled the sword. The blade glinted and caught lightning flashes. In seconds, her clothing was sodden and stuck to her, but she didn't even think of going inside.

The bizarre reality of her situation struck her hard. She was holding Joan of Arc's sword! And somehow it was bound to her!

On top of the building, with the sounds of modern life echoing through the concrete caverns of the city, Annja went through the sword forms again. This time she elaborated, bringing in different styles. Her feet moved mechanically, bringing her body in line with the sword.

No matter how she moved, the sword felt as if it were part of her. When she was finished with the forms, breathing hard and drenched by the rain, she closed her eyes and placed the sword away from her.

She felt the weight of the sword evaporate from her hand. When she opened her eyes, the weapon was gone. Another breath, eyes still open, and she reached out for the sword. In a flash, the sword was in her hand.

Despite her familiarity with the process now, she still felt amazed. If it's not magic, she asked herself, what is it? She had no answer.

Giving in to impulse, Annja held the sword in both hands high over her head. Almost immediately, lightning reached down and touched the tip in a pyrotechnic blaze of sparks. For a moment, the blade glowed cobalt-blue.

Annja dropped the sword, grateful she hadn't been electrocuted.

When she inspected the sword, it was unmarked. If anything, the blade seemed cleaner, stronger. Energy clung to the weapon. She felt it thrumming inside her.

Soaked and awed, Annja stood for a moment in the center of the city and knew that no one saw her. She was invisible in the night. No one knew what she held. She didn't even know herself. She breathed deeply, smelling the salt from the

Atlantic, and knew she'd somehow stumbled upon one of the greatest mysteries in history.

"Why me?" she shouted into the storm.

There was no answer, only the rolling thunder and lightning.

OF COURSE THE IDEA CAME to her in the middle of the night. That was when her subconscious mind posed a potential answer to one of the riddles that faced her.

She sat up in bed and found the sword lying on the floor. I've got to protect this sword, she told herself.

Though after the blade had been hit by lightning and hadn't been harmed or allowed her to come to harm, she didn't think much could destroy it.

The sword was destroyed once, she reminded herself. Roux had told her that. She had seen the pieces. But why was it back now?

Slowly, she visualized the pieces in the case at Roux's house. She drew her fingers along the sword's spine, trying to link to whatever force tied her to the weapon.

Part of the sword had been the charm she'd found on the warrior who died bringing down La Bête. Somewhere inside that sword, the mark that had been struck on both sides of that piece of fractured metal still existed.

In her mind's eye, she lifted the image of the wolf and the mountain to the surface of the blade. On the other side of the weapon, she brought up the die mark of the Brotherhood of the Silent Rain.

Thunder cannonaded outside, close enough to make the windows rattle.

Annja focused on the sword. She traced her fingers along the blade. This time she felt the impressions of the images.

Opening her eyes, she looked down. In the darkness she couldn't see the images she felt. Then lightning blazed and lit up her loft for a moment.

There, revealed in the blue-white light, the image of the wolf and the mountain stood out in the smooth grain of the steel. When she turned the blade over, the die mark of the Brotherhood of the Silent Rain was there.

She grabbed one of the digital cameras she used for close-up work. She took several shots of the images.

When she was satisfied that she had all that she needed, she stared at the imperfections on the blade. She ran her fingers over them again, feeling how deeply they bit into the metal.

The sight of them, the feel of them, was almost unbearable.

She willed the sword away, back into wherever it went when it was not with her. It faded from her hands like early-morning fog cut by direct sunlight.

Taking a deep breath, she reached into that otherwhere and drew the sword back. Light gleamed along the blade. The marks had disappeared.

A quick check of the images on the digital camera revealed that the shots she'd taken still existed. She put the sword on the bed and turned her full attention to the camera images.

Was the sword weak while it was shattered? Annja wondered. *Or had it allowed itself to be marked? And if it had allowed itself to be marked, why?*

She set to work.

22

Using the software on her computer, Annja blew up the images of the wolf and the mountain. After they were magnified, she saw there were other images, as well. The detail of the work was amazing.

The shadowy figure behind the bars was better revealed. Although manlike in appearance, the figure was a grotesquerie, ill shaped and huge, judging from the figure of the man standing behind him.

With her naked eye, Annja had barely been able to make out the second figure. Once the image was blown up, she couldn't miss him. He wore the armor of a French knight. A shield bearing his heraldry stood next to him.

Annja blew up the image more, concentrating on the shield.

The shield was divided in the English tradition rather than the French. That surprised Annja. The common armchair historian assumed that all heraldry was the same, based on the divisions of the shield that English heraldry was noted for. But the French, Italians, Swedish and Spanish—as well as a few others—marked their heraldry differently.

This one was marked *party per bend sinister*—diagonally from upper right to lower left. The upper half showed the image of a wolf with its tongue sticking out. The animal didn't have much detail, but Annja got a definite sense of malevolence from the creature. The lower half of the shield was done in ermines, a variation of the field that represented fur. Ermines were traditionally black on white.

The design was unique. If it hadn't disappeared in history, there would likely be some documentation on it.

Annja cut the shield out of the image with the software, cleaned up the lines as much as she could and saved it.

Logging onto alt.archaeology, she sent a brief request for identification to the members. She also sent an e-mail to a professor she knew at Cambridge who specialized in British heraldry. She also followed up with a posting to alt.archaeology.esoterica.

What was a British knight doing at a French monastery of an order of monks that had been destroyed?

Annja returned to the image.

The shadowy, misshapen figure had another drawing under it. Annja almost missed the discovery. The image had been cut into the metal but it was almost as if it had been scored there only to have the craftsman change his mind later.

Or maybe he was told not to include it, Annja thought.

She magnified the image and worked on it, bringing it into sharper relief with a drawing tool. In seconds, she knew what she was looking at. A lozenge.

Annja sat back in her chair and stared at the image, blown away by the possibilities facing her. The shadowy figure wasn't a man. It was a woman.

The lozenge was heraldry to represent female members of a noble family. Designed in an offset diamond shape that was taller than it was wide, a lozenge identified the woman by the family, as well as personal achievements.

This particular lozenge only had two images on it. A wolf salient, in midleap, occupied the top of the diamond shape. At the bottom was a stag dexter, shown simply standing. A crescent moon hung in the background with a star above and a star below.

Annja repeated her efforts with the postings, sending off the new image, as well.

Back aching from the constant effort, Annja decided to take a break. She quickly dressed and went out into the rainy night, surprised to find that dawn was already apparent the eastern sky.

ANNJA HEADED for the small Italian grocery store several blocks from her loft. The Puerto Rican bodega she favored was closer, but it wasn't open at such an early hour. She didn't mind as she wanted to stretch her legs.

She loved being in the middle of the city as it woke around her. Voices cracked sharply. Cars passed by in the street, horns already honking impatiently.

Stopping by the newsstand, she picked up a handful of magazines—*Time, Newsweek, Scientific American, People, Entertainment, Ellery Queen Mystery Magazine,* and *Magazine of Fantasy* and *Science Fiction.*

She liked to keep up with current events. The entertainment and fiction magazines were guilty pleasures. If she hadn't been able to occasionally borrow from fictional lives in the orphanage, she sometimes wondered if she'd have made it out with the curiosity about the world and the past that she now had.

At the grocery store, she passed a pleasant few minutes with the owner, who loved to talk about her children, and bought a small melon, eggs, fresh basil, a small block of Parmesan cheese and garlic bread. She also picked up a gallon of orange juice.

Back at the loft, Annja let herself in through all five locks. She was startled but not entirely surprised to find Garin seated at her desk. Her eyes immediately strayed to the bed, but the sword was nowhere to be seen.

"You're looking for the sword?" Garin seemed amused. He wore a black turtleneck, jeans and heavy black boots. A leather jacket hung on the back of the chair.

"How did you get in?" Annja demanded. She stood in the open door, ready to flee immediately.

"I let myself in," he said. "I did knock first."

Suspicion formed in Annja's mind. She had the definite sense that he'd waited for her to leave, then broke in.

"You weren't here," Garin said.

"Odd that I happened to miss you," Annja said.

Garin smiled. "Serendipity. You can never properly factor that into anything."

"You could have waited for me to get back," Annja pointed out.

"And stood out in the hallway so that your neighbors would gossip about you?" Garin shook his head. "I couldn't do that."

Deciding that she didn't have anything to fear from the man—at least for the moment—Annja walked into the kitchen area and placed the groceries on the counter.

"Breakfast?" Garin asked.

"Yes." Annja took a big skillet from the wall.

"We could order in. I noticed there are some places nearby that deliver," Garin said.

"I've eaten restaurant food for days," Annja replied. "Here and in France. I want to cook." She put the skillet on the burner to warm, then cracked eggs into a bowl.

Glancing over her shoulder, Annja saw that he looked amused. She resented his presence in her home, the fact that he had broken in, and she was distrustful of him. Still, she couldn't just pretend he wasn't there when she was about to eat.

"Have you eaten?" she asked.

"No. I just got in from LaGuardia." Garin sat at the desk. "But that's all right. You go ahead."

"Nonsense. There's enough for both of us. More than enough."

"That's very kind of you. Can I help?"

Annja chopped the basil and Garin grated the Parmesan. She mixed both with the eggs, then poured olive oil into the skillet. "Have you really lived over five hundred years?" she asked, suddenly aware of feeling comfortably domestic with this mysterious stranger.

Garin smiled. "You find that hard to believe?"

Annja didn't answer. She sliced the garlic bread and the melon.

"You know what happened to the sword, don't you?" Garin asked. "You've got it."

Annja poured the eggs into the skillet, then popped the bread into the toaster.

"Where is the sword?" Garin asked.

"It disappeared," Annja replied. "Somewhere outside Paris."

Grinning, he said, "I don't believe you."

"We share a trait for skepticism." Annja scrambled the eggs. "Would you care for some orange juice?"

Garin walked around the loft, gazing at all the things Annja had collected during her years as an archaeologist. "You have a nice home," he said softly.

Annja had deliberately left the bread knife close at hand. So far, Garin didn't appear to be armed. "Thank you," she said, watching him closely.

"I know you're lying about the sword," Garin said, looking at her.

The bread slices popped out of the toaster. She laid them on plates, buttered them. "That's not a polite thing to say to someone about to serve you breakfast."

"The sword was on the bed when I arrived," Garin told her.

For a moment, Annja felt panic race through her. She concentrated on the eggs, removing the skillet from the heat. *If he'd taken the sword, he wouldn't be here now.*

"It disappeared when I tried to touch it," Garin said.

"Maybe it was just a figment of your imagination," Annja said, flooded with relief.

Garin shook his head. "No. I've seen that sword before. And I've lived with its curse."

"What curse?" Annja asked.

Approaching her but staying out of arm's reach, Garin leaned a hip against the kitchen counter. "A story for a story," he told her. "It's the only fair way to do this."

Annja dished the scrambled eggs onto the garlic toast. She added slices of melon.

"Very pretty," Garin said.

"I prefer to think of it as nourishing." Annja handed him his plate.

Garin looked around. "I don't see a dining table."

"That's because I don't have one." Scooping up her own

plate and orange juice, Annja walked to the window seat. She thought about the Mercedes Garin had driven in Lozère. "Probably isn't exactly the lifestyle you're used to," she said, feeling a little self-conscious.

"Not the lifestyle I now have," he agreed. "But this is a lot better than I started out with."

Annja folded herself onto one end of the window seat. "Where did you grow up?"

"One of the city-states in Germany. A backwoods place. Its name is long forgotten now." Garin sat and ate his food. "I was the illegitimate son of a famous knight."

"How famous?"

Garin shook his head. "He's been forgotten now. But back then, he was a name. Famous in battle and in tournaments. I was the only mistake he'd ever made."

For a moment, Annja felt sorry for Garin. Parents and relatives who simply hadn't wanted to deal with kids had dumped them at the orphanage. It was an old story. Evidently it hadn't changed in hundreds of years.

If Garin could be believed.

"I like to think that my father cared for me in some way," Garin went on. "After all, he didn't give me to a peasant family as he could have. Or let my mother kill me, as she'd tried on a couple of occasions."

Annja kept eating. There were horrible stories throughout all histories. She wasn't inured to them, but she had learned to accept that there were some things she couldn't do anything about.

"Instead," Garin went on, "my father gave me to a wizard."

"Roux?" That news startled Annja.

"Yes. At least that's what men like him were called in the

old days. Once upon a time, Roux's name was enough to strike terror in the hearts of men. When he cursed someone, that person's life was never the same again."

"But that could simply be the perception of the person cursed," Annja said. "Zombies created by voodoo have been found to be living beings who are so steeped in their belief that their conscious minds can't accept that after their burial and 'resurrection' they are not zombies. They truly believe they are."

"What makes the sword disappear?" Garin asked, smiling.

"We weren't finished talking about you." Annja took another bite of toast, then the melon, which was sweet and crisp.

"I was nine years old when I was given to Roux," Garin went on. "I was twenty-one when he allied himself with the Maid."

"He allied himself with Joan of Arc?"

Garin nodded. "He felt he had to. So we traveled with her and were part of her retinue."

"Fancy word," Annja teased, surprising herself.

"My vocabulary is vast. I also speak several languages."

"Joan of Arc," Annja reminded.

"Roux and I served with her. He was one of her counsels. When she was captured by the English, Roux stayed nearby."

"Why didn't he rescue her?"

"Because he believed God would."

"But that didn't happen?"

Garin shook his head. "We were…gone when the English decided to burn her at the stake. We arrived too late. Roux tried to stop them, but there were too many English. She died."

Annja turned pale. It was all too fantastic to be believed,

yet she didn't feel any sense of danger—just curiosity. Who is this man? she wondered. What is going on?

"Are you all right?" Concern showed on Garin's handsome face.

"I am. Just tired."

He didn't appear convinced.

"What about the sword?" Annja asked.

Garin balanced his empty plate on his knee. "It was shattered. I watched them do it."

"The English?"

He nodded. "Afterward, Roux and I realized we were cursed."

Annja couldn't help herself. She smiled. Anyone could have read about the legendary sword. The details were open to interpretation or exaggeration, as all historical accounts were. Where will this elaborate hoax lead? she wondered.

Then she remembered how Bart McGilley had told her that the fingerprints—*friction ridges*—she'd pulled from the euro Roux had given her belonged to a suspect in a sixty-three-year-old homicide. She thought about the sword.

"Who cursed you?" she asked.

Garin hesitated, as if he were about to tell her an impossible thing. "I don't know what Roux thinks, but I believe we were cursed by God."

23

After Garin finished his story, Annja sat quietly and looked at him. The fear that he had felt all those years ago—and, in spite of herself, she did believe him about the five hundred years—still showed in his dark features.

"You helped Roux look for the sword?" Annja asked.

Garin shook his head. "No."

"Why?"

"I was angry after Joan's death and I had no idea there would be consequences if the pieces of the sword weren't found."

Annja had to admit the man had a point. "So when did you start to believe?"

"About twenty years later."

"When you didn't age?"

"No," Garin answered. "I aged. A little. It was when I saw Roux again and saw that he hadn't aged. I began to believe then. I'd thought he would be dead."

"So he has looked for pieces of the sword for over five hundred years?"

Garin nodded. "He has."

"And you didn't help?"

"No. I tried to stop him. I tried to tell him that as it stood, we could live forever. I was becoming wealthy beyond my grandest dreams."

"That was when you started trying to kill him."

Grinning, Garin asked, "Wouldn't you? If you were promised immortality by simply not doing a thing, wouldn't you take steps to make sure that thing didn't happen?"

Annja didn't know. She regarded Garin with renewed suspicion. "Why are you here now?"

"I'm still interested in what happens to the sword." Garin shrugged. "Now that it is whole again, does that mean I no longer have untold years ahead of me?"

"Noticed any gray hairs?" Annja asked.

He smiled at her. "Your humor is an acquired taste. When you were in Roux's face, I found you delightful. Now I feel that you have no tact."

"Good. But keep in mind that I fed breakfast to a man who broke into my home." Trying not to show her anxiety, Annja took her plate and Garin's to the sink.

"Tell me about the sword," Garin said.

Turning, Annja leaned a hip against the counter and crossed her arms over her breasts. "What do you want to know?"

"Mostly whether it can be broken again."

Annja shook her head. "Honesty's not always the best policy."

"I've *never* thought it was."

She grinned at that.

"If I had lied," he asked, "would you have known?"

"About this? Yes."

"I already know about the sword," Garin pointed out. "I could have left before you returned."

"After you happened to arrive while I was out."

"Of course."

Annja respected that. He could have done that. She reached out her right hand, reached out into that otherwhere and summoned the sword. She held it in her hand.

Garin's eyes widened as he got to his feet and came toward her. "Let me see it."

"No." Annja leveled the sword, aiming the point at his Adam's apple, intending to halt him in his tracks.

In a move that caught her totally by surprise, Garin tried to grab the blade in his left hand and slam his right forearm down to break it. Instead, his hand and arm swept through the sword as if it weren't there.

Annja reacted at once, throwing out a foot that caught Garin in the side and knocked him away. He scrambled to his feet and fisted the bread knife on the counter.

As Garin brought the bread knife around, Annja took a two-handed grip on the sword and slashed at the smaller blade wondering if it would pass harmlessly through. The bread knife snapped in two, leaving Garin with the hilt in his hand.

Annja planted the sword tip against his chest right over his heart. The material and flesh indented. Maybe Garin couldn't touch the sword, they both realized, but the sword could touch him.

"Are we done here?" Annja asked.

Garin swept his left arm against the blade to knock it away, but again his arm passed through. His effort left him facing Annja, his chest totally exposed to her retaliation.

Annja pressed the sword against his chest. "I've fed you

breakfast," she said evenly. "I've overlooked the fact that you broke into my house. I'm even willing to forgive you for trying to break my sword."

"Your sword?"

"Mine," Annja responded without pause or doubt. The sword was hers. It had chosen her. That much was clear. "But if you ever make an enemy of me, if you ever try to kill me like you did Roux, I'll hunt you down and kill you."

"If I try," Garin promised, unwilling to back up another inch, "you'll never see me coming."

"Then it would be in my best interests to kill you now, wouldn't it?"

Garin stood stubbornly against the sword.

Annja pressed harder, watching the pain flicker through his features and hate darken his eyes. He stumbled back, then turned and walked away. She let him retreat without pursuit.

Garin wiped at the blood seeping through his shirt. "How much?" he demanded.

"For what?" Almost casually, as if she'd been doing it forever, Annja balanced the sword over her right shoulder.

"To break the sword."

Annja shook her head. "I'm not going to break this sword."

In truth, she didn't know what would happen if she tried. An image of the lightning bolt passing through it filled her mind.

She had a definite feeling that whatever happened if she tried to destroy the sword wouldn't be good. Also, she felt that she would be betraying the spirit of the sword. Joan of Arc had led people in a war against oppression with it.

"I could give you millions," Garin said. He waved to encompass the loft. "You wouldn't have to live like this."

"I happen to like the way I live." Annja watched the dark calculations take place in his eyes.

"You love knowledge," he said finally. "With the money I could give you, *would* give you, you could go anywhere in the world. Study anything you like. With the best experts money can buy. You could open up any door to the past you wanted to."

The idea was tempting. She believed Garin could provide that kind of money. She even believed he would.

"No," she said. As if to take the temptation out of his hands, she willed the sword away.

He came at her without warning, rushing at her low and grabbing her hips as he shoved her back against the stove. He fumbled for one of the knives in the wooden block by the sink. Grabbing a thick-bladed butcher's knife, he raised it to strike.

Freeing her right arm from Garin's grasp, Annja drove the heel of her palm into his nose. Blood spurted as the cartilage collapsed.

He yowled in pain and tried to hang on to her. His knife hand came down.

Annja twisted and avoided the knife. The blade thudded deep into the countertop. She reared up against him, forcing him back.

Shifting, she butted him aside with her hip, heel stamped his foot, head butted him under the chin, and brought an elbow strike into line with his jaw.

Garin stepped back, his black eyes glassy. He punched at her but she slapped his arm aside. Then he caught her with an incredibly fast left hand.

Annja dropped as if she'd been hit with a bag of wet cement. Her senses spun and for a moment she thought she was going to pass out.

Garin came after her immediately. On the ground, she knew from experience, his greater size and weight would take away every advantage her speed and strength gave her.

She rolled backward and flipped to her feet in the center of the loft. Annja only had to think of the sword for a split second and it was in her hand. Stepping back, right leg behind her left, hilt gripped firmly in both hands, she readied the sword.

Garin halted, completely out of running room.

All Annja had to do was swing. But he'd stopped his aggressions. *Will it be murder?* she wondered.

"Are you going to kill him, then?" a raspy voice suddenly asked.

Circling slowly, Annja maintained her grip on the sword. She turned just enough to see Roux standing in the doorway.

"Don't either of you respect a person's privacy?" Annja asked.

"I knocked. No one answered. Then I heard the sounds of a scuffle." Roux entered unbidden. "I thought it best if I investigated." He closed the door behind him.

Okay, Annja thought, at least I know he's not a vampire.

Roux took off his long jacket. He wore a casual tan suit. "Are you going to kill him?" he asked again as if the question was a typical greeting.

Garin watched her carefully. He kept his hands spread to the side, ready to move.

Annja continued to slowly circle, never crossing her feet, so she wouldn't trip. She stopped when Roux was behind Garin.

"I don't know yet," Annja admitted.

"My vote is no," Garin said.

"You tried to kill me," Annja said, "right after I told you that I would kill you if you tried."

"I really didn't think you meant it," he said.

"You would have killed me."

Garin was silent for a moment, then nodded. "Probably."

"Miss Creed," Roux said.

"Do you want to kill him?" Annja asked. Maybe that would be better. Although it would still be in her loft. She wondered if she could talk the old man into killing Garin somewhere else.

"No," Roux answered.

"Why not? He's tried to kill you, too."

"I've been like a father to him. It doesn't seem fitting."

"He's tried to *kill* you," Annja said in exasperation.

"Ours has been a...difficult relationship at best," Roux said. "That's the way it is between fathers and sons."

"I'm not your son," Garin snarled.

"You were as close as I ever had," Roux said. He looked around. "May I sit, Miss Creed?"

"Could I stop you?"

"Not if you intend to continue menacing Garin with the sword." Roux sat in the window seat. "Is that melon?"

"Yes."

"May I help myself?"

"Sure," Annja replied, not believing he'd actually asked. "I'm trying to keep the homicidal maniac from killing us."

"I'm not a homicidal maniac," Garin objected. "If you'd just let me destroy that sword—"

"Apparently you can't," Annja taunted. At the moment, after he'd tried to kill her twice, she didn't mind acting a little superior.

"—we could all walk out of here happier," Garin finished.

"I wouldn't be happier," Roux said. He looked for a plate, found one in the cabinet and put melon pieces on it. He returned to the window seat. "I spent five hundred years and more looking for the pieces of that sword. I don't care to repeat that experience any time soon."

"We're immortal, Roux," Garin growled.

"Not immortal," Roux replied. "If she'd cut your head off the day she met you, you'd have died."

"You know what I mean."

"I do." Roux ate the melon with obvious gusto. "This is quite good."

"Why are you here?" Annja asked.

"I thought maybe you might have come looking for me before now," Roux said. "I thought surely you would be curious about the sword. Since you didn't, I thought perhaps it was best if I came looking for you."

"Why?"

"Because of the sword, of course. I knew it couldn't have just disappeared. After you got away and the sword never showed up again, I knew it had gone with you."

"How?"

"As I said, it didn't turn up again at my house." Roux frowned. "Which, I might add, may never be the same again. Why did the Brotherhood of the Silent Rain attack my house?"

"They were after the charm I found in La Bête's lair," Annja said. "How did the sword come with me?"

"Magic. Arcane forces. Some psychic ability on a higher plane," Roux said. "Take your pick."

"Which do you choose?"

"I know why the sword came with you," the old man said.

"Why?" Annja asked.

"Destiny."

Annja was speechless.

"You were destined to hold that sword, Annja Creed," Roux said. "Otherwise you wouldn't have found the last missing piece or me. And, judging from the years I've spent searching for that final piece, no one else could have found it. If you'd found the piece but not me, you wouldn't have found the rest of the sword. Therefore it's destiny."

It was a lot to take in at one time. Annja had trouble dealing with the whole concept. But here she stood, with the sword pressed to the throat of the one man who wanted desperately to destroy it.

She tried to remember when she'd last felt that anything made sense.

She looked at Garin. "Sit over there by the desk."

"Sure." As though he'd just been invited to tea, Garin walked over to the desk and sat.

"We're all three bound by Joan's sword," Roux said. He held up a hand. "May I?"

"I don't think that's such a good idea," Annja said.

"From what I gather, Garin can't touch the sword."

"No."

"It would be interesting to find out if I can."

Annja hesitated.

Roux waved his hand impatiently. "If I didn't want to ask you, I'd simply shoot you and take it off your body."

"You don't have a pistol," Annja said.

Lifting his jacket, Roux revealed the small semiautomatic leathered beneath his left arm. He dropped the jacket to hide the pistol again. "Please."

Reversing the sword with a flourish, Annja laid the blade over her arm and extended the hilt to him.

Roux took the sword easily. He examined it carefully. "This is truly exquisite. You can't see where any of the breaks were."

Tense, Annja waited. She didn't like the idea of anyone else holding the sword.

"Here you go, Miss Creed." Roux passed the sword back. "Do you want to tell me how you did that vanishing trick back at my house?"

Gripping the sword, Annja willed it away. The weapon faded from sight.

Roux grinned in wonder. "Splendid!"

Garin cursed. "You're a fool, old man. Now that the sword is whole again, we're no longer cursed to walk the earth after it. We're no longer immortal."

"Long-lived," Roux argued. "Not immortal. Long-lived. And that remains to be seen, doesn't it?" He looked at the kitchen area. "Do you have anything to drink?"

"Orange juice," Annja said. "Or tea."

"Juice, if you please."

Annja got a glass and filled it with orange juice. She took it to Roux. "What's your interest in this?"

"In the sword?"

She nodded.

"I don't know that I have one," Roux replied. "The sword is complete. I'm not sure what happens now. "

"I know about the curse."

"I suppose you do." Roux sipped his drink. "At any rate, it may well be that my part in this whole affair is over. I truly hope that it is. I have other pursuits I'd like to follow. I'm going to be playing in a Texas Hold 'em Tournament soon and I've qualified for a senior's tour in golf."

"Did you know you're listed as a suspect in Doris Cooper's murder?" Annja asked.

"No. Though it doesn't surprise me."

"Did you do it?"

"No."

"Did Garin?"

"I don't even know anyone named Doris Cooper," Garin protested.

"I don't know," Roux said. "Doris was a good person. Too trusting, perhaps, but a good person."

"Why didn't you try to clear your name?" Annja asked.

"Hollywood was a rat's nest in those days," Roux said. "If the Los Angeles Police Department was determined to pin the woman's murder on me—and I tell you right now that they were—they would have done it. I left the country as soon as I knew they were looking for me." He paused. "Do you want to talk about things that have no bearing on where you're going or what you're going to do? Or do you want to discuss the sword?"

Before Annja could answer, the phone rang. She considered letting the answering service pick up, but she decided she wanted a few minutes of diversion. Things were coming at her too quickly.

"Hello?"

"Miss Creed?" The voice was urbane, accented, and almost familiar.

"Yes," Annja said. "Who is this?"

"Corvin Lesauvage. We met briefly in Lozère."

"I remember you, Mr. Lesauvage," Annja replied. Her thoughts spun. Glancing at Roux and Garin, she saw that both of the men were listening with interest. "You were trying to have me abducted, as I recall."

"Yes, well, I've had to reconsider that. I still want that charm you found and I've had to find new leverage to achieve that goal."

"I don't have the charm," Annja said. "I told you that."

"Then you'll have to get it, Miss Creed," Lesauvage said. "Because if you don't, Avery Moreau will die and his death will be on your head."

24

For just a moment, the loft seemed to spin around Annja. She stood with effort, remembering the young man who had been her guide in Lozère.

"What are you talking about?" she asked.

"If I don't get that charm, Miss Creed," Corvin Lesauvage said, "I'm going to kill Avery Moreau. Do you have Internet access?" His voice oozed self-satisfaction.

"Yes."

"Log on, please, and go to this Internet address— LesauvageAntiquities.com."

Waving Garin away from the desk, Annja opened the Web page. It was attractive, neat and precise, with everything in place. The casual peruser knew immediately that Lesauvage Antiquities did business in appraisal and research, as well as purchases and sales of antiques. It was a nice cover for a man who was a drug runner, thief and murderer.

"The Web link I'm about to give you is masked," Lesauvage said. "You'll have to be quick."

Annja didn't say anything. Roux had gotten up and stood behind her, whether out of interest or to help protect her from any attempt Garin made, Annja didn't know.

"Click on appraisals, then hit the F12 key immediately," Lesauvage ordered.

Annja did.

The Web page cycled, then stopped. A window popped up and asked for an ID and password.

"Okay," Annja said.

"Good. The ID is 'Avery.' The password is 'Mort,'" Lesauvage said.

Mort was French for "death." Reluctantly, Annja entered the keystrokes.

Another window opened. This one filled with a video download that took forty-three seconds. When it finished, it opened and played.

There was no audio, but the video feed was clear enough. Avery Moreau, tied up and dressed in some garish costume, lay on a flat rock in a cave. Blood covered his face. There was too much blood for it to be his without some obvious sign of injury.

Wearing a similar costume but with a mounted-deer-head helmet, Lesauvage entered the camera's view. He raised a knife, then drove the blade down into Avery's left hand, all the way through to the rock beneath.

Avery jerked in pain and screamed. Even without the audio, Annja could hear his agony and fear.

Garin swore.

Thankfully, the video ended.

Annja was breathing deeply. "What do you want, Lesauvage?"

"As I told you, I only want the charm. Bring it to me and I will let Avery Moreau live. If you do not, I will kill him.

Make your travel arrangements. Once you know when you will return to Lozère, let me know. I can be reached at this number at any time." He gave her the number and the phone clicked dead.

Annja cradled the handset.

"A threat?" Roux asked.

"Lesauvage is going to kill Avery Moreau if I don't bring the charm back."

"Well, that's a shame," the old man said, "but you can't be expected to save everyone."

"I'm not going to let him die," Annja said and immediately started looking on the computer for flight possibilities.

Roux stared at her. "You can't be serious. That man is a villain of the basest sort."

"I know the type," Annja said.

Garin grinned at her. "So you're going to rush off and play the savior."

"I'm not going to let Avery Moreau die." Annja backed up all her files on the charm, the heraldry and the Brother-hood of the Silent Rain onto an external hard drive.

"Lesauvage will kill you," Roux protested. "The sword will be lost again."

"One can only hope," Garin said.

"I'm not planning on dying," Annja said. She looked for her suitcase, then realized it was still at the Lamberts' bed-and-breakfast outside Lozère.

All right, then, I'm already packed. All I have to do is live long enough to collect my luggage.

"Don't be foolish," Roux said. "You don't even have the charm."

"I took pictures of it," Annja said. She brought them up on the computer.

"How did you do that? You didn't have time to photograph it like this in Lozère."

"I summoned it up on the sword," Annja explained as she stuffed gear into her backpack.

"It's still part of the sword?"

"I don't know. Maybe." Annja lifted the phone.

"Call the police in Lozère," Roux urged. "Let them know what is going on."

"Do you remember Police Inspector Richelieu?" Annja asked.

"Yes."

"He shot Avery Moreau's father."

"Whatever for?"

"Gerard Moreau was a thief. He broke into the house where Richelieu happened to be entertaining the wife."

"It wasn't the inspector's wife, was it?" Roux said.

"No." Annja dialed information and asked for the number to Air France.

"Excuse me," Garin said.

Annja looked at him.

"I've got a private plane. Actually, a Learjet, at La-Guardia."

"You'd let me use your jet?" Annja asked, surprised.

"If it's going to allow Lesauvage to kill you more quickly, certainly." Garin appeared quite earnest.

"You're going with us." Annja hung up the phone.

"Us?" Roux repeated.

"We're not finished talking about the sword, are we?" Annja asked the old man.

"Perhaps," Roux said.

"Fine," she told him. "Then you can stay here. If Garin and his pilot jump out of the plane somewhere over the

Atlantic and I go down, you can hope you don't have to wait another five hundred years for the sword to wash up on some beach."

Roux grimaced. "If I was certain my part in all of this was finished, I wouldn't entertain this at all."

"Why am I going?" Garin asked.

"Because I don't trust you not to have someone fire a heat-seeking missile at us while we're en route. If you're along for the trip, I figure that's less likely to happen." Annja didn't know if Garin could actually get his hands on something like that, but she wouldn't put it past him.

"That's *your* reason to get me to go," Garin said. "*I* don't have a reason."

"If you go," Annja said, "maybe you'll get to see Lesauvage kill me."

Garin thought about that briefly. "Good point."

GARIN'S PRIVATE JET WAS outfitted like a bachelor pad with wings. It was divided into three sections. The cockpit was the most mundane thing about the aircraft. The living quarters and the bedroom shared equal space and came with a personal flight attendant.

Annja sat in one of the plush seats. Equipped with a wet bar and the latest in technological marvels, including a sixty-inch plasma television and a Bose surround sound system, in-flight entertainment was no problem. There was also a satellite link for phones and computers.

The bedroom, which Annja had not seen and had no intention of seeing, contained a king-size bed.

Garin and Roux had settled into their seats and started watching a televised poker championship.

Hooked up to the Internet, Annja continued her research

into the Brotherhood of the Silent Rain and the charm. Those were at the heart of the mystery before her.

There were new postings at alt.archaeology and alt.archaeology.esoterica.

Two were from Zoodio.

Hey! I traced that shield heraldry you posted. Interesting stuff.

From what I found out, the shield belonged to a British knight named Richard of Kirkland. He was thought to be a great-grandson of one of the English soldiers that burned Joan of Arc at the stake in France.

A chill passed through Annja. She hadn't expected the hit to be tied so closely to Joan.

Supposedly, the great-grandfather's luck turned sour after he got back from France. Devotees of Joan swear he was cursed.

Anyway, that curse seems to have passed down to his great-grandson, who somehow got himself titled along the way. He had a daughter in 1749 who was supposed to have horrible birth defects.

If you're not careful when you do your research, you'll find entries that list her as dead. She even has a gravesite in a private cemetery outside London. Her name was Carolyn. In 1764, Sir Richard of Kirkland took his daughter to the Brotherhood of The Silent Rain.

Why not an abbey? Annja wondered again.

Some reports say Carolyn died in 1767 when the monastery was destroyed. Hope this helps.

It did and it didn't, Annja ultimately decided. She skimmed through the list of sources he'd included. Many of them were on personal Web sites so she was able to check them out.

She saved the Web links to Favorites, then read the next posting by researchferret@secondlook.org.

Zoodio has it wrong. Sir Richard's daughter wasn't his daughter after all. She was his *wife's* illegitimate child. While Sir Richard was off fighting in one of the wars, his wife was having an affair with one of the inbred members of the royal family. Which was why there were so many birth defects in the child.

The wife also tried to abort the child, and even the church got involved because of all the political unrest the baby would cause.

Despite everything everyone did, the baby went to term. When Sir Richard got home, knowing that he wasn't the father—can you imagine how pissed this guy was, out risking his life, and his wife's shacking up?—he probably had to be restrained from killing the baby and his wife.

The church, trying to cover its own ass, told Richard that a demon had fathered the child. They arranged for the baby girl, when she got to be fourteen, to go to the Silent Rain monastery. Can you say cop-out?

"Annja?"

Startled, she looked up and saw Roux standing there. "What?"

"Would you like something to eat?"

"Whatever you want to nuke in the microwave will be fine."

"No nuking," Roux responded. "There's a full galley."

"Do you think it's safe?" she asked. "I mean, he could poison the food."

Roux smiled gently at her. "I'll make sure that doesn't happen."

"All right."

"What would you like?"

"Surprise me."

Roux nodded. He started to turn away.

"Hey," Annja said.

The old man turned back around to her. "What?"

"You've really lived over five hundred years?"

He smiled and shook his head. "My dear girl, I've lived far longer than you can even imagine."

Whatever, Annja thought, thinking the comment was sheer braggadocio. "Did you know a knight named Sir Richard of Kirkland?"

"An English knight?"

Annja nodded.

"I knew of such a man, but I never knew him personally. He was—"

"English. I know. I got it. English was bad back then."

"Yes." Roux's blue eyes twinkled. "He was a tournament champion all over Europe. And he fought in a few skirmishes. There was something about a child that besmirched his reputation. A child born out of wedlock, I believe."

"A child the church contended was spawn of the devil," Annja said. "And she was locked up in the Silent Rain monastery."

"Truly?" Roux seemed amazed.

"Yes."

"Why wasn't she taken to an abbey? Several of the female children born in brothels were taken there."

"I don't know."

"If you find out—"

Annja nodded. She returned to her reading.

"I'll go and attend to our lunch," Roux said. "Then, at some point, you and I need to discuss what's going to happen with the sword."

Three spam entries followed the one by Researchferret. Then Zoodio had posted again.

I missed that one. Good catch.

Interesting. I looked at the data you sent to support what you posted, Researchferret. And I found something you missed.

According to the journals of Sister Mary Elizabeth of a local London abbey, the sisters took in a fourteen-year-old girl early in 1764.

Sir Richard's name isn't mentioned. Neither is the girl's. But it does say she's the illegitimate child of a tournament hero and thought to be the daughter of the devil.

Sounds familiar, huh?

Annja silently agreed.

Also truly weird are the murders that occurred in the abbey in 1764.

That instantly caught Annja's attention.

Early in 1764, January and February, two nuns, then a third, were beaten to death in the basement of the main building. The rumor was that an insane man had broken into the building and killed the nuns while looking for church silver or donations to pilfer.

However, Sister Mary Elizabeth notes that the strange girl the abbey had taken in murdered the nuns. According to her entries during those days and the days that followed, the girl had been restrained in the basement, had gotten loose, and had beaten the nuns to death *with her bare hands.*

Yikes!

This story gets creepier and stranger the more I look into it. More later.

Of course, that entry started a flurry of postings that included Jack the Ripper theories and led to the Loch Ness Monster before taking a detour through the twilight zone.

25

Roux brought Annja a plate while she was still sorting through the entries.

Reluctantly, Annja pushed the computer off to the side and flipped out the tray built into the seat. She surveyed the plate for the first time while she was spreading a linen napkin across her lap.

A small steak shared space with a baked potato and a salad. The steak was grilled.

"No poison, I assure you." Roux sat in the seat next to her and set up his own plate. He tucked a napkin into his shirt collar. "I trust you like steak?"

"Yes." Annja cut the meat and found it sliced easily.

"From the last time we shared a meal, I knew you had a robust appetite. Judging from the way most young people your age eat, missing meals when you get busy and such, I thought a solid meal was called for."

"This steak is grilled," Annja said in amazement. She'd never had a steak actually grilled in midflight.

"Garin has always been one for whatever is new and flashy," Roux admitted. "I found his galley is equipped with all manner of culinary accoutrements."

"And it has a grill, too." Annja poked fun at the old man's verbosity.

Roux got the joke and smiled. "Although not my native language, I find that English does have its charm. So does French."

That surprised Annja. "French isn't your native language?"

"No. Why? Do I sound like a native when I speak it?"

"Yes."

Knife and fork in hand, Roux attacked his steak. "What have you discovered about the charm?"

Briefly, Annja brought him up-to-date.

"What are you going to do?" Roux asked when she was finished.

"Find out the truth about what happened all those years ago," Annja said. "Discover who the prisoner was in the monastery and what happened to her. Why the monastery was destroyed. Why the monastery still exists even though it's been destroyed. Why the monks of that monastery want the charm. Why Corvin Lesauvage wants the charm."

"Don't forget, you want to save this young man, as well."

"Avery Moreau. I haven't forgotten."

"Quite a shopping list." Roux abandoned his plate and leaned back to digest his meal.

"It is," Annja admitted. "But it's what I do."

"Look for truths in the past?"

Put that simply, Annja had to admit her job sounded too altruistic. "I love learning about the people who lived in the past. Who they were. What they did. Why they did it. Where they lived. How they saw the world and their places in it."

"You only left out 'when.'"

Despite her tension, Annja smiled. "'When' is sometimes part of the mystery, too. Carbon dating is pretty exact, but you don't always have it, and the results can be off enough to seriously screw with a theory."

"You're a classically trained archaeologist?"

"I am, but I've also got degrees in anthropology and ethnography."

"Good. I know it's hard for a traditional archaeologist to find work inside the United States and in most parts of the world these days. The focus tends to be on culture rather than things."

"You know about archaeology?" Annja was surprised.

"I know a lot about a great many things. I was with Dr. Howard Carter while he was doing his exploration of the Valley of the Kings in Egypt."

"That was in the early 1900s." Annja still couldn't believe they were talking about a period a hundred years ago, or that Roux might actually have seen it.

"Yes. Though Howard didn't find the tomb of Tutankhamen until 1922." Roux smiled. "I was there. It was a most gratifying moment. The man who funded the search, Lord Carnarvon, had very nearly given up on Howard. But Howard, for the most part, remained certain he was about to find the tomb. And he did. It was most impressive. The world will very probably never see the like again."

"I hope that's not true," Annja said. "Egypt grabbed everyone's attention, especially the British after Napoleon's army found the first pyramids there during the war. But there are other things out there we can learn."

"You're probably right. The world has forgotten more than anyone alive today will ever know." Roux talked as if he were an authority on that line of thinking. He was silent for a moment.

"What about the sword?" Annja asked.

Roux looked at her. "What do you mean?"

"I mean, why me?"

"My dear girl," Roux said, "the sword *chose* you."

"FROM THE VERY FIRST TIME I met Joan," Roux said, "I knew she was destined for greatness." In his mind's eye, he could see her again, proudly riding the great warhorse and carrying the banner. He had never—or, at least, very seldom—met anyone like her. "When you've been alive as long as I have, you tend to recognize such things."

"You've never stated your age," Annja said.

Roux grinned. He discovered he liked dueling with the young woman seated next to him. Not only was she beautiful, but she possessed mental alacrity, as well.

However, she was still naive in many ways. He hoped to be able to occasionally use that to his advantage. He had served the command he had been given. Now his life was his to do as he pleased.

"Nor will I state my age," Roux said. "But I do forgive your impertinence in your not-so-subtle attempt to find out."

She smiled at him, rested her elbows on the chair's arms and steepled her slender fingers to rest her chin.

Looking at her, Roux knew she was going to break many men's hearts. She was too beautiful and too independent—too driven—not to.

And now she carried Joan's sword, and everything that such a calling brought with it. That taken into account, and the looming confrontation with Lesauvage and the Brotherhood of the Silent Rain, she might not live to see the end of the week.

"As I said," Roux returned to his story, "I met Joan and I was very much taken with her. I saw that she was going to be a...*force*. No other word can match what I saw in her."

"You were a fan," Annja said. Her tiger's eyes gleamed with humor.

"I was," Roux admitted. "I was quite taken with her. But it was the power invested in her that drew me the most. The company of others has seldom been a preoccupation for me."

"Except for the part about hearing your own voice, I've noticed."

Roux grimaced. "There used to be an appreciation for storytelling."

"There still is," Annja said. "But now it also includes brevity. Getting to the point. That kind of thing."

"I believe Joan was supposed to help the balance," Roux said.

"What balance?"

"The balance between good and evil."

Annja paused, thinking, her brows tightly knit. "With a big *G* and a big *E?*"

"Exactly. The cosmic balance. A turning point between order and chaos." Roux sighed and still felt hugely guilty even after more than five hundred years and the vexing job of finding all the sword pieces. "But the world was cheated of her presence far too early."

"Because you got back to her late."

Roux shifted uncomfortably in his seat. Across the room, Garin lounged on a full-sized sofa and enjoyed the conversation, smirking the whole time.

"I wasn't the one who threw her up on that bloody stake and roasted her alive," Roux snapped. His own guilt was one thing, but he bloody well wasn't going to have it shoved on him by someone else.

Annja was quiet for a moment. "No," she said finally, "I suppose you weren't."

"That's right."

"So what's supposed to happen now?" Annja asked.

Roux was quiet for a moment, knowing what he was about to say would have a lasting impact on the young woman. At least, it would as long as she lived.

"I believe that the inheritor of Joan's sword is going to have to live up to that same potential," Roux said. "You're going to be asked to intercede on the behalf of good. Or not, if you so choose."

That shocked her. He saw it in her eyes. She was silent and still for a moment.

"That's ridiculous," the young woman finally said.

"Is it?" Roux gazed at her. "Yet, here you are, racing to the rescue of some unknown young man who actually may have set you up to be kidnapped while we were in the mountains."

"I'm not going because of the sword."

"Then why are you going?"

"Because I don't want Avery Moreau to die."

"Why? You don't truly know him. He may already be dead. More than likely, he betrayed you to a vicious enemy. You'd be a fool to do anything to help him." Roux leaned back. "Furthermore, you could call and let the local police deal with the matter."

"The sword has nothing to do with this."

"Perhaps not. Perhaps by your very nature you're quixotic. I submit to you, Miss Creed, that is probably the very reason the sword chose you."

Annja was silent for a moment, blinking as if she was dazed. Then she said, "You can't be serious."

"Of course not," Roux said. "I'm just leading you on a wild-goose chase. And the sword can't really appear and disappear just because you want it to. And it didn't somehow reform itself from pieces when you touched it. All those things are lies."

A troubled look flashed in her eyes. "It also drew a lightning strike from the sky."

Roux was intrigued. "When?"

"Last night. On top of my building."

"You left the sword lying on top of a building?"

"I was holding it at the time."

Roux's eyebrows lifted. "Lightning struck the sword while you were holding it?"

"Yes."

"And you were undamaged?"

Annja nodded.

"This is fascinating. May I see the sword again?"

She held out her hand, paused a moment, then drew the sword from thin air.

Roux accepted the weapon as she handed it to him. He examined the blade. "It's unmarked."

"I know. Doesn't make a lot of sense, does it?"

"Neither does the fact that it shows no sign of ever having been shattered." Roux held on to the sword, wondering what other properties might manifest. Then it faded from his grip. He looked at her. "You did that?"

Annja nodded. "I guess I did. I was feeling…uncomfortable with the way you were holding on to the sword."

So stealing the sword, should he ever decide to do that, was out of the question. Roux felt challenged. He couldn't help wondering what would happen to the sword if Annja Creed were suddenly dead.

Roux happened to glance over at Garin, who smiled broadly. Roux knew he had spent too many years with his apprentice; Garin knew exactly what was crossing his mind. The old man was just thankful the young woman didn't have the same expertise.

ANNJA STARED at the lozenge. The heraldry beside the shadowy figure on the obverse of the coin was key to unlocking the mystery. She felt certain of that.

The diamond-shaped image containing the leaping wolf, the stag at rest and the crescent moon with a star above and below, had to mean something.

She continued searching through the pages of heraldry. Patience was one of the first and best skills an archaeologist learned.

THE RING OF HER cell phone startled Annja out of a near doze. She fumbled to find the device and catch the call.

"Hello."

"May I speak to Ms. Annja Creed, please?" a crisp British voice asked.

"Graham," Annja said.

"Ah, Annja. I wasn't sure at all if it was you. You sound as though you're talking from the bottom of a well. Come to think of it, the last time I spoke with you, you *were* talking to me from the bottom of a well. Didn't you get out?"

Annja smiled. Professor Graham Smyth-Peabody was professor emeritus at Cambridge University. He was in his early eighties and taught only those classes he wanted to during times he wished. Tall and distinguished-looking, he was a frequent guest on talk shows when discussions of British royalty were the subject.

"I did get out of the well," Annja said. That had been in the Bavarian countryside pursuing the lost loot of a highwayman. She hadn't found that, but she still occasionally sifted through the information she had about the event.

"Have you found another, then?" Smyth-Peabody laughed at his own wit.

"Actually, I'm flying on a private plane," Annja said.

"Jet," Garin growled. He sat on the couch with a drink in his hand. His disposition hadn't improved.

"Your publisher must really like you," the professor said. He hesitated. "You're able to afford a private plane because of the book, right? You haven't suddenly decided to start losing your shirt like that other young woman on that dreadful program on the telly?"

"No," Annja said. "I manage to keep my shirts on."

"Jolly good. I understand why you do those pieces for that program, but you should keep your naughty bits to yourself."

Despite the tension and all the trouble waiting on her in Lozère, Annja had to laugh. The professor was in rare good form.

Papers rustled at the other end of the phone connection. "I've managed to identify the heraldry you e-mailed me," the professor said.

"You could have e-mailed me back."

"Of course, of course. But I shall own up to a bit of curiosity here. I've found something a bit incongruous."

Annja pushed out of her seat and paced the short length of the jet's living room. "The shield bears markings of Richard of Kirkland," Annja said.

"Yes, yes. Quite right. So you've identified that."

"It makes me feel better to hear you agree with the answer I've received."

"He was knighted in 1768."

The monastery outside Lozère was burned down in 1767. Experience had taught Annja not to overlook coincidence. "Why was he knighted?" she asked.

"According to the documentation I found, it was for special services to the crown."

"What services?"

"I'm afraid it doesn't say, my dear."

"You would think the conferring of a knighthood under George III would have been important enough to record."

"Indeed," Smyth-Peabody agreed. "Perhaps it even was. But you have to remember, George III wasn't called the mad king for vacuous reasons. The man had porphyria, a most debilitating affliction that ultimately ruined his health and rendered him mad as a hatter. And there was a lot going on during his reign. He undermined the Whig Party, including Pitt the Elder, fought the French for seven years, then turned around and fought you Americans, not once but twice, staved off another attack at political control by the Whigs under Pitt the Younger, and managed to fight Napoleon's efforts at world domination twice."

"Those campaigns were managed by the Duke of Wellington."

"Quite. But they were under George III's reign. Perhaps he wasn't aware of what was going on by that time, but his royal historians were kept busy nonetheless."

"Point taken." Annja sighed. History and archaeology were sometimes at odds with each other. Then when a research project brought in other branches of science, things became even more convoluted.

"You are aware he had a daughter?" Smyth-Peabody asked.

"Carolyn," Annja said.

"Yes. Do tell me there is something I've left to amaze you with?"

"I'll let you know when we get there. Tell me about Carolyn."

Smyth-Peabody cleared his throat. "Sir Richard's daughter was born to his wife while he was tending the king's holdings in the New World."

"Richard wasn't in France?"

"No. He was one of the king's primaries during engagements in King George's War. You Americans refer to it as—"

"The French and Indian War," Annja said. "From 1757 to 1763."

"Yes. A rather melodramatic name, don't you think?"

Annja's mind flew. "Did Richard see any action in France?"

"No. According to the texts I've been through, Richard spent his whole military career marshaling forces in America. Until his death in 1777 at the Battle of Brandywine Creek when General Howe's troops forced the Continental Congress from Philadelphia."

"Richard never served in France?"

"I never found mention of it. I didn't know that was an important detail. I suppose I can go back through the research."

"What about Richard's wife?"

"Victoria, yes. By all accounts, she was rather a handful. She was married at fourteen to Richard, who was twenty years her senior."

Annja wasn't surprised. Marriages were often arranged for officers in the British military. Poor working-class parents wanted to get rid of a mouth to feed and hoped that a daughter, who wasn't allowed to work, might find a good home.

"Evidently being married to Richard didn't agree with her," the professor continued.

"What makes you say that?"

"She *did* have the affair behind her husband's back. After she lost the baby, I'm sure things weren't any easier."

"The baby didn't die."

Smyth-Peabody was silent for a moment. "Are you quite sure?"

"Yes. I'll forward the documentation on to you."

"In everything that I read, the child died and was buried in a private cemetery on family land outside London."

"Was the cause of death mentioned?"

"I inferred there were massive birth defects. There was, in one of the resources I investigated, some reason to believe there were instances of inbreeding within Victoria's family. Perhaps even incest."

"Where did you get that?"

"From the newspapers. They were little more than gossip sheets at the time."

The jet hit a downdraft. For a few seconds, Annja felt weightless. Then her stomach flipped and gravity held her in place again.

"What about the lozenge?" Annja asked.

"It never existed. Or, I should say, it never existed in the form that you showed me." The professor paused and the computer keys clacked. "The wolf design?"

"Yes."

"That was one that Sir Richard had ordered designed for his wife. She was going to be given her own coat-of-arms on the birth of their first child. The lozenge was never struck."

"The stag was part of the design?"

"No. The stag belonged to Sir Henry of Falhout."

"Could he have been Carolyn's father?"

"He died in 1745 while at sea in a tragic accident. It would have been quite impossible."

"Did he have a son? The coat-of-arms would have descended to him."

"Sir Henry did have a son, but he was only eight at the time Carolyn was born."

"What about brothers?" Annja kept trying to make sense of the puzzle. The image of the lozenge wouldn't leave her thoughts. Someone had initially thought to put the inscription on the charm, then had decided—or been told—not to. It had to be important.

"Sir Henry did have two younger brothers. The youngest brother died while fighting the French in 1747."

"What about the other brother?"

"I've not found anything out about him. He seems to have disappeared," the professor said.

"No family fortune to care for?"

"Remember, dear girl," the professor said, "this is Britain. We had the law of primogeniture here. Only the eldest male issue shall inherit family estates. Once Sir Henry had a son to carry on the family name, the rest of the family got nothing."

"Then who would use his heraldry?"

"I don't know. I shall keep looking and endeavor to find out. But as it stands at the moment, I'm at a loss to explain it."

"Thanks, Graham," Annja said.

"Of course, dear girl. I am yours to command. I have only one request."

"Yes."

"Once you decipher this puzzle, come to England and share the story with me. It's been too long since I've seen you."

"I will," Annja said, and hoped she survived the encounter with Lesauvage to do that.

26

"Annja."

Waking with a start, Annja lifted her hands in front of her in a defensive move. She blinked, focused and saw Roux standing in front of her.

"What?" she asked. Her throat was dry.

"We're descending. We'll land in a few minutes."

Annja felt the shift in the jet then. "Thanks." She put her seat belt on again.

Roux looked guilty. "I feel bad for waking you. You've hardly been asleep at all."

"I'll be fine." Annja uncapped a bottle of water and drank. The truth was, she didn't know how much longer she could keep going. It seemed as if the past few days had all turned into one exhaustive blur.

"May I?" Roux gestured to the seat next to her.

"Sure."

Roux sat and belted himself in. "I plan on accompanying you." He paused. "Unless you have an objection."

Annja thought about it. She really didn't want to be on her own facing Lesauvage and possibly the Brotherhood of the Silent Rain.

"It's going to be dangerous," she warned.

Roux favored her with a small smile. "Now that you have the sword, I should wonder if you will ever know peace again."

Annja lay back in the seat. "I hope you're wrong."

"You could give up the sword." He regarded her with idle speculation.

For a quiet moment, Annja thought about it. She could give up the sword, simply lay it down and walk away. But she knew she wouldn't. That wasn't her way, and...the sword had felt entirely too right in her hand.

"No," she said. "I can't."

"I'M NOT GOING."

Standing at the door of the jet, the noise of the airport loud in her ears, Annja looked at Garin.

Hands clasped behind his head, he lounged, barefoot, on the sofa.

"I thought you couldn't wait to see me get killed," Annja said.

Mirthlessly, Garin grinned at her. "If I go with you, I might be tempted to help you. If I did, I wouldn't be helping myself, would I?" He shook his head. "No. I'll sit on the sidelines for this one, and wait to see how it turns out."

Without a word, Annja ducked through the door and went quickly down the steps to the tarmac. Roux followed her, carrying a slim, dark wood walking stick. He exchanged no words with Garin. After more than five hundred years of being mentor and student, then enemies, what was left to say?

A jet screamed through the air overhead. Annja looked up into the night and adjusted her backpack over her shoulder.

Eyes were watching her. She was sure of that. She wondered if she would ever see Garin again.

THREE MEN WAITED outside the gates, near the baggage claim area. They were better dressed than the motorcycle riders but they were the same kind of stock.

"Miss Creed," one of them said.

Annja stopped. "Who are you?"

"Mr. Lesauvage sent a car for you."

"I prefer my own car," Annja said.

"Mr. Lesauvage," the man said more harshly, *"insists."*

"He can call me and arrange a meeting place." Annja stared at him. "I insist."

The man stepped forward and grabbed Annja's upper arm. She reacted without thinking, opening her fist and popping him in the throat.

Buckling, gasping for breath, the man staggered away. The second man reached for her, but she shifted, grabbed his arm and bent it behind him, then lifted his arm high between his shoulders and rammed him into the nearest wall. Senseless, he collapsed.

The third man took one step, then Roux swung the walking stick up between his legs. Mewling with pain and grabbing himself, the man dropped to the floor.

Roux adjusted his collar and tie. Frowning, he gazed at the rapid approach of the security people. "Well, so much for the quiet arrival."

IT TOOK almost an hour to straighten out the mess with airport security. In the end, one of Lesauvage's men claimed to have staggered drunkenly into Annja and caused the misunderstanding. Annja had supported that by saying she might have overreacted. The security chief let them go with a stern warning, and probably because he didn't want any further paperwork than he already had.

"Have you always been this way?" Roux asked while they stood at the car-rental desk.

Annja was quiet for a moment. Then she looked at him. "I grew up in an orphanage. You learn not to let people push you around in there. If circumstances were different, if I didn't already know that Lesauvage was slime, maybe I would handle this a different way."

The agent brought a set of keys to a Nissan Terrano 4X4. The cost was extra, but Annja wanted the off-road capability.

"But Lesauvage is a criminal," Annja went on, "and circumstances aren't different. I'm preparing for war."

Roux smiled and shook his head. "You remind me so much of her at times. So focused. So deliberate. So convinced of your own righteousness."

"Of who?" Annja signed the agreement and left the desk. She knew whom Roux meant, but for some reason she wanted him to say it. That way maybe he'd remember that he'd been too late last time and would put forth greater effort.

Roux fell into step beside her. "Of Joan."

For a moment, the image of the burning pyre filled Annja's head. "Joan's dead."

"I know," Roux said. "I was going to remind you of that."

ANNJA WAS KEYING the ignition when her cell phone rang. Fumbling it from her backpack, she answered.

"Miss Creed," Lesauvage said.

Annja paused with the Terrano in gear. All around her, people arrived and departed the busy airport even this late in the evening. All of them had places to go, were starting journeys or ending them.

And what are you doing? she wondered. Starting one or ending one? She didn't know.

"We'll meet outside Mende," Annja said with cold deliberation. She tried to sound as though she weren't about to throw up.

"I sent a car for you," Lesauvage stated.

"I declined. Move on to your next point." Annja couldn't believe how forceful she was being. Maybe it was from watching all those adventure movies with Sister Mary Annabelle when the other nuns were away. Or maybe it was just that in this situation a whole lot of dialogue wasn't needed.

"I could kill Avery Moreau," Lesauvage threatened.

"And I could get on the next plane out of here." Glancing back over her shoulder, Annja spotted the three men moving toward her. "Call your men off."

"We're going to do this my way," Lesauvage said.

"No," Annja said, "we're not." She broke the connection, tossed the phone onto the dashboard and looked at Roux. "Buckle up."

Without a word, the old man did. But a faint grin pulled his lips.

Annja shoved the transmission into reverse and backed toward Lesauvage's three men. Trapped in the ruby-and-white glow of her taillights, they tried to run. She managed to clip one of them with her rear bumper and send him sprawling into a parked car. The alarm roared to life and lights flashed.

The other two men ran to help their companion to his feet.

They tried to run to their car, but public parking was a long way from rental parking.

Annja switched on her lights and merged with the departing traffic.

The phone rang again.

Grabbing the phone, Annja said, "Be polite."

"Where," Lesauvage asked, "do you want to meet?"

Annja named a kilometer marker a short distance from the city. Then she hung up again.

For a short time, Roux let her drive in silence, long enough to get onto the loop around Paris so they could head south. Finally he said, "You realize, of course, that Lesauvage and his men will outnumber you when you reach that destination."

"Yes." Annja made herself try to believe that she wasn't sleepy and that driving was taking all of her attention.

"What do you plan to do?"

"I don't know," she replied, "exactly." She paused. "Yet. This is still a work in progress."

"You're trusting that Lesauvage won't kill you."

"He won't." Annja thought that through. "He can't. He wants the charm and whatever secrets it possesses."

"Once he has it, he may well kill you. Us."

Annja looked at him and smiled. "Are you worried about us? Or *you?*"

"Both, actually." Roux regarded her. "I'm fascinated by you. I'd like very much to see what you do with Joan's sword."

Me, too, Annja thought. Then she turned her attention back to her driving. The rendezvous was hours away.

"IT APPEARS we have a tail," Roux announced when they were three kilometers north of their destination.

"We've had one for the past half hour," Annja said.

"We'll not be arriving unannounced," Roux stated.

Annja looked at him. "I could let you out."

Roux gave her a crooked smile. "No. I've seen myself through worse than Corvin Lesauvage."

"You mean Garin?"

Roux studied his hands. "I mean much worse than Lesauvage or Garin." He wouldn't say any more.

Annja glanced in the rearview mirror again and watched the car holding steady at the same speed it had for the past thirty minutes. She still hadn't been able to tell how many men were in the car.

It didn't matter, though. There would be a lot more waiting with Lesauvage.

A roadside sign announced the rest stop she'd chosen was only two kilometers distant.

PULLING OFF the highway, Annja drove into the rest stop. The building was off to the right with a small park behind it. Security lights marked the parking area in front of the building and at the north side.

Lesauvage waited on the north side. A sleek black BMW looked like a predatory cat hunkered down between two stalwart Renault Alpines. Only a short distance behind them, a cargo van sat solid and silent. A dozen motorcycles were spread around the cars. They had the whole end of the parking area to themselves.

Annja's cell phone rang.

"Yes," she said.

"I see you, Miss Creed," Lesauvage announced. "Do come in. There is no need for further game play. You will not leave this area unless I allow it. And I will kill Avery Moreau just to show you that I mean what I say."

The tail car, flanked by two others, pulled in behind Annja. One came alongside on the left and blocked the exit lane. The other two remained behind her. Their lights shone through the Terrano's back glass.

Annja remained where she was. As she stared at the cars and motorcycles ahead of her, Lesauvage got out of the BMW and stood in front of the vehicles. He held his cell phone to his ear and smiled broadly. His sandy hair caught gold fire in the light.

"At this point, Miss Creed," Lesauvage said, "you truly have no choice."

Without replying, Annja closed the cell phone and shoved the device into her backpack. She drove the SUV toward the BMW.

Roux gripped the suicide handle above his head. "You purchased the optional insurance, didn't you?"

"I never go anywhere without it," Annja said as she put her foot down harder on the accelerator. She drove straight for the BMW. The cell phone shrilled for her attention but she ignored it.

Lesauvage turned abruptly and waved to the BMW's driver. The man engaged the transmission and squealed backward, sliding out of the protective custody of the two Renaults. In his haste, the driver ran over one of the motorcycles.

Annja braked and skidded to a halt between the two Renaults.

"Well," Roux said in a calm voice as he released his hold, "I'm sure we wouldn't have enjoyed a more welcome response before this anyway."

Quivering a little inside, knowing that she was laying her life—and Roux's—on the line, Annja nodded.

One of the men wearing motorcycle leathers ran and jumped onto the Terrano's hood. He landed in a kneeling position with a deadly machine pistol in his hands. Annja didn't recognize the weapon, but she knew it for what it was.

"Don't move!" he shouted in accented English. "Keep your hands on the steering wheel!"

Annja did.

"And you, old man," the thug went on, "you put your hands on the dash!"

"Impertinent twit," Roux growled.

For a moment fear ran rampant in Annja's stomach. She felt certain Roux was not going to do as he'd been ordered. Then, thankfully, he put his hands on the dash.

Lesauvage stepped to the Terrano's side and gazed into the vehicle with a hot-eyed glare. A tense moment passed. Annja returned the man's gaze without batting an eye.

"Get them out of the car," Lesauvage ordered.

MINUTES LATER, Annja sat on the floor in the back of the cargo van. Her hands were cuffed behind her. Roux sat near the double doors at the back. His hands were also cuffed. He sat impassively, watching the exchange between Annja and Lesauvage.

You have no business being here, Annja told herself again. The statement was now a litany that spawned over and over again in her head like a video-game monster.

But every time she looked at Avery Moreau, sitting shaking and frightened across from her, she knew she couldn't have stayed away.

"You did not bring the charm, Miss Creed." Corvin Lesauvage paced the carpeted rear deck of the van.

Annja made no reply.

"What did you hope to accomplish?" Lesauvage demanded.

"You would have killed Avery Moreau if I hadn't come," she said.

"Yes."

Avery looked up at Lesauvage. The young man held his injured hand cradled in his lap. Red streaks along his forearm showed the onset of infection. Even though Lesauvage had wounded him, Avery still looked surprised by the man's quick admission.

"So here I am," Annja said.

"What good are you?"

"I memorized the charm," Annja said. "I know what it looks like. Do you?"

Lesauvage drew back his hand to strike her. Annja didn't flinch, fully expecting to feel the weight of the blow.

"Don't," Roux said. There was something in the old man's voice that stayed Lesauvage's hand.

The criminal stepped away, fastening his gaze onto Roux. "You should have stayed out of this, old man."

"Perhaps," Roux replied. "But, then, you don't know who you're trifling with, do you?"

Annja watched Lesauvage. This wasn't like the final tense moments in a movie where the villain laid out his plans for conquest. In the movies, the script kept the villain from killing the captured heroes. Annja was desperately aware that there was no such script here.

Joan of Arc died at the hands of her enemies, Annja thought. For a moment she believed Lesauvage was going to kill Roux.

"What do you want?" Annja asked.

Visibly restraining himself, Lesauvage took a deep breath

and turned to face her. The constant roar of the tires against the pavement filled the van. They were obviously headed for a destination, but Annja had no clue what that might be.

"How familiar are you with the Brotherhood of the Silent Rain, Miss Creed?" Lesauvage asked.

"I know they represented the church and were known for keeping to themselves," Annja said. "They worked on scholarly pieces for the church libraries and were self-sufficient. I know they also took a stand against the French noblemen who wanted to continue the Wild Hunt. I know their monastery was destroyed in 1767. I assume that was done by the same French noblemen they displeased."

"It was," Lesauvage said. "But that monastery was destroyed and the monks slain for more than mere interference."

Annja waited. She'd baited him. She could see that. He loved knowing more than she did and he couldn't hold that knowledge back.

"The Brotherhood of Silent Rain wasn't just against the Wild Hunt," Lesauvage said. "They also protested the search for the Beast of Gévaudan, saying that the creature was imagined and the poor people were killed by the noblemen only to justify the Wild Hunt."

"Why would they do that?" Annja asked.

"Because," Lesauvage said, "they were providing safe harbor for La Bête. The beast was living among them."

27

"How do you know La Bête was living at the monastery?" Annja asked.

Lesauvage showed her a grin, then lit a Gaulois cigarette and breathed out a plume of smoke. "You're not the only one who does research, Miss Creed."

"Not to be offensive," Annja stated evenly, not truly caring if the man took offense, "but you hardly seem the sort to crack a book."

"I didn't." Lesauvage stared at her coldly. "All my life I've been told that a knight named Benoit of Mende, nicknamed 'the Relentless' because he never gave up on anything he set his mind to, found out that the monks of the Brotherhood of the Silent Rain were providing shelter to La Bête. He blackmailed the monks into giving him a huge ransom."

"Instead of telling others who might help kill the beast?" Roux asked.

Lesauvage grinned. "Benoit was truly a man after my own heart. Always looking after himself."

"How did he find out the monastery was sheltering La Bête?"

"He was a master of the Wild Hunt. No beast—no man—was safe once Benoit took up the trail." Lesauvage's eyes gleamed with excitement at the telling. "He followed the creature back there in 1767. The following morning, he went to Father Roger, who was master of the monastery, and told him they would have to pay for his silence. Reluctantly, the monks agreed. And they began to gather up the gold and silver Benoit exacted for his price. But he knew they would try to betray him. After all, everyone knows you can't trust the English."

"The English?" Annja repeated.

"Father Roger was English. He was banished to the Brotherhood of the Silent Rain years before for some transgression against the church."

"What transgression?"

Lesauvage shrugged. "Does it matter?"

Annja knew it did. Lesauvage was missing a large part of the story, but she thought she had it. "Go on."

"Thank you," the man said sarcastically. "At any rate, knowing he couldn't trust the English, Benoit arranged to accept delivery of the ransom. He and his men fled from the monastery that day. A sudden storm rose up and chased them down the mountain."

"What mountain?" Annja asked.

"Up in the Cévennes," Lesauvage said. "That's where we're going now. We'll see how well you remember the charm."

Annja didn't respond. "You're looking for the treasure."

"But of course. On his way down the mountainside, Benoit fully expected to be attacked by the monks. What he had not counted on was being pursued by La Bête. He thought to outmaneuver the monks, though. There are some old Roman ruins up in the Cévennes."

"Several of them are at Nîmes," Annja said.

"You know of them? Excellent. But there are several others. The Roman legions marched everywhere through France on their way to conquer the rest of the known world. They left garrisons, temples and buildings everywhere they went. Quite the builders, the Romans. Benoit chose to hide his treasure in those ruins."

"And you believe it's still there?" Annja shook her head.

"I do."

"That was 240 years ago."

Lesauvage glared at her. "The treasure was never found. Benoit and ten of his finest knights, accompanied by twenty peasants, raced down the mountain with La Bête on their heels. Benoit had counted on having the day to help him. Instead, the sky had turned dark and rain lashed the forest. The horses skidded and tumbled, hardly worth attempting to ride."

"On the ground, in full armor, the knights were sitting ducks for La Bête," Annja said.

"They had no chance," Lesauvage said. "La Bête was among them in minutes. Benoit said that he heard the screams of his men as they were slain."

"I guess he didn't stay to help them," Roux said dryly.

"Benoit was no hero," Lesauvage said. "He was a fighter. He stayed and fought only when he knew he was going to win. Against the rain, unhorsed and on the treacherous slopes of a forested mountain, he knew he could not win. His only victory lay in survival, being able to live to reclaim his fortune. So he ran."

As Annja listened to the man's words, she imagined what

the battle must have been like. She'd seen La Bête's huge
body in the cave. Trapped in their armor in the mud as they
had been, instead of secure on horses, the knights had little
chance.

"In the end, the knights were all slain," Lesauvage said.

"What happened to the peasants?" Annja figured she
already knew, but she had to ask.

Lesauvage grinned. "After they'd helped hide the treasure
in the ruins, Benoit and his men killed them. Well away from
the hiding area, of course."

Roux growled a curse.

"Secrets, you see, are hard to keep when they're shared
so broadly," Lesauvage said.

"I take it Benoit didn't die," Annja said.

"No," Lesauvage agreed. "Benoit didn't die. The storm
that poured out its fury and took away his fighting terrain also
offered him a means of escape. A stream runs at the foothills
of the Cévennes near the ruins. With the arrival of the storm,
the stream swelled and overflowed its banks, becoming a
raging torrent."

Annja had been in mountains caving when flash floods
had struck. She'd always been amazed at how much water
was dumped during a sudden storm.

"Benoit shed his armor as he ran, knowing his only chance
was the stream." Lesauvage flicked ash from his cigarette. "He
reached a cliff overlooking the water. Before he could jump
La Bête overtook him." Lesauvage smiled. "They fought.
Benoit was armed with only a knife. He didn't fare well. But
he wounded the beast enough that he was able to escape and
leap into the stream. La Bête tried to follow, but couldn't
swim."

"Why didn't Benoit recover his ransom later?" Annja asked.

"Unfortunately, Benoit was not only injured by La Bête, but also by the plunge into the river. He was in a coma for nine days. Everyone thought he was dead. Then, on the morning of the tenth day, he woke to find that he had suffered a spinal injury that robbed him of his legs and most of the use of his arms."

Annja waited, knowing Lesauvage was doling the story out as he wanted to.

"Condemned to his bed, Benoit still intended to have both his ransom and his vengeance against the monks," Lesauvage said. "He rallied the other knights who shared his interest in the Wild Hunt and told them that the monastery of the Brotherhood of the Silent Rain was giving shelter to La Bête."

"They believed him?" Annja asked.

Lesauvage shrugged. "Either way, they were going to be rid of the monks and their insistence that the Wild Hunt be stopped. They took up arms and destroyed the monastery, pulling it down stone by stone and burning what was left. For his revenge against the monster, Benoit struck a secret deal with the most renowned knight in all of Gévaudan at the time, Scarlet Didier, whose blood was made of ice water and whose thirst for action was unquenchable."

"He agreed to hunt La Bête?"

"When it wasn't found at the monastery, yes."

"Why?"

"For money, of course. Benoit had claimed a coin from the monastery. A piece of metal stamped with the Brotherhood of the Silent Rain's symbol. On the other side, Benoit crafted an image of a wolf and a mountain."

Annja waited.

"That image," Lesauvage said, "is a map to the treasure. Benoit gave the charm to Scarlet Didier and told him he would give him the secret of the map after he had killed La Bête and brought back the creature's head."

"Scarlet Didier didn't come back from that hunt," Annja said. She remembered the dead man holding on to the spear in the cave.

"No. After Didier went up into the mountains, he was never heard from again," Lesauvage said. "Three days after Didier left, Benoit had a relapse caused by an infection. He died a week later, never regaining consciousness."

"You expect that treasure to still be there after two hundred years?" Roux asked in a manner suggesting that Lesauvage was insane or a fool.

"It was never found," Lesauvage replied.

Roux snorted in open derision. "More than likely the monks took it back."

"The treasure was never found at the monastery," Lesauvage argued.

"Then it never existed." Roux's conviction was damning.

Lesauvage wheeled on the old man and struck him with his fist. Roux's head turned to the side. When the old man turned to face his tormentor, he glowered at him.

"No man," Roux said in a quiet, deadly voice that barely rose above the steady whir of the tires, "has ever laid a hand upon me without paying the price in blood. I will kill you."

Bending down, Lesauvage shoved his face close to Roux's. He raised his voice. "Marcel," he called.

One of the guards stepped forward.

"Tie that length of chain around the old man's leg," Lesauvage directed.

The big man knelt and carried out the order. The oily black chain left smudges on Roux's pants.

"Now open the cargo doors."

Marcel opened the cargo doors. The highway passed in a dizzying rush. Trees stood black and dark against the moon. One of the Renaults, flanked by motorcycles, followed closely.

"When I tell you to," Lesauvage said, "heave the old man out the cargo doors. If he somehow is missed by the car or survives the impact, we'll keep dragging him until there's nothing left of him."

The big guard nodded and seized Roux's bound feet. He dragged and pushed the old man to hang poised over the edge. Roux never said a word.

Horrified at the prospect of what was happening, Annja tried to break free of her bonds. The metal cuffs felt loose, but she could not break them.

She pictured the sword in her mind's eye and reached for it. But somehow she couldn't manage to take the hilt up into her bound arm. It was as if the sword were suddenly behind a glass wall.

Frustrated, Annja said, "If you hurt him, you might as well kill me."

Lesauvage threw up a hand, freezing his minion in place. "Are you that brave?" he asked.

"If you're going to kill him," Annja said, "I know you'll kill me. If I know you're going to kill me, why should I help you?"

"What do you propose?"

"Leave him alone," Annja suggested. "Once we get up into the mountains, I'll help you find the ransom Benoit hid."

"You'll help me anyway." Lesauvage leered. "I've got a taste for torture. Breaking you could be a delight."

Swallowing the fear that threatened to engulf her, Annja made herself stare back at Lesauvage. Don't let him see that you're afraid. He's like any other predator. Keep him off balance, she thought.

"Breaking me will take time," she promised. "And what do you do if you go too far? Do you want to lose time and take the chance on losing the information I have?"

Lesauvage stood. "Pull the old man back inside and close the door."

The guard did that. Immediately the road noise inside the van diminished.

"Now," Lesauvage said to Annja, "here's the deal you reaped. The first time I get the impression that you're lying to me, I'm going to kill all of you. And I'll take my time while I'm doing it." He paused. "Is that understood?"

Annja nodded, not trusting her voice.

"Good," Lesauvage said.

LITTLE MORE than an hour later, they were up in the Cévennes mountains. They left the BMW, Renaults and van at the base of the mountains.

Lesauvage checked the GPS locater he carried, then gave directions to his team. All of them were heavily armed. From his conversation over the cell phone, Annja knew that he had a helicopter standing by. Evidently Lesauvage planned to use the helicopter to transport the treasure and for a quick exit.

"Are you going to continue to be his captive?" Roux whispered. He stood beside her against the van.

"I don't have much choice," Annja said.

"You have the sword," Roux hissed.

"The sword isn't exactly available at the moment."

Roux glanced at her in consternation. "What do you mean?"

"I can't get to it." Annja flexed her hands behind her back. The cuffs held her arms in place. "I reach for it, the way I always have, only it won't come."

"But it's there?" Roux asked.

"It feels like it is."

Lesauvage returned, closing and pocketing his cell phone. At his command, one of the men placed Roux on the back of his motorcycle.

Annja was seated on another. Avery Moreau, looking feverish and exhausted, was placed on the back of a third.

Only a moment later, they were tearing across the night-darkened terrain, heading steadily up into the Cévennes Mountains.

THE MOTORCYCLE CARAVAN reached the ruins over an hour later. The long ride left Annja's legs in agony. She hadn't been on a motorcycle in a while and being handcuffed while riding kept her in an uncomfortable position.

Near the top of the mountain, they found the remains of an old Roman garrison. Judging from its position, the stronghold had once existed as a checkpoint along a trail that led over the mountain.

In its time, the garrison had probably looked formidable. Now it looked like the scattered blocks of a giant child. Forest growth had shot roots into the mortar, gained hold and was inexorably pulling the structure into its destructive grip. One day, if no move was made to preserve the garrison, it would crumble, devoured by vegetation.

Lesauvage and his men carried powerful flashlights. The driver in front of Annja helped her off the motorcycle but wasn't gentle about it. She stood on wobbly legs, but her strength quickly returned.

Roux and Avery appeared to have the same problem for a while longer.

"There is a cave inside the mountain," Lesauvage said.

Annja had already known there would be. The Romans had used every advantage the land they built upon would give them, then manufactured others. Having a cave meant having a place to store provisions, as well as retreat to.

"Hasn't the cave been explored?" Roux asked.

"Hundreds of times," Lesauvage answered, gazing at Annja in open speculation.

"Then you're on a fool's errand," Roux snapped.

"For your sake," Lesauvage said, "I hope not."

Like you're going to set us free, Annja thought derisively. But the idea of the cave captivated her thoughts. Even places that had been investigated for hundreds of years sometimes turned up surprises. Often secrets weren't revealed until the searcher knew what to look for.

She pictured the charm in her mind again. The hanged wolf stood out against the background of the mountain.

Why a wolf? she wondered. Why was it hanged?

"Miss Creed?" Lesauvage prompted.

"I'll need my hands," she said.

Lesauvage hesitated, then nodded at one of his men. Two others kept their weapons leveled at her. The cuff around one wrist was removed only long enough to bring her arms in front of her, then was once more secured.

But during that moment, Annja had reached out and touched the sword. It was there. She just couldn't take it from that otherwhere with her hands bound.

"I need a flashlight," Annja said.

Lesauvage handed her a flashlight. Lightning stabbed across the sky. The wind changed directions and rose in intensity. The temperature seemed to be dropping a few degrees.

Good thing you don't believe in omens, Annja told herself. She switched on the light and walked through the remnants of the checkpoint and into the cave beyond.

BROTHER GASPAR WOKE in the stone niche that served as his bed. He heard his name repeated, then looked over at the doorway where one of the young monks stood holding a single candle.

"What is it?" Gaspar asked, pushing himself into a sitting position.

"Lesauvage and the American woman have returned to the mountains." The yellow glow of the candle flame played over the young monk's tense features. "They're at the Roman checkpoint where Benoit was believed to have hidden the ransom he extorted from our order."

"Why?"

"I don't know."

For a moment, Gaspar sat wreathed in his blankets. The caves were always damp and chill. He had never questioned where God had chosen to assign him, but he sometimes longed for the day when he would know a warm bed at night.

"Get everyone ready," Gaspar said. "Let's go see what they found."

After the young monk left to wake the others, Gaspar wondered if all the secrets they had protected were on the verge of finally coming out. Over the years of its existence, the church had covered up many things. Men served God, and men were always made of flesh and blood. And flesh and blood were doomed to be forever weaker than faith.

28

Annja followed the narrow passage, having to duck twice. Not wide enough for two men to walk abreast, the passageway formed a bottleneck that would have been suicidal for an opposing force to attempt to breach.

Almost twenty feet in, the passageway opened into the first cave chamber.

Playing her flashlight beam around, Annja discovered the cave was a near rectangle thirty feet wide and about fifty feet long. The ceiling averaged about fifteen feet up, but dipped as low as five feet.

Her foot slipped over the edge of a hole and she barely caught herself.

"Careful, Miss Creed," Lesauvage admonished.

Pointing the flashlight down, Annja discovered she'd almost stepped into a hole nearly five feet in diameter and at least six feet deep.

"It's a trap," Lesauvage explained.

"I know." Annja shone her beam around and discovered

that the pits made a checkerboard mosaic across the front of the cave entrance. Some of them were filled in with dirt, debris and rocks.

"Back in the days of the Roman soldiers," Lesauvage said, "I'm told stakes were placed in the traps to impale the unsuspecting. The stakes are long gone now, of course."

Annja stepped around the pits; stakes or not, they'd make a nasty fall.

At the back of the cave, she found three passageways. All of them led to smaller caves. She guessed they'd been used as storage areas and barracks.

Puzzled, she played the flashlight beam over the cave walls and ceiling again. Bats clung to stalactites that had been chipped and broken off at uniform height.

"What are you looking for?" Lesauvage asked.

"A way out," Annja answered. "It doesn't make sense that Roman soldiers would plan on falling back into a cave they couldn't escape from. There has to be a way out." She started testing the walls.

"People have looked for that treasure in the caves for years," Lesauvage said angrily. "If there had been a secret door in one of the walls or the ceiling, it would have been found."

Annja ignored the comment. Discoveries had been made in what were believed to be "explored" areas before. She just had to put her mind into finding the solution.

"Perhaps," Roux suggested, "the monks already reclaimed the treasure all those years ago. It could be they didn't tell anyone so the search would continue as an exercise in frustration. And to remind everyone that no one could steal from the church. The Vatican liked the idea of divine justice and curses overtaking thieves who robbed them." He stepped into the last cave with a flashlight and helped her look.

Annja wondered why Roux was helping, then decided maybe his own curiosity had prompted him to action.

"They could have," Annja agreed. "This wasn't the best hiding place for Benoit to attempt to stash the ransom."

"There was no other place for him to hide it in the time that he had," Lesauvage said. "It was this place—or no place."

"Perhaps he never got a treasure at all," Roux suggested. "The tale about the treasure could have been merely a way for him to get his vengeance."

"The knights all resented the Brotherhood of the Silent Rain," Lesauvage said. "They needed only the smallest excuse to tear down that monastery."

Annja went back to the second cave, ignoring the fact that Lesauvage's men held guns on her. Her mind worked to solve the problem she'd been presented. She was drawn more into that effort than in being afraid. Something chewed at the back of her mind and restlessly called attention to itself.

"Benoit swore that the charm held the answer to the hiding place," Lesauvage said.

Annja stumbled over a depression in the ground. Aiming the flashlight down, she saw a round hollow.

"Perhaps we should look outside," Roux said.

Lightning flashed, invading the caves for a moment. Almost immediately, thunder shook the earth. Loose rock tumbled from the ceiling and skidded down the walls.

"This isn't gonna cave in, is it?" Avery asked nervously.

Lesauvage sneered at the young man. "You wanted revenge for your father. Don't you realize you need a spine for that?" He cursed. "Instead, you came to me, imploring me to unleash my Wild Huntsmen on Inspector Richelieu."

Annja looked at the young man.

Tears ran down Avery's face and dripped from his scruffy

chin. He spoke in French. "He killed my father! I saw him do it! It's not fair that everyone thinks he's a hero! My father wasn't even armed. He was just a thief, not a murderer." He wiped at his face with his bandaged hand. The handcuffs gleamed in the flashlight's beam.

Annja felt a surge of compassion for the young man. She'd never known her parents. She couldn't imagine what it would be like to watch a parent's murder.

"Stop your damned sniveling, child," Lesauvage commanded. "Otherwise I'll have you taken out and shot."

"No," Annja said.

Lesauvage turned on her. "I'm getting tired of your continued insistence on giving the orders around here, Miss Creed. You've not done as I've asked and brought the charm, and now you're wasting my time."

"I don't have the charm," Annja said. "I told you that. You choose not to believe me. I can't help that. I've offered you the best help that I can."

Smiling, Lesauvage pointed his pistol directly between Annja's eyes. "I won't kill you, Miss Creed. Not yet. But I am going to kill one of these two men if you don't have some degree of success." He paused. "Soon."

Unflinching, Annja stared across the barrel of the pistol. Lesauvage's men shifted uneasily behind him.

"Choose one of them," Lesauvage ordered. "Save one. I will kill the other."

"I need a shovel," Annja said.

Lesauvage blinked at her. "What?"

"I think I know what the charm referred to," she said.

"Tell me."

Annja pointed to the depressions in front of the smaller caves. "These were traps at one time."

Surveying the ground, Lesauvage nodded. "So?"

"I think at least one of them is more than that." Excitement filled Annja as she thought about the clue her subconscious mind had given her. "You and I have been speaking English. Avery spoke in French."

"How has that any bearing?"

"Because it made me think of what these traps were originally called. Have you heard of the word *loophole?*"

"As in a legal maneuver?" Lesauvage sounded impatient.

"As in the origin of the word," Annja said.

Lesauvage glared at her. "I don't care for a lesson in wordplay."

"You should. Two hundred and forty years ago, wordplay was everything in entertainment. Puzzles, limericks, jokes and brainteasers took the place of television and video games. When I work a dig site, I have to keep that in mind. Words can have several meanings, not just the superficial ones. The hanged wolf on the charm was a clue, and it was an icon. A picture of the word Benoit perhaps didn't know how to write."

"A loophole was an opening in a defensive wall on a structure or a cave in the forest," Roux said, smiling as if he knew where Annja was going. "A way a traveler might check for wolves lying in wait outside the wall. Or, as they were known in French, *loupes.*"

"That's right," Annja said. She gestured toward the trap. "Pits like these were used back in the days of Julius Caesar. He wrote about them in his *Commentaries on the Gallic Wars.* But do you know what they're called in French?"

Lesauvage shook his head.

"*Trou de loup.*"

"Wolf trap," Lesauvage said.

"Yes. The charm had a picture of a hanged wolf on it," Annja said. "But maybe it wasn't a hanged wolf. I think it was a trapped wolf."

Lesauvage looked down at the *trou de loup* beneath Annja's feet. "Get her a shovel," he ordered. "Get them all shovels."

ANNJA DUG. The effort brought a warm burn to her arm, shoulder and back muscles. The chill of the cave left her.

The work went easily. Someone had filled in the wolf traps a long time ago, but the earth wasn't solidly packed. The shovel blade bit down deeply each time. Roux and Avery dug out the other two pits.

Annja reached the bottom of her pit first. Stakes had impaled a victim hundreds of years ago. Bones and a few scraps of fabric testified to that. She knew the time frame from the few Roman coins and a copper bracelet she dug up on the way to the bottom. The coins, bracelet and the bones were all that were left. The stakes had splintered long ago. When they had been placed all those centuries ago, the Romans had hammered the stakes into bedrock.

Lifting the shovel in both hands, Annja drove the blade down against the bedrock. Satisfied it was solid, she tossed the shovel out and climbed from the pit.

Lesauvage looked at her.

"It's solid," she replied.

"If you're wrong about all three," Lesauvage taunted, "at least you'll have your graves dug."

Annja ignored the comment. They had freed her from the handcuffs. In her mind she had reached out and touched the sword. It was there, waiting.

"How are you doing?" she asked Roux.

"Almost there." Grime stained Roux's face as he worked by lantorn light. He turned another shovelful of dirt from the wolf trap. "You do realize that simply losing the treasure wasn't enough to keep the Brotherhood of the Silent Rain in hiding. They were, and still are, one supposes, being punished."

"I know. I have a theory about that, as well. They weren't ostracized by the church for their failure to protect the gold and silver they lost," Annja said.

"It was because of La Bête." Roux took a handkerchief from his pocket and wiped his face.

"Yes."

"Then they did give the beast shelter."

Annja nodded. "They did."

"But whatever on earth for?" Roux asked.

"The clue to that is in the lozenge," Annja said. "In the heraldry that was almost marked for the shadowy figure on the charm."

"Do you know who that figure was?"

"I think I do."

Lesauvage stepped forward and cursed. "Enough talk. More digging."

Annja tapped on Avery's shoulder. The young man's wounded hand had bled through the bandages and formed a crust of dirt.

"What?" Avery asked.

"Let me do it," Annja said.

He scowled at her. "I can do it." Stubbornly, he pushed the shovel back into the dirt.

"You'll be lucky if you don't bleed to death at the rate you're going," she pointed out.

"Go away."

Stepping forward, Lesauvage said, "Get out of there. You're digging too slowly."

Eyes tearing with emotion, looking scared and confused, Avery climbed from the hole. He threw the shovel back into the half-dug pit and started cursing.

Quick as a snake, Lesauvage slammed his pistol into the side of Avery's head. Dazed and hurting, the young man dropped to the ground. He rocked and mewled in pain, holding his head, bleeding down the side of his face. Crimson drops fell from his jawline to the stone floor of the cave.

Anger surged through Annja, but she knew she had to contain it for the moment. At the bottom of the wolf trap, she paused a moment and reached for the sword. The leather-bound hilt felt rough beneath her fingers.

Then she drew back her hand and started to dig. Now wasn't the time. But soon.

For a time only the sounds of the storm and the two shovels cleaving the earth existed. Thudding impacts competed with the rumbling that sounded as if it were on top of the mountain.

A moment later, Roux's shovel struck something hollow. "Here," he called.

Annja vaulted out of the pit where she worked and crossed the cave. Roux tapped the shovel several times, causing the hollow thump each time.

Looking at Roux's pit, Annja immediately noticed the difference between it and the two she'd worked in. The ones she'd dug tapered like inverted cones. As she'd neared the bottom, the excavation had been harder because the earth had been previously unworked.

Roux's pit had obviously been completely dug out. He kept shoveling, working around a stone oval that fitted onto mortared stoneworks below.

"Is that a tunnel?" Lesauvage asked.

"Maybe," Annja answered. "It could also be a well. The Roman soldiers would have wanted a water source if they were besieged."

More of Lesauvage's men shone their beams into the hole Roux had made.

Within minutes, the old man had completely dug out around the oval. He leaned back against the wall. Perspiration soaked his clothing.

Fear swarmed inside Annja. They were nearing the point of no return. Soon, Lesauvage would no longer need them. If the treasure was revealed beneath, she was certain they'd be shot immediately.

"Get that cover off," Lesauvage ordered.

"I can't," Roux replied. "It's too heavy." He levered the shovel under the stone oval and demonstrated the difficulty he had in raising it only a couple inches.

"We need ropes," Annja said. She directed the flashlight up at the ceiling. There, almost hidden in the shadows, an iron ring was pounded into the ceiling. If it had been found in the past, it might have been mistaken for use with heavy supply loads.

"Get the ropes," Lesauvage ordered. He grinned at Annja. "Very good, Miss Creed."

MINUTES LATER, Annja had tied a harness around the stone oval, then connected that to a double-strand line running through the iron hook mounted in the ceiling. Lesauvage put a team of men on the rope. Together, they pulled and the stone lid slowly lifted from the hole. The sound of running water echoed inside the cave.

Anticipation fired every nerve of Annja's body.

When the lid was clear, Lesauvage walked to the edge of

the wolf trap and aimed his flashlight beam. The yellow cone of illumination melted the darkness away.

"What's that sound?" Lesauvage asked.

"Running water," Annja said. "There's probably a stream or groundwater running down there. Like I said, the soldiers would have wanted a steady supply of freshwater."

"How far down?"

Holding her flashlight, Annja climbed down into the wolf pit. She shone the light around and spotted rusty iron handles covered with fungus set into the wall.

"Do you need a rope?" Lesauvage asked.

"No." Annja threw a leg over the edge of the pit and started down. Her boots rang against the iron handles. Three rungs down, one of them snapped off beneath her weight, nearly rusted through.

She almost fell, only hanging on with her hands.

The tunnel walls showed tool marks. Someone had cut through the solid rock into the shallow stream below. Cold air rushed up around Annja, chilling her.

She thought about the tunnel. The Romans, or whoever had constructed it, had known the stream was there. They hadn't drilled blindly through the rock in the hopes of hitting water.

They found it sometime before they decided to dig down to it, Annja realized. And if they found it before they dug down to it, there had to be another entrance.

That gave her hope. She finished the climb and dropped into the stream. The water came up to her calves, but her boots were tall enough to keep her feet dry.

She aimed the flashlight up the stream and down. The tunnel was almost eight feet across and barely five feet in height.

Upstream? Or downstream? She wasn't sure. Her flashlight didn't penetrate far enough to show her much.

A gleam of white suddenly caught her attention. Mired in the dirt and clay that coated the rock, scattered bones lay in disarray.

Enemies? Annja wondered. Or soldiers no one else cared enough to bury?

Amid the death, though, the dull gleam of metal reflected the flashlight beam. She knelt and dragged a hand through the running water, closing her hand on some of the smaller objects she touched.

When she lifted her hand, she held three gold coins and two silver ones. One of the gold ones bore the insignia of the Brotherhood of the Silent Rain.

"Miss Creed?" Lesauvage called.

"I'm here." Annja pocketed the coins and returned to the tunnel. When she looked up, Lesauvage was shining his light into her eyes.

"Well?" he asked.

"I'm coming up. Douse the light."

For a moment Lesauvage hesitated, obviously struggling with whether he wanted to obey.

"Please," Annja called up. "I can't see the rungs."

That near admission of helplessness salved Lesauvage's pride somewhat. "Of course." He moved the light away.

Annja glanced down, trying to will the spots from her vision. Then she noticed a single green leaf riding the stream.

Upstream, she thought, smiling. There's nowhere else that leaf could have come from. She felt certain another opening existed upstream. The storm's fury had probably torn leaves from the trees, and at least one of them had found its way into the cave.

She took hold of the rungs and climbed. At the top, she clambered out of the wolf trap.

"Well?" Lesauvage asked.

Roux and Avery stood near the wolf trap. The young man looked anxious. Roux wore an irritated look, like someone who'd been asked to stay on long after a party had lost its charm.

Annja looked at Roux and spoke in Latin, trusting that for all his hauteur, Lesauvage hadn't learned the spoken language. He might have learned to read bits and pieces, but surely not enough to speak it.

"We can escape down there," she told Roux. "Upstream. Take the boy."

Roux nodded, looking slightly less irritated.

Lesauvage pointed his pistol at Annja's head. "What the hell did you say?"

Without a word, Annja took the coins from her pocket and tossed them to the middle of the stone floor. Enough light existed to catch their golden gleam.

"The treasure's down there." Annja pictured the sword in her mind as she switched off her light and shoved it into her pants pocket. "It's in the stream. You're rich."

Drawn by greed, Lesauvage and his men looked at the coins, swiveling their flashlight beams.

"Now," Annja said in Latin.

Roux grabbed Avery and shoved him toward the hole. The boy yelped in fear and tried to get away, but the old man's strength proved too much for him. Avery disappeared, falling through the wolf trap with Roux on top of him.

Cursing, Lesauvage raised his pistol again. "Kill them!" he shouted.

Annja closed her hand around the sword and pulled.

29

As soon as the sword was in the cave with her, Annja's senses went into overdrive. It was like time slowed down and everyone was moving in slow motion.

She swung the sword, cutting through Lesauvage's pistol before he could fire, hitting the barrel and knocking the weapon off target. When he fired, the yellow-white muzzle-flash flamed in a spherical shape and the bullet ricocheted from the ceiling.

The other men had trouble aiming at her for fear of hitting Lesauvage. She stepped toward him as he tried to point his pistol at her again.

Planting her right foot, Annja pivoted and slammed her left foot into the center of Lesauvage's chest, knocking him back into his men. Machine pistol-chatter filled the cave with a deafening rattle that defied the sonorous cracks of thunder. Ricochets struck sparks from the wall, and two of Lesauvage's men went down with screams of pain.

Annja ran for the wolf trap and dropped to the bottom of

the pit. Bullets cut the air over her head and slammed against the stone oval hanging from the ropes.

Reacting instinctively, as if the sword had been part of her for her whole life, Annja swept the blade from her hip and launched it at the double-stranded line.

The sword sailed straight and true through the rope. Stepping over the tunnel's edge, she dropped and landed in the stream below, bending her knees to take the shock.

Lying in the rush of water, Avery and Roux stared at her in surprise.

In the next instant, the ropes parted and the heavy stone oval slammed down onto the tunnel. The fit wasn't exact. Flashlight illumination leaked through the cracks. It was enough to show that Lesauvage's men were wasting no time about pursuit.

"The sword." Roux pushed himself to his feet.

Annja reached into the otherwhere for the weapon and was relieved to find it there. "I've got it," she said.

"Did you get any of their weapons?" Roux asked.

"No."

The old man cursed and shook his head. "At the very least you could have slain one of them and taken his weapons."

"Next time," Annja said. "If you want, you can wait for them down here. They'll probably get that tunnel opened again in a minute. You can get all the weapons you want."

Roux glared at her. "She was never a wiseass."

"I'm not Joan," Annja said. She turned her attention to Avery.

The young man looked as though he was in shock and about to pass out. He cradled his wounded hand in his good one.

"Can you run?" Annja asked.

"I...I think so."

"Upstream," Annja said. "There should be another way out." She took the lead, splashing through the water. She set the flashlight to wide angle.

Behind them they could hear Lesauvage's men wrestling to remove the heavy stone oval.

"What makes you think there's another way out?" Roux asked. "I trust you haven't been here before?"

"I saw a leaf float past me. It came from outside."

"It could have passed through an underwater opening. For all you know, this stream could run for miles underground."

"I hope not." Annja followed the slope up into the heart of the mountain.

The way got tricky and footing was treacherous. There were sinkholes along the way that plunged them up to their chests in near freezing water. They scrambled out and kept going. The rock ran smooth as time and fungus had made it slippery. Again and again, they fell with bruising impacts that left them shaken. They kept moving, certain that Lesauvage and his men would follow.

Annja tried to make sense of the direction they were heading, but she had to give up and acknowledge that they were lost. She listened, but she couldn't tell if they were being pursued.

Maybe not, she thought hopefully. With the treasure right there, Lesauvage wouldn't let anything else stand in his way.

She kept running.

CORVIN LESAUVAGE WAS in heaven. Hanging from the rungs set into the wall, he played his flashlight beam over the treasure that Benoit the Relentless had dumped into the Roman garrison's hiding place all those years ago.

It didn't matter to Lesauvage how Benoit had managed to find the place. Maybe he'd learned of it while searching for La Bête. Or perhaps one of his men had known about it.

The fact was that everyone who knew about it now was dead.

Except for Annja Creed, Avery Moreau and the hard-eyed old man who had accompanied her.

Lesauvage reconciled himself with the knowledge that they wouldn't get down off the mountain in the storm. He wouldn't allow that to happen. If they told the authorities about his ill-gotten gain, it could cause him no end of problems.

He stared at the gleaming precious metals in the glare of his flashlight a moment longer, then he climbed the rungs back up to the cave. His men awaited him.

"We hunt," he declared.

They all grinned and howled in eager anticipation. Quickly, they took up the old Celtic chant he'd taught them in the cave beneath his house. Then they took the special concoction of drugs he'd created, which he told them contained ancient magic. It was mostly speed with a mild hallucinogenic, enough to make them physically able to push themselves past the level of normal human endurance and never know any fear.

Within minutes, they were all high, edgy and ready to explode. Eager to kill.

"They're down there," Lesauvage said, feeling the drug's effects himself. He felt impossibly strong and invincible. Almost godlike. "I want them dead."

Dropping back through the wolf trap, Lesauvage lowered himself into the stream. He didn't know which way to go. Closing his eyes, he tried to sense his prey, but there were no signs of them.

He reached into the water and came up with a gold coin. He laughed a little, feeling the heavy weight of it in his hand. The coin had two sides. One was blank. The other held the symbol of the Brotherhood of the Silent Rain. He designated the insignia "heads" and flipped the coin.

The gold disc whirled in the air. Lesauvage slid a hand under it and looked down at the symbol lying in his palm.

It was heads.

"This way," he told his men. They headed upstream.

Baying and laughing, the Wild Hunt took up the chase.

BROTHER GASPAR STOOD back for a moment while two of the young monks entered the Roman garrison. Cold rain pelted him, a barrage of hostility fueled by nature. He fully expected an exchange of gunfire within the cave at any moment.

Instead, the two monks returned. They were armed with pistols, rifles and swords.

"There is something you should see," one of them said.

Brother Gaspar followed the monks into the cave. He saw the stone oval suspended over the wolf trap at once. Peering down into the hole while another monk pointed his flashlight, Brother Gaspar saw the water and the gold and silver below.

"Benoit's ransom," Brother Gaspar said. "I'd thought it lost forever." He looked up at the young monk. Then he noticed a dead man sprawled on the floor. "Who is that?"

"One of Lesauvage's men."

Brother Gaspar knew that Lesauvage and his men had not left. Their motorcycles were still parked outside. "What happened to him?"

"He was shot," the young monk said. He touched a spot between his own eyes. "He was dead when we got here."

"They're in the tunnel below." Brother Gaspar looked down at the water. "Where does it lead?"

The young monk shook his head. "We've tapped into an underground stream as a well. Perhaps it's another one."

"And perhaps this one leads to the one we use." Brother Gaspar realized that the monastery had been left virtually undefended. He turned from the wolf trap. "Take half of your men into the tunnel. Follow them. The others will return to the monastery with me." He hurried out into the storm, once again hating the secrets that bound him to his life in this horrible place.

The treasure had been found. Did that mean that Father Roger of Falhout's dreadful secret had been discovered, too?

Brother Gaspar lifted his robes and ran as fast as he was able. Nearly 240 years ago, some of the terrible secrets the Vatican had chosen to hide had spilled out. Over a hundred deaths had resulted because of that choice.

How many more lives would be sacrificed to keep the secret?

LIGHTNING FLARED overhead, exploding inside the cave like a light bulb shorting out.

Glancing up, shielding her eyes against the spots that danced in her vision, Annja saw a hole nearly a foot across at the roof of the cave they were in. The hole was almost twenty feet above them.

"There," Roux said, pointing.

"I see it," Annja replied.

Lightning strobed the sky again, igniting another flare that danced across the water swirling at their knees. The water level was rising, and that concerned her. A flash flood would drown them.

"We can't get up there," Roux said, slapping the slab of rock that framed the cave.

Judging from the walls, the cave had been carved by constantly flowing water thousands of years ago. The result was a smooth surface that couldn't be climbed.

"Then we keep going," Annja said. Heading upstream once again, she ran, knowing that Avery Moreau was growing steadily weaker and the flashlight beam was growing more dim.

LESS THAN FIFTEEN minutes later, Annja found the source of the water. A cistern had formed within the mountain. The hollow half bowl collected water in a natural reservoir, but with the current storm, it had exceeded capacity.

However, the thing that drew Annja's attention most was the light that bled through the cracks where the cistern had separated from the cave roof. A waterfall of glistening water poured into the lower cave.

"Light," Roux said.

"I see it." Warily, Annja drew her sword and moved closer.

The light source was stationary, not the flickering randomness of the lightning. And it was pale yellow, not flaring white.

Cautiously, she made her way up the pile of broken rock that had spilled over the cistern's side. Holding the sword in one hand, trying to avoid as much of the water as she could, Annja peered through the crack.

A room lay beyond. It was another cavern actually, but someone had built a low stone dam to help trap the water in the cistern. Plastic five-gallon water containers sat in neat rows beside the dam. Candles burned in sconces on the walls.

"What is it?" Roux asked.

"A room," Annja answered.

"Someone is living there?"

"Several someones from the look of things," Annja answered. The cold was eating into her now. She was beginning to feel as if warmth had never existed.

"Is there a way in?" Roux asked.

Annja tossed him the flashlight. He caught it before it hit the water.

Avery Moreau leaned against the wall nearby. He held his arms wrapped around himself. His teeth chattered and his breath blew out in gray fogs. "He's going to kill us, you know. Lesauvage. He won't let us escape because we know too much."

"Hang in there, Avery," Annja said.

Reluctantly, the young man nodded. He heard her, but he didn't share her hope.

Hefting a large stone block, Annja took a firm hold and swung it at the cistern's edge. The impact sounded like a cannon shot inside the cave.

The third time she slammed the stone into the cistern, the side cracked. Then sections of the cistern tumbled to the cave floor and the stream below. Water deluged Annja, knocking her from her feet.

Roux tramped through the sudden increase in the water level and pinned her with the flashlight beam. "Are you all right?"

"I'm fine." Annja pushed herself to her feet. She was soaked and the cold ate into her like acid.

The broken section of the cistern wall drained most of the water. Annja knew whoever had purposefully created the larger reservoir from the natural one wouldn't be happy with the damage she'd done.

Catching hold of the cistern's edge, she heaved herself up and in. Kneeling, she offered her hand to Avery and pulled him along, then did the same for Roux. She took a candle-powered lantern from a hook on the wall.

Stone steps, shaped from the bones of the mountain, led out of the cistern room. Annja was certain they followed the meanderings of a cave shaft—with occasional sculpting, as testified to by the tool marks on the walls—but there was function and design.

When she waved the lantern close to the steps, she found impressions worn deeply into them.

"Whoever lives here has been here for a long time," she observed.

"It's a monastery," Roux said. His voice echoed in the stairwell.

"What makes you so sure?"

"Can you imagine anyone else living like this? Cloistered. Underground. With only the rudimentary amenities. And you said you didn't know where the Brotherhood of the Silent Rain came from." Roux looked around. "I think you can safely say that you do now."

THREE TURNS LATER, Annja came upon a door to the right. She tried it and found it unlocked.

I guess there's no need to lock doors on a subterranean fortress no one knows about, Annja thought. She followed the door inside.

The cavern was long and quiet. Spiderwebs filled the open spaces of the roof. Rectangular openings in the walls occurred at regular intervals.

Annja held the lantern up high. Another doorway stood at the opposite end of the cave.

"What is this place?" Avery asked. His voice sounded brittle.

"A cemetery," Annja said.

The young man stopped in his tracks. "We shouldn't be in here, should we?"

"No," Annja agreed. "But we are. This could be the shortest route to an exit." She didn't really think so, but there were questions she needed answered. She walked to the closest wall and began examining the coffins.

All of them were crafted of flat stones mortared together in rectangular shapes left hollow for the bodies. Once the dead were interred, the lids were mortared on, as well.

Annja brushed at the thick dust that covered them, searching for identification marks. Near one end of the coffin she was examining, she found a name carved into one of the rocks:

Brother Gustave
1843–1912

"What are you looking for?" Roux joined her in the search, working on the other side.

"Father Roger." Annja moved on to the coffin above the first one she'd inspected.

Rats, no doubt drawn into the caves by the ready supply of food kept on hand by the monks, scattered across the top of the coffin. She didn't want to think about what the rodents would have done to the bodies if they'd gotten inside.

"Who was he?" Roux asked.

"He was head of the monastery in 1767 when it was destroyed." Annja read the next inscription, but it wasn't the one she was looking for, either.

Reluctantly, Avery joined in the search. He approached another wall of coffins tentatively.

"'Roger' isn't exactly a French name," Roux said.

"It's English." Annja went to the next stack and swept dust from it, as well. "He was once Roger of Falhout."

Roux looked at her then. "Wasn't he the man whose heraldry is represented on the lozenge?"

"No. That heraldry belonged to his brother, Sir Henry. And to Sir Henry's father before him. Roger was Sir Henry's younger brother. One of them, anyway."

"But he wasn't entitled to the heraldry because of the law of primogeniture," Roux said, understanding.

Avery turned to them. "I don't know what that law is."

"Basically," Annja said, moving to the next coffin, "it's a law that keeps the family farm from being split up. Say a man has three sons. Like Sir Henry's father. The eldest son, Sir Henry, inherits all the family lands and titles. At the time, it took a lot of land to field a knight, and knights were the lifeblood of a king's army."

"That's not true anymore," Avery said.

"No, but it was when Father Roger was around." Annja frightened away another rat and read the next inscription. "Fathers had to have a system to keep brothers from fighting over the lands. So a simple method was devised. The first son inherited the land. The second son was given to the military. The third son was given to the church."

"And if there were more?"

"They were apprenticed to master craftsmen as best as could be done," Annja said.

"Roger was a third-born son," Roux said.

"Right," Annja agreed. "He was given to the church."

"Which wasn't without its own problems," Roux said.

"England had fought the Roman influence for six hundred years before the Anglican Church was declared."

"Henry VIII closed the Roman Catholic abbeys and monasteries during his reign," Annja added, "and supported the Anglican Church. Father Roger, as evidenced by his presence here, was Roman Catholic."

"Why did they send him here?" Roux asked.

"As punishment."

"For what?"

"I think he fathered Carolyn. The girl who was born while Sir Richard of Kirkland was over in the New World fighting the French and the Indians."

"What makes you think that?"

"Why else would the Falhout family heraldry be on the lozenge?"

Roux had no answer.

30

"I think the Roman Catholic Church found out about Father Roger's indiscretion with Sir Richard of Kirkland's wife," Annja went on. "And once they did, I think the Vatican shipped Father Roger here before the affair caused any further problems in London."

"Such as Sir Richard coming home and killing him?" Roux suggested.

"Yes. King George III would have backed one of his knights in such a matter, and the Roman Catholic Church could have lost even more ground in England. They'd already lost a lot by that time."

"So it was better to hide the problem than to deal with it," Roux said.

"Hiding the problem *was* dealing with it. But I think they had more to hide than they'd originally believed." Annja moved to the next stone coffin. "They also had Carolyn to hide."

"The child?"

Annja nodded. "The daughter of Father Roger and Sir Richard's wife. Some of the reports I read suggest that she showed signs of inbreeding, but I believe that was a cover-up, an attempt to point the blame elsewhere. I think Carolyn's condition was caused by something worse than inbreeding."

"What?" Roux dusted off another coffin.

"Have you heard of Proteus Syndrome?"

"The disfigurement that created the Elephant Man?"

"Yes. Joseph Merrick's X-rays and CT scans were examined by a radiologist who determined that the disease was Proteus Syndrome."

Roux turned and faced her. "You think Carolyn had Proteus Syndrome?"

"Yes. More than that, I think she was La Bête." All the pieces came together in Annja's mind. She was certain she had most of it now. "I saw that creature in the cave where I found the charm. It looked almost human. At least, aspects of it did."

"But Proteus Syndrome is debilitating and life-threatening," Roux argued. "It creates massive tissue growth. Merrick's head was too misshapen and too heavy for his body. He died at twenty-seven, strangled by the weight of his own head."

"Does Proteus Syndrome always have to present negatively?" Annja asked. "Couldn't it sometimes be an unexpected change and growth that makes a person stronger?" She looked at Roux. "I saw all those pieces of this sword become one again. I think that's harder to believe than my suggestion about Proteus Syndrome."

"You believe the disease turned her into an animal?"

Annja took a deep breath. "We'll never know if it was her

condition or the treatment she received as a result of it. That's an argument for the nature versus nurture people. Sir Richard disowned Carolyn and cast her from his house. Her mother never visited her in the abbey. And the nuns—" She shook her head, thinking about the afflicted child. Sometimes things hadn't been easy in the orphanage where she'd grown up, but the conditions had to have been a lot better than in the eighteenth century. "The nuns couldn't have known how to treat her or what to do."

"They would have believed she was demon spawn," Roux said quietly. He shrugged. "In those days, the church believed everything, and everyone, who was different was demon spawn."

Annja silently agreed.

"Carolyn killed the sisters in the abbey where she was first kept," Roux said. "You have to wonder what triggered that, but I'm afraid I could hazard a guess. The human mind has its breaking points."

Annja was surprised. She hadn't known the old man had been truly listening to her while she'd pursued the truth. "Yes. Then they faked her death and shipped her here."

"To be with her father."

"Yes."

"As further punishment?"

Shaking her head, Annja said, "I think Father Roger wouldn't allow any harm to come to his daughter. He forced the church to send her here."

"How did he do that?"

"I don't know. I only know that he must have. Otherwise she wouldn't have been here." Annja moved on to the next coffin. "Once here, Carolyn must have grown bigger, stronger *and* more intelligent. Or possibly she was always intelligent. Either way, she learned to escape from the monastery."

"She was La Bête," Roux said, understanding.

"I believe so. If you look at those pictures I took of the corpse in the cave where I found the charm, you can see the misshapen limbs and body. Proteus Syndrome didn't occur to me then, but it did later."

They kept searching.

"Here it is, then." Avery brushed layers of dust from a stone coffin.

Joining him, Annja held her candle lantern closer to the inscription.

Father Roger
1713–1767
Cursed by God
Condemned by Believers

Below the inscription was a carving of the standing stag that matched the one on the charm. Annja placed the candle lantern on the coffin and brushed at the dust, exposing the top to see if there were any more inscriptions.

Emotions swirled within her. There was excitement, of course. There always was when she made a discovery. But it was bittersweet this time. She couldn't help thinking about the innocent child afflicted with a disease no one had understood or even known existed at the time.

"The grave diggers always get the last word," Roux said. "Not very generous, were they?"

"Or very forgiving," Annja agreed quietly.

"He was a sinner," a strong voice filled with accusation announced.

Annja spun, summoning the sword as she turned. Light splintered along the sharp blade.

A man in his sixties stood in the doorway. He was wearing monk's robes. A dozen more flanked him.

"I suppose," Roux whispered, "in retrospect we truly should have posted a lookout to keep watch."

"Next time," Annja promised.

"More than merely being a sinner, though," the old monk said, "Father Roger was an embarrassment to the Vatican. They had empowered him to act on their behalf in London. England had already stepped away from much of the Roman Catholic Church's auspices. News of Father Roger's perfidies would have made things even worse. You were wondering how he got his bestial child transferred here when by all rights she should have been taken out and euthanized."

"I was," Annja admitted.

The monk stepped into the mausoleum. The other monks followed. Light from their lanterns and flashlights filled the arched cavern.

"Father Roger wrote out a document detailing his transgressions," the monk stated. "He admitted to carrying on with a married woman and fathering a child by her." He shook his head. "It was more than the Vatican wished to deal with. Sir Richard of Kirkland, the cuckolded husband, and Sir Henry, Father Roger's brother, were landed gentry. Men who were important to the king."

"The Vatican didn't want to run the risk of the king's wrath," Annja said.

"That's correct. Neither of the knights knew the truth of the child's heritage. Sir Henry would not have accepted his brother's expulsion from the church. So the decision was made to bring Father Roger to the Brotherhood of the Silent

Rain. He could have lived out the rest of his days making books. Instead, he saw to sowing the seeds of his own doom by blackmailing the church into bringing that dreadful creature here."

"Who are you?" Annja asked.

"I am Brother Gaspar," the old monk said. "One of the last of those who safeguard the secrets that nearly escaped our monastery all those years ago."

"Looking back on things," Annja said, "with over a hundred people dead, I'd say your 'secret' got out on a regular basis."

"Regrettable, but true," Brother Gaspar said. "If I had been leader of the order at that time, Father Roger's child would not have escaped."

"Would you have killed Carolyn?" Annja demanded.

The old monk's answer came without hesitation. "Yes."

"She was a child," Annja protested. "Children aren't born evil."

"By all accounts, she was a child of the devil allowed entrance into this world by the sin committed by her mother and father. She was a murderess and a monster." Fire glinted in the old monk's eyes. "Don't you dare try to tell me what she was. All of my order since that time have lived our lives in darkness here within this mountain because of her and her blasphemous father."

"Why did you stay here after the monastery was torn down?" That was the only part Annja hadn't been able to resolve.

"That's none of your business," Brother Gaspar snapped.

"Father Roger left his record," Roux announced. He looked at Annja. "That has to be the answer, of course. No one at the monastery would hear his confession. Or if they would, perhaps he thought it wouldn't matter. No one here worried about Father Roger's eternal soul. In their eyes he was already damned to hell."

"Is that it?" Annja asked. "Is that why you people have been stuck here?"

For a moment, she didn't think Brother Gaspar was going to answer.

"Unfortunately, that's true. One of the documents, his confession, was found at the time of his death. He died during the destruction of the monastery. It wasn't until later that the document was found among his papers."

"I don't see the problem," Annja said.

Brother Gaspar shook his head. "It was clearly marked as the second copy." He shrugged. "I think it was habit for Father Roger to number his copies. The monastery worked on books here. Handwritten and illuminated. We still do. It's a habit to number all versions."

"For all these years that the monastery has gone underground, you've been searching for the original copy?" Annja asked.

"Yes. We won't be permitted to leave this place until we have secured that copy. Or confirmed its destruction." Looking at her, Brother Gaspar lifted an eyebrow. "You have been so clever so far, Miss Creed. Finding the lost treasure. Finding this place when it has been secret for all these years. Figuring out the truth of La Bête. Locating the charm that Father Roger wore. I would have hoped you could divine where Father Roger's missing documents were."

"Father Roger wore the charm?"

"Before Benoit took it, yes." Brother Gaspar paused. "I'd heard Benoit took Father Roger's charm and fashioned it into a map of sorts."

"He did."

"No one at the monastery ever saw it. We thought it lost forever."

"It was around the neck of the man who killed La Bête. Carolyn."

"Was it?" That appeared to surprise the old monk. "You have been quite resourceful."

"I'm good at what I do," Annja said.

"On any other subject," Brother Gaspar said, "I would probably offer you accolades on your diligence and devotion to your craft. I would warn you about putting other pursuits ahead of God, but I would congratulate you." He paused. "Unfortunately, all I can show you for your endeavor is imprisonment."

"What?" Avery exploded. "We've done nothing wrong! The treasure is still where we found it! We only came here because we were trying to escape Lesauvage!"

"But you know too much," Brother Gaspar explained patiently. "I can't afford to let you leave."

At his signal, the monks lifted their weapons and took deliberate aim.

Annja looked over her shoulder at the other door. Three monks stood there with pistols and swords. Cowls shadowed their faces.

"Now," Brother Gaspar said, "your choice is to come willingly…or be shot and interred in this mausoleum. Which will it be?"

Avery looked at Annja. Fear widened his eyes.

"Easy," she said. "Roux?"

"I have him," Roux stated quietly.

"The sword, Miss Creed," Brother Gaspar commanded. "Throw it down, and any other weapons you might have, or we'll take them from your lifeless bodies."

After a momentary hesitation, Annja lowered the sword
to the mausoleum floor and slid it across. The weapon
stopped in the center of the room.

"Very good," Brother Gaspar said. "Now—"

Hoarse shouts cut off the old monk. Sharp bursts of
gunfire followed. One of the monks standing out in the
hallway twisted and went down, his face ripped to bloody
shreds.

"Kill them!" Corvin Lesauvage shouted out in the
hallway. "Kill them all!"

"Roux!" Annja yelled as she turned toward the other door.
She reached for the sword and suddenly the intervening
twenty feet were no longer there; the sword was in her hand.

Launching herself forward, Annja slashed the sword
across two of the assault rifles. The impacts knocked the
weapons from the hands of the men.

The third man aimed his weapon and pulled the trigger.

Annja went low, just under the stream of bullets that
hammered the stone floor and threw splinters and fragments
in all directions. She swept the man's feet out from under him
in a baseball slide that tangled them both up for a moment.
Before the man could recover, Annja slammed the sword hilt
into the side of his head. His eyes turned glassy and he
sagged into unconsciousness.

Rolling to her feet, Annja avoided one man's outstretched
arms, then popped up with a forearm that caught him under
the jawline. He flew back against the stone wall and collapsed.

The third man drew a long knife and sprang at her. Annja
fisted his robe and fell backward, planting a foot into his
stomach and tossing him back into the center of the mausoleum.

Rolling to her feet again, Annja saw Roux shove Avery Moreau out into the hallway, then bend down to slide a pistol from one of the monk's robes. After he tossed the weapon to Annja, he took another pistol and an assault rifle for himself. He palmed as many magazines as he could find for the weapons and shoved them into his pockets.

Annja headed into the hallway as Brother Gaspar and the monks fled their positions and flooded toward them. Bullets slapped the cave walls and ricocheted overhead, filling the air like an angry swarm of bees.

Roux knelt like a seasoned infantryman and aimed his assault rifle low. He fired mercilessly. Bullets chopped into the wave of fleeing monks, turning the middle of the mausoleum into a deadly no-man's-land. As flashlights and lanterns hit the ground, the illumination was extinguished and the room turned dark.

Peering around the corner of the doorway, Annja spotted Lesauvage and his men racing into the mausoleum. Most of the monks were down. Brother Gaspar lay draped over one of the stone coffins, dead or dying.

Lesauvage laughed like a madman and strode through the large room as if he were invincible. Bullets had smashed two of the coffins open and the withered bodies inside had spilled onto the bloodstained floor.

Roux withdrew. He released the magazine from the assault rifle and shoved another one into place.

"Go," he told Annja. "We can't stay here."

Annja turned. She realized then that she'd left her candle lantern on one of the coffins. Thankfully the hallway was lit. She held the pistol in her left hand and the sword in her right. She pushed her left hand against the small of Avery Moreau's back, urging him into motion.

"Run," she said. "As fast as you can."

The young man ran and Annja passed him, taking the lead. The hallway twisted and turned. She tried to keep a mental map going in her mind but quickly grew uncertain.

The footfalls of Lesauvage and his men thundered through the cave tunnels in pursuit.

THE DRUG COCKTAIL BLAZED hotly within Corvin Lesauvage. He strode through the mausoleum and looked at the dead monks lying around the cave.

A few of his men were down, as well. Two of them were dead. Another sat holding an arm across his midsection trying to keep his intestines from spilling out.

"Damn!" the young man said. "Look at this!" He gazed at his bloody guts shifting inside his embrace. "This can't be all me!" He threw his head back and howled with laughter, as if it were the funniest thing he'd ever seen. "Somebody help me!"

Lesauvage walked over to the man and gazed down at him coldly. "You're dying," he said.

"I know!" The man laughed again, but tears skidded down his face.

Taking deliberate aim, Lesauvage squeezed the trigger and put a round into the man's mouth. It took him nearly a minute to wheeze and choke to death on his blood. The death wasn't as merciful as Lesauvage had intended.

Still, it was finished.

"What did you do?" another man asked.

"He was dying," Lesauvage explained.

Several of the men were in the process of tearing open the stone coffins. Corpses littered the mausoleum.

Lesauvage fired a round into the ceiling. The detonation drew everyone's attention.

"They were monks!" Lesauvage roared. "They won't be buried with anything worth the time it takes to bust open those coffins!" He waved his pistol. "Find the woman! We don't need a witness to talk about what we've done here!"

Howling with gleeful anticipation, the Wild Hunt once more took up the chase, pounding through the doorway where Annja Creed had fled.

31

Annja's breath tore hotly through her lungs as she ran up the next flight of stairs. Halting at the top of the stairs, she took up a position by the opening, listened intently for a moment, then realized she couldn't hear anything over the sounds of the Wild Hunt closing in on them.

She whirled around the opening and dropped the pistol out before her. She held her sword arm braced under her gun wrist.

The next cave was a library. Books lined handmade shelves mixed with plastic modular shelves. Furniture consisted of large pillows and tent chairs. Candelabras heavy with partially burned candles and bowls of wax occupied tables in the cave.

Life as a monk of the Brotherhood of the Silent Rain hadn't been easy.

Curiosity pulled at Annja's attention. She couldn't help wondering what kind of books were on those shelves. Copies of books from around the world wouldn't have interested her as much as personal journals and collections of observations during the past few hundred years.

"Annja."

Roux's voice drew her from her reverie. She glanced behind her and found that Avery and Roux hadn't joined her. Turning back to the stairway carved in the sloping tunnel floor, she looked down and saw them huddled on the last landing. Men's laughter and threats cascaded around them like breakers from an approaching storm front.

"I can't...do it," Avery wheezed, shaking his head. He doubled over and retched. "I can't...breathe...can't run... no more."

Roux didn't look very good, either, but he was still moving.

"If you stay here, boy," the old man said. "They'll kill you."

"I...*can't!*" Avery doubled over and retched again.

The voices grew louder.

Running down the steps, Annja shoved the pistol into her waistband at her back, then grabbed Avery and threw him across her shoulders in a fireman's carry. She'd thought she'd barely be able to move with the extra weight. Instead, Avery felt light as a child.

"You can't carry him," Roux objected.

"I can't *leave* him," Annja responded. Holding her free arm over his arm and leg, she started up the steps. She expected her body to protest. Instead, it seemed to welcome the challenge.

She turned the corner at the library, then rushed through the doorway on the other side. Another flight of steps awaited her. She went up, hoping that the entrance to the monastery was in that direction.

She was just starting to breathe harder. She was surprised by the strength, stamina and speed that she had—even while carrying Avery Moreau. Where had it come from? The sword?

Or had the sword only awakened something within her?

Annja put the questions out of her mind and concentrated on escape. If she survived, maybe she could figure out what it all meant.

Like the Roman garrison cave, the entrance to the main chamber used by the Brotherhood of the Silent Rain was narrow. Once they reached it, she had to put Avery on his feet and shove him ahead of her.

A faux wall covered the opening. Latches held it in place.

Annja opened the door.

Beyond, the storm continued with renewed fury. Gray rain ghosted across the mountain in sheets as neatly as marching soldiers. Annja felt the chill of the rain even before she stepped out into it.

"Which way?" Avery asked, holding his arms across his body.

Roux played the flashlight around. The ground was stone. No path existed.

Of course there's no path, Annja thought. They'd have to be careful about their comings and goings. They couldn't afford to be seen.

"Down," Annja said.

Roux took the lead, making his way as fast as he dared. The yellow beam of the flashlight revealed the weakening batteries.

Avery followed, hunched over and moving more slowly.

We're not going to make it, Annja thought grimly. The certainty almost made her sick. She'd come all this way, solved most of the puzzles that were presented, and she was going to die inches short of the finish line.

Lightning flared, filling the sky with white-hot incandescence.

Below, not more than a hundred yards away, a road ran down the mountain. Even as Annja recognized it, she spotted five motorcycles speeding into view. Another blaze lit the night. Annja knew the men were after them.

At that moment, they saw Roux and Avery.

The motorcyclists pulled up short and unlimbered assault rifles, pulling them quickly to their shoulders.

"Roux!" Annja yelled.

The old man looked up and saw her standing on the mountainside. Then he saw the motorcycles. He reacted instantly, grabbing Avery and pulling him to ground behind a copse of trees and boulders.

The motorcycle riders howled like beasts. Rain and shadows turned their faces into those of snarling animals. They brought the rifles around in her direction.

Annja ran, hoping she could keep her footing, and plunged toward the brush to her right. Bullets ripped after her, tearing through the leaves and branches.

Knowing if she stopped she was only going to be pinned down, then attacked from above and below as Lesauvage and the rest of his men emerged from the monastery, Annja kept moving. She threw herself through the brush, heart hammering inside her chest. She knew she was moving fast; everything was in slow motion around her again.

She tripped over a loose rock and fell, sliding through the brush at least ten yards on the wet surface before she could roll to her feet. She steadied, whipping through branches and plants, skidding across loose rock.

One of the motorcycle riders pitched sideways, knocked down by rounds from Roux's rifle.

Ten yards out, almost running into a hail of gunfire from the other riders, Annja ran up onto a boulder, took two steps across it and launched herself into the air, hoping that the dark night and the rain would help hide her. She flipped, drawing the sword, then spreading her arms out to her sides to help maintain her balance while keeping her feet together.

Lightning blazed overhead and tore away the darkness.

Annja knew the men saw her as she fell toward them. Their faces filled with awe and fear.

"An angel!" one of them cried. "An angel with a sword!"

It was the drugs, Annja knew. They'd caused the man's hallucination and preyed on his fear.

She landed among them. She swept the sword out, cutting a diagonal slash through one man's weapon as he fired. The rifle blew up in his face and threw him backward.

Moving forward, Annja kicked the next motorcycle's handlebars, sending it crashing into the one beside it, taking down both riders.

The fourth man fired, missing Annja by inches as she whirled. She lashed out with the sword again, turning it so the flat of the blade caught the man along the temple and knocked him out.

I won't kill them, she told herself. Not unless I have to. Somehow that thought made a difference.

The fifth man dodged back, then dropped like a puppet with its strings cut. He hit the ground and rolled onto his back. A bullet from Roux's stolen rifle had torn out his throat. His chest jerked spasmodically twice, then he went slack.

Move, Annja told herself. Don't think about him. Deal with it later. Get everybody out safe now.

Annja grabbed the nearest motorcycle and pushed it

upright. When she pulled in the clutch and touched the electronic ignition, the engine grumbled to life.

Roux ran toward her, dragging Avery after him.

"You could have gotten yourself killed with a damned fool stunt like that," the old man shouted.

"It worked," Annja replied. "There wasn't a lot of time. There still isn't." She pushed the motorcycle toward him. "Can you ride?"

"Yes. You live five hundred years, you learn a few things." Roux reloaded the assault rifle and slung it over his shoulder. Then he threw a leg over the motorcycle and climbed aboard. He glanced at Avery. "Can you ride, boy?"

"No." Avery looked like a drowned rat.

Roux sighed. "This mountain is going to be difficult at best. Carrying double is foolish." Then he shook his head. "I'm getting foolish in my dotage. Climb on, boy."

"Thank you." Avery climbed on back of the motorcycle.

"Get a good grip," Roux told him.

For just a moment, Annja couldn't help but think about Garin's story, about how his father had sent him off on horseback with Roux all those years ago. There was something paternal about Roux that she hadn't seen before.

"Here." Annja clapped a helmet on Avery's head that she'd taken from one of Lesauvage's riders.

Roux looked at her. "Can you ride one of these mechanical nightmares?"

Annja smiled at him, seeing the concern in those electric blue eyes. "Yeah," she said. "I can. Probably better than you can."

Roux harrumphed his displeasure. "Well don't get over-confident and get yourself killed. There are still things we should talk about."

Lightning threw crooked white veins across the troubled sky. Movement along the ridge higher up caught Annja's attention.

Lesauvage and the survivors of his group fanned out along the mountainside.

"Go," Annja said.

Roux revved the motorcycle's engine and took off. Clutching him tightly, Avery hung on. Bullets raked the stones and the muddy earth where the motorcycle had been.

Taking advantage of the distraction Roux's escape afforded her, Annja retreated to another of the motorcycles. She righted it, started the engine and threw a leg over while it started forward. She stood on the pegs, cushioning the rough terrain and muscling the motorcycle to keep it upright in the mud and on the slick stone surfaces exposed between the earth and vegetation. She focused on Roux, spotting his headlight and following it along the trail.

Because he was riding double, Roux struggled with the motorcycle. Avery had no aptitude for riding. He swayed wrong or stayed straight up as Roux handled the motorcycle, creating even more difficulty.

Glancing over her shoulder, Annja saw that Lesauvage and two other men had recovered the three remaining motorcycles. They sped along in pursuit, closing the distance quickly.

We're not going to make it, Annja realized. Between the storm and Avery, we can't escape. She cursed herself for not disabling the other motorcycles, then realized that she'd only been thinking forward, not backward.

When Roux disappeared in front of her for just a moment, a desperate plan formed. Annja crested the hill Roux had just passed over, then switched off her motorcycle and ran it into the brush off the trail into the shadows. The droning engines of the pursuit motorcycles filled her ears.

She waited nervously. She breathed deep, blinking the rain from her eyes, concentrating on what she had to do. Reaching behind her, she removed the pistol from her waistband and waited.

The three motorcycles whipped by, never spotting her in the darkness.

Coolly, Annja lifted the pistol and fired at the last motorcycle's back tire, placing her shots just below the flaring ruby taillight. On the fifth or sixth shot, the rear tire blew.

Slewing out of control, the motorcycle went down in a skidding heap, shedding the rider and pieces of the fenders and body.

The pistol blew back empty. Out of ammunition, Annja tossed the weapon away. Then she pressed the electronic ignition and the engine roared to life as her headlight came on. She twisted the accelerator and let out the clutch so fast she almost lost the motorcycle.

She was speeding along the trail, standing on the pegs again as she slitted her eyes against the rain. Her face stung and her vision occasionally blurred, but she held the motorcycle to the course. She gained ground quickly, but knew she was going to arrive too late when she saw Roux lose the motorcycle. Roux and Avery tumbled across the ground, trying to get up even as Lesauvage and the remaining rider bore down on them.

Roux stood but appeared dazed. Avery didn't get up.

Lesauvage and the other rider roared past them and came around in tight turns, putting their motorcycles between Roux and the one he'd lost.

Roux fumbled for the assault rifle draped over his shoulder. Somehow he'd managed to hang on to it.

Lesauvage pulled his pistol from his shoulder holster and took aim. At that distance, there was no way he could miss.

"Lesauvage!" Annja screamed.

The other rider raised his assault rifle, bringing it up on a sling.

Annja hit the same rise that had dumped Roux and Avery. But she twisted the accelerator, gaining speed, then yanked back on the handlebars.

The motorcycle went airborne. Throwing her body sideways, Annja turned it with her, performing a tabletop aerial maneuver she'd seen on X Games.

Not wanting to be trapped under the weight of the motorcycle, Annja released it and kicked free of the pegs. The motorcycle rider dodged to one side as her bike crashed into his and they bounced away in a rolling mass that exploded into flames.

Annja landed hard on the ground. Out of breath, her lungs feeling paralyzed by the impact, she managed to push herself to her feet.

The motorcycle rider rose up on his knees, cursing foully. He pulled the assault rifle to his shoulder.

Without thinking, Annja summoned the sword and threw it.

Glittering in the sudden flare of lightning, the sword seemed to catch fire as it looped end over end. It struck the gunman full in the chest, driving him backward, his heart pierced by the blade.

For a moment, everything was frozen.

Lesauvage stared at the dead man in disbelief. Then he started laughing. "That was stupid!" he roared. "You threw away your weapon!"

From more than thirty feet away, Annja reached for the sword. It faded from sight where it still quivered in the dead man's chest.

The sword was in her hand.

The confidence drained from Lesauvage's features. He lifted his pistol and took a two-handed grip on it.

Annja rose, knowing it would do no good to run. He would only shoot her in the back. She held the sword in front of her, the blade bisecting her vision, her left foot in front of her right.

She thought about Joan of Arc dying on the pyre. Annja didn't want to die, but if she were going to and she couldn't die old and famous and in her bed with a man she loved, this was how she wanted it to happen, looking death in the eye.

"You brought a sword to a gun fight," Lesauvage sneered. He fired.

Annja saw the muzzle-flash rush from the pistol barrel. She even believed she saw the bullet streaking toward her, knowing there was no way it was going to miss her. She waited to feel it bite into her flesh.

But her hands moved instinctively, tracking the projectile. Incredibly, she saw sparks as the bullet hit the sword, felt the vibration race through her hands, then heard the bullet whiz within inches of her ear.

Annja was already moving toward Lesauvage instead of away from him. She threw herself into a flying kick, sailing above Lesauvage's next round, then lashing out with her left foot when she came within range.

The kick drove Lesauvage from his feet, knocking him backward. He lost the pistol before he slammed against the boulder behind him.

When Annja stood, she held the sword to Lesauvage's throat.

He stared at her over the blade as lightning blazed and burnished the steel. The sound of the rain drowned out everything but the hoarse rasp of their breathing.

"Kill him," Roux directed, limping up. Blood threaded down the side of his face, diluted by the rain.

"I can't," Annja said. She couldn't even imagine taking a man's life in cold blood.

"He would have killed you."

"He didn't."

"He tried to kill you."

Annja trembled slightly. "That wouldn't make killing him right."

Roux grinned and shook his head. "I hate moral complications. Wars and battle should be so much simpler." He bent down and picked up Lesauvage's pistol, taking time to wipe the mud from it. "You have to realize that you've made an enemy here."

"Like you did with Garin?"

"No, that's different," Roux said. "Garin made an enemy of me. If he had the chance to kill me, I truly think he would." He nodded toward Lesauvage. "This one, if he gets the chance, will kill you someday."

Annja lowered her sword and stepped back. She glared at Roux. "I'm not a murderer."

"There are," Roux said, "worse things to be." He shot Lesauvage between the eyes.

Lesauvage pitched forward onto his face. The back of his head was blown off.

"Thankfully," Roux continued as if he hadn't a care in the world, "I'm none of those things."

Annja wheeled on him, looking at him and realizing that she didn't know him, and certainly didn't know what he was capable of. She held her sword ready.

Roux tossed the pistol away and spread his arms, leaving his chest open to her attack. He smiled benignly. "Lesauvage still has other drug-crazed fools in the mountains tonight. Do you want to argue about this right now?"

Annja knew he was right. They still had to escape. "No," she said in a hard voice. "But we *will* talk about this at a later date."

"I look forward to it," Roux said. "There's a lot you're going to have to learn. If you want to survive your destiny."

Ignoring him, Annja turned back to the two surviving motorcycles.

Avery Moreau sat huddled in a ball and looked consumed with fear.

She righted one of the motorcycles, threw a leg over, started it and looked back at the young man. "Come on. Let's get you safe."

Slowly, Avery climbed onto the motorcycle with her. He wrapped his mud-covered arms around her, shaking with terror as he held on.

Annja didn't wait to see if Roux could manage. Even though he was limping and banged up, she felt certain the old man could fend for himself. She accelerated and raced down the mountain, hoping to get out of the cold and the wet soon.

epilogue

Annja Creed swam with an easy stroke. As soon as her feet touched the sandy bottom, she stood and walked out of the ocean. She was conscious of dozens of male spectators watching her, maybe wishing she'd gone topless instead of wearing the bright red bikini she had on, and for a moment she luxuriated in the harmless attention.

She crossed the beach, basking in the heat after the cool of the sea, knowing that her tan was unblemished by scratches or bruises. She had healed quickly from her minor injuries.

Annja thought the sword had somehow enhanced her, but Roux didn't believe that was true. He wished she knew who her parents were. But if anyone had ever known, all that information had been lost when New Orleans drowned during the hurricane in 2005.

Roux was sitting in a chaise longue near hers when she

returned to her seat. A large, colorful umbrella shaded both chairs.

"Enjoying the afternoon?" Roux asked.

"Yes." Annja wrapped a towel around her waist and sat. "There's not much of it left."

"Ah, well," Roux said. "That only means the evening and all the nightlife won't be far behind."

"I'm not much for nightlife," Annja said. "I prefer quiet places and just a few people." She gazed at the crowd scattered along the oceanfront. "Personally, I could do with a more secluded beach."

"I know of several good ones," Roux said. "I'd be happy to take you there sometime."

Annja slipped on her sunglasses and regarded the old man warily. They had talked a little about Roux's murder of Corvin Lesauvage. At best, though, they'd agreed to disagree. Roux had ultimately decided that she didn't have to kill anyone she didn't want to kill, and he didn't have to spare anyone he didn't want to let live. Under the circumstances, and since Roux pointed out that he'd lived in such a manner for centuries, she had shelved the argument.

"Would you?" Annja asked.

"Well," Roux said, "not right away. I'm going to be playing poker soon. I'm not about to give that up." He took a cigar from his jacket and lit up. "Have you given any thought to staying for a while?"

"I have." For the past three days, while waiting anxiously to see how the events that had happened up in the Cévennes would touch her, Annja had slept, read and swam, hardly leaving the spacious hotel suite Roux had arranged for her.

"And?"

"I'll spend some time," Annja said.

"Splendid," Roux enthused.

"A short while."

"Good. Because I don't want you underfoot while I'm playing poker."

"Have you heard from Garin?" she asked.

"No, but I still check for traps routinely." Roux patted the arms of the chair. "And I suddenly realize this isn't really a good place to be if he's hired an assassin."

"Maybe Garin doesn't really want you dead as much as he claims."

"Truthfully," Roux said, "I think the sword being reassembled has him spooked. He probably wants it destroyed more than he wants me dead. At least for now. Until he discovers whether the sword's reemergence is going to have an effect on him. If it does, who else is he going to talk to about it?"

A server passed by and Roux ordered drinks. In short order, they were delivered.

"Thank you," Annja said, lifting her glass.

"My pleasure."

Annja sipped, enjoying the cool, clean taste of the fruit and alcohol. With the wind skating under the umbrella and the sand warm around her, the mountain seemed very far away.

"Did you arrange for an attorney for Avery Moreau?" she asked.

"I did. I understand Inspector Richelieu is about to be temporarily suspended while an investigation into the death of Avery's father is conducted."

"What about Avery?"

Roux shrugged. "I don't know. Even after all these years,

I still find that I can't judge people well. They constantly surprise you."

Annja silently agreed with that. Life was full of surprises. She sipped her drink again and smiled. "I've been thinking about Father Roger's confession. The one that he threatened the Vatican with."

"And?"

"I think I know where it is."

Roux shook his head. "I'm quite certain it doesn't exist."

Annja sipped her drink again and remained silent.

After a while, Roux's curiosity got the better of him. "Enough with the mystery. Tell me what you think."

"Are you sure you want to hear? I mean, you do think you're right."

"Of course I do. But I'm willing to entertain a possibility of it being somewhere else."

"It's in Carolyn's grave."

"Where you found the last piece of the sword?" Roux asked.

"No," Annja said. "In the false grave she was given in England. In Sir Richard of Kirkland's holdings. Or whoever has them now. I think he hid the truth in a lie."

Roux smiled. "If he did, that was very clever."

"There's only one way to find out."

"Does it look like there's a bit of grave robbing in your future?"

"No," Annja replied. "I thought maybe you, using some of your money and influence, could arrange for an exhumation of Carolyn's grave in England."

"So you could broadcast it on that tawdry television show you do pieces for?"

"I thought about that, actually. I mean, I could propose a whole new possibility about who and what the Beast of Gévaudan was. It could be a good move."

"Yet you're undecided about doing it," Roux said.

"No, I'm decided. I'm not giving this story to *Chasing History's Monsters*. Though it is tempting to allow Father Roger his final jab at the Vatican."

"The man did break his faith with God and the church," Roux pointed out. "Not to mention disrupting a marriage."

"I think he was punished enough for that. So was Carolyn."

Roux nodded. "You're probably right." He smoked his cigar for a time and they sat in silence.

Annja sipped her drink and studied the foaming white curlers rushing in from the sea. "What am I supposed to do with the sword?" she asked.

"What do you mean? It's your sword now. You do with it whatever you wish to do with it," Roux stated.

"But shouldn't I do something special with it? Become— I don't know—*something?*"

Roux looked at her seriously. "Annja Creed, you are someone special. The sword only allows you to act on your natural gifts with more authority. You have a destiny ahead of you that no one in this world has ever had. You've not been given the sword to be another Joan of Arc. She did what she had to do." He paused. "You have to figure out what it is you're supposed to do like everyone else, one day at a time."

Annja looked at him and felt he was telling the truth. Roux had lied about things in the past and would again in the future, but she knew he wasn't lying now.

"Thank you," she said. She moved the umbrella and lay back in the warm sun. She thought about everything she should be doing—all the cataloging of the things in her loft, the certificates of authenticity she had to do, the trip she wanted to take to North Africa, the next story she'd have to pitch to Doug Morrell—and somewhere in there, she dropped off to sleep.

Her destiny stretched out before her. There was no need to rush to meet it. It was waiting for her.

TAKE 'EM FREE

2 action-packed novels plus a mystery bonus

NO RISK

NO OBLIGATION TO BUY